The WARTIME CHOCOLATE MAKER

BOOKS BY GOSIA NEALON

THE SECRET RESISTANCE SERIES
Her Secret Resistance
The Resistance Wife
Daughter of the Resistance

STANDALONE NOVELS
The Codebreaker Girl

Gosia Nealon

The
WARTIME
CHOCOLATE
MAKER

bookouture

Published by Bookouture in 2025

An imprint of Storyfire Ltd.
Carmelite House
50 Victoria Embankment
London EC4Y 0DZ

www.bookouture.com

The authorised representative in the EEA is Hachette Ireland
8 Castlecourt Centre
Dublin 15 D15 XTP3
Ireland
(email: info@hbgi.ie)

Copyright © Gosia Nealon, 2025

Gosia Nealon has asserted her right to be identified as the author of this work.

All rights reserved. No part of this publication may be reproduced, stored in any retrieval system, or transmitted, in any form or by any means, electronic, mechanical, photocopying, recording or otherwise, without the prior written permission of the publishers.

ISBN: 978-1-83618-262-7
eBook ISBN: 978-1-83618-263-4

This book is a work of fiction. Names, characters, businesses, organizations, places and events other than those clearly in the public domain, are either the product of the author's imagination or are used fictitiously. Any resemblance to actual persons, living or dead, events or locales is entirely coincidental.

For Kasia, Mateusz and Ryan.
The love between a mother and her children is eternal...

One word frees us of all the weight and pain in life. That word is love.

> Sophocles

PROLOGUE

My father's office smells of a fleeting sweetness: burned sugar mixed with flowers and fruits. In a way, it reminds me of my own life... I want so badly to forget his betrayal, so I close my eyes and pretend that the last six years never happened.

For a short moment, I drift back to being a little girl who's watching her papa preparing various mixtures of chocolate. I often perched on a tiny stool for hours while he described different flavors with such passion. My happiness lifted every time he asked me to taste something new, calling me his sweet tooth.

I gently push aside my thoughts and blink away my tears, forcing my mind back to here and now. Still, Papa's words ring out strong in my memory, explaining that when roasting is done right, it brings out the distinctive chocolate aroma in cocoa beans. While lighter roasted beans taste more fruity, darker ones have more bitter flavor.

I pick a cocoa bean from a small, electric oven, and chew it, enjoying its creamy taste with delicate hints of caramel. I munch on it, trying to place the flavors, decide the right ingredients to go with it. Perhaps some vanilla with small notes of cinnamon? Every new batch has distinct flavors and aromas, so not all cocoa beans go well with the same seasonings and ingredients, or the same proportions.

Because of the war, every mixture must have a simple but catchy taste, and only hours of experimenting with different flavors can assure this.

I invest all my senses into my new chocolate mixture, so for a moment I fail to register a gentle tap on the door. The thought that it must be Sebastian causes my heart to beat fast from a combination of excitement and fear. This man is like a complicated cipher machine, one I struggle to solve.

"Look at you," he says and smiles down at me, "already working on our chocolate creations."

The word "our" isn't missed on me. "I've finished the delivery schedule, so I thought I'd tackle some of my other duties."

His intensely blue eyes, shades of ocean on sunny days, linger on my lips and refuse to move away.

In this very moment it feels as if he's kissing me. Every fiber of my being is hot-blooded and excited. But I turn away to the table behind me and bring my mind back to the soothing chocolate scent in the air. Its warmth and richness of oils has this calming effect on my nerves. I close my eyes and inhale deeply, yearning to be far away from him.

"Katharina," he whispers, making me even more aware of his closeness. "I'm glad that you are back. I've missed you."

I embrace myself to compose my face and then swirl back to him, not knowing what to do with that awkwardness between us. I begin fixing his tie, my hands flirtatiously close to his chest. "I've missed you too."

The truth is that I don't want him, and I despise the physical attraction I feel for him. When it comes to this man, everything good ends with his handsome looks...

He takes my hand in his and kisses the knuckles, sending

jolts of electricity through my skin. "You belong here, my dearest. I will always protect you and all your secrets are safe with me. Please, be assured of that."

All my secrets? "I have nothing to hide," I say with an innocent look. It feels as if I'm balancing on a thin line here, trying to remember my Polish mother's words that he's our only protector from the Germans and that my little brother's future lies in his hands. If not for her reasoning, I would never have agreed to work in this factory.

Now I'm forced to play this game with him where my every wrong move might prove deadly. It reminds me of a chess competition we're both determined to win.

A sarcastic smile curls on his mouth, but he changes the subject. "Please, don't run away from me this time—" His words are cut by the screeching sound of the opening door, which reveals a uniformed man.

"Here you are, Richter," Bruno says but bows at me. "Please, Katharina, forgive me the lack of manners but I have a rather urgent matter I must discuss with your boss."

When they are gone, I exhale with relief but his mention of "all my secrets" boggles my mind again. What does he know about me? Is it possible that he's merely referring to what happened between my father and myself all those years back?

That's all it must be, I resolve, because if he knew about my involvement with the Polish Resistance, I would be already dead at the hands of the Gestapo.

ONE

KASIA: HOME

Six months earlier, June 1943, Gdańsk—a port city on the Baltic coast

I missed my father's funeral on purpose...

I could not stomach the sight of German dignitaries swarming at his coffin. I knew they would be there in their craven, over-adorned uniforms paying their respects to honor his devotion to Hitler. They think Papa was one of them. Was he? I still don't know the answer to that. But I do know it's more complicated than one would think.

With my trembling hands, I push an iron gate and walk the dirt path toward our villa, surrounded by Mama's majestic garden. Sweet scents of peonies make me slow down to take a deep breath. It's the smell of my childhood, so ideal but also elusive.

The front door swings wide open and a blond boy flees down the stairs and runs into my embrace. Warmth soars through my heart at the realization that he does remember me, after all. It's been five years since I moved to Warsaw.

With tears in my eyes, I hold him tight. "I missed you so much, my little Kornel," I say and kiss the top of his head.

He wiggles his way out from my arms. "I'm not little anymore, sister. I'm ten," he says in German, and I hear a clear echo of our father's voice as he speaks his language. Then he peers around. "You must be careful not to speak Polish when out here in Danzig," he whispers this time in Polish, his mother tongue, and mine.

Since the start of this awful war, I prefer to call my city in the Polish way, Gdańsk, not the German Danzig. But before I get a chance to answer, my throat constricts even more at the sight of Mama in a black dress edging our way. Her now-bony figure and the deep wrinkles under her hazel eyes make me wonder for a second if it's truly her, but my heart knows better. It's just that she looks so pale and fragile.

This time I run straight into her arms. "Oh, Mama..."

"Kasia, my girl." She draws her hand down my hair and a moment later she whispers, "Let's go inside, I have supper for you."

The so-familiar scent of chamomile brings a surge of warmth to my heart. Everything in this home looks the same, from our oak furniture upholstered in champagne-gold fabric to the collections of leather-bound books that Papa stacked so carefully onto shelves.

After leaving my suitcase in my old bedroom, which hasn't changed a bit, I devour Mama's potato pancakes. They are piping hot, just the right side of greasy and salted to perfection. I take another, dip it in sour cream and sigh in satisfaction. I only had a sliver of dry black bread before leaving my aunt's flat in Warsaw and heading to the train station.

We talk as if in desperate need of making up for lost time. Soon Mama tells Kornel to fetch Maciek, our black cat, from the garden while she makes a chamomile tea.

"How's my sister doing?" Mama asks from across the

kitchen table. She now sits with a handkerchief in her hand, wiping her tears. I'm not sure if she's crying after Papa or these are tears of happiness at my return. My mother always tended to hide her emotions, so seeing her like this unnerves me.

"She's doing the best she can but life in Warsaw is very hard since the war began." Ciocia Lucyna took me in when I left Gdańsk after refusing my father's demands. She's been like a mother to me, though her cheerful personality is so different from Mama's usual gloominess.

She sighs. "These are the terrible times we live in."

I pour tea into our glass cups, watching as fragments of chamomile flowers float in the liquid. Then I cast my gaze to my left where Kornel sits with Maciek curled on his lap and a book in his hand, not caring about the rest of the world around him. It seems that he loves to read as much as I do.

"I'm surprised that Kornel remembers me," I say with a slow smile.

Her lips quirk. "He keeps a photograph of you under his pillow."

"So sweet of him." I don't tell her that it's what I've been doing too during the years of separation—sleeping with our family picture under my own pillow.

She nods but changes the subject back to one more doleful again. "I worried that you would decide to stay with Lucyna and never return to Gdańsk."

I lean forward and take her hand in mine. "When I received the awful news, I arranged to return as soon as I could because I wanted to be here with you through it all. I'm sorry I missed his funeral."

She shrugs and treats me to a knowing look. "Don't beat yourself up for it. Just know that he loved you."

I turn my gaze away from hers, unable to contradict the softness in her eyes. If she'd only heard his last words to me, she wouldn't be saying this. But she must sense my unease because she continues, "At first, your papa was very angry at you but as time passed by, he understood that he'd been too harsh. By then, the war was already here, so we thought you were safer with Lucyna in Warsaw anyway." She blinks rapidly as if to chase away a new batch of tears. "Now it has all changed."

It's a lie, I know, told to soften the bad memories. But I keep my thoughts to myself. Mama has enough to deal with now. I also don't ask her why she never took the time to visit me with Kornel before the war. I know the answer. She was too afraid to stand up to Papa, so she cut her ties with me instead. For a very long time I couldn't forgive her for this, but in time I learned to live with it. Not everyone was born to be brave, definitely not my mother.

"How did Papa die?" I ask, even though I dread to hear the answer directly from her. The telegram I received did not state the cause of his passing.

"Heart attack." She dabs at her eyes with the handkerchief and blows her nose. "Dr. Fischer said it was instant and he didn't suffer."

She loves him, and I do too, despite all he put me through. Will I ever be able to forgive him, though? In some ways, I already have, but there is so much sadness lingering around my heart that I can't bring the good moments into my memories.

For a while she sips her tea and looks absent-minded. "It's good you're here because soon we'll have a guest over for dinner."

Judging by her frowning face, she isn't looking forward to that meeting. "Anyone I know?"

She looks down at her hands and sweeps an imaginary crumb from the table. "It's your father's business partner."

"I had no idea that Papa had a partner," I say. I have been wondering lately how things are going to be now he's gone. I'm pretty sure the Germans won't allow Mama, as a Polish-born woman, to take over the ownership of the factory.

"One year after you left, your father combined our factory with Sebastian Richter's. He was afraid that in the event of war breaking out, he would be forced to close, and Sebastian has powerful connections in Berlin thanks to his uncle."

Just hearing the name *Richter* sends cold shivers down my spine. "What will happen now?"

"Sebastian will tell us, but it doesn't look good. I have some money hidden in the house, but our bank accounts were seized. I'm certain that the factory is already lost to us too but I'm hoping Sebastian will show some mercy." Careworn, she pushes a strand of hair off her face. "I pray they will not turf us from our home and send us away."

I shake my head. "They can't do this." The moment I say it, the absurdity of it angers me. The truth is that they will do whatever they want.

"It's what they did with so many Poles here in Gdańsk when the war started. They evicted them from their homes and sent either south or straight to camps. The ones allowed to stay, now live in cellars and serve as a labor force. It's only Germans who are living in their villas and fine townhouses."

I'm not surprised at my mother's words. I'd heard about all of this, the horror stories of women and children dragged out into the street, their homes ransacked. I knew, too, that the Nazis' agenda right from the beginning was to murder the Polish intelligentsia and forbid the younger generation from learning. They want them to conform to their hideous, lowly view of Poles, so they're nothing more than illiterate slaves. This is why it gladdens me so to see my little brother, even now, curled up with a book.

"You must be careful when you're out to never speak Polish outside of this home. Remember your real name is Katharina, not Kasia," Mama continues. "You must show yourself to be a proud German woman, your father's descendant."

Katharina. While I was growing up, Mama always spoke

Polish to me and called me Kasia, but Papa was German and for him I was Katharina. For myself, I'm not so sure. I grew up within two cultures, a minority already within my city's population—which was eighty percent German and only twenty percent Polish. But Mama was so educated and cultured, part of the Polish intelligentsia—attending salons and art galleries and poetry readings. All that started to change when the National Socialists took over in 1933. Then Papa urged Mama to act in public like she was a German woman, to stay away from those discussing philosophy and politics and art. Even though he didn't agree with Hitler's views, or the behavior of the NSDAP, at some point he joined his party. I told myself he was afraid of losing the family's only source of income—the chocolate factory—if he stood against the Nazi party or was even perceived to be neutral. And now it turns out his business partner has powerful connections in Berlin. The thought of it makes me sick to my stomach.

"You're right, Mama," I say, knowing that the ability to pretend is a huge weapon in today's world. "Did Papa trust Sebastian?"

Her eyes reflect traces of pain and shame. "He seemed to, but your father changed since the war started. He became a fast believer in this awful ideology. And he trusted that being on their side might save us all."

My heart sinks still further. I'd wanted to believe that Papa wasn't completely brainwashed, but Mama's words are making me question my convictions. How wrong I'd been.

"I'm hoping that Sebastian will have the decency to offer you a position in the factory. He did mention that to me at the funeral, pointing to the fact that he owes it to your father to assure our safety."

I snort. "I don't want anything from him."

Mama twists her wedding ring and gives me a pleading

look. "It's our only hope," she implores. "We need him to protect us. You must obey, please, darling, for Kornel."

I almost roll my eyes. If she knew about my activities in Warsaw, she wouldn't be so sure about me saving our family. I can only pray the authorities know as little as she does.

"We should leave Gdańsk," I say, briskly. "We can stay with Ciocia Lucyna. She has enough room for all of us."

Her chin trembles. "Your father worked so hard for us to have this home and family business. We can't abandon it. Once the war is over, it will be rightfully ours again."

I answer with a small nod. "Fine, Mama." I don't dwell on the subject any longer as this conversation exhausts me. But one thing is for sure—if I end up working at Papa's factory, I will be using my work in ways that Sebastian Richter never intended or foresaw.

After the years spent in my aunt's lively apartment, being at home like this, with my father's oak furniture, paintings, and music—which now all seem so pompous and oppressive—reminds me so vividly that I am half German. But the Nazi-driven Germany that has created the hell on earth, one we're all trying to survive, is nothing to me.

I will resist it.

For I am half Polish too, and my heart belongs to Poland and her freedom.

TWO

KASIA: THE PAST COMES CALLING

July 1943, Gdańsk

Being back home feels right but Papa's absence lurks at me from every corner. Everything here reminds me of him, like the velvet upholstered armchair he always sat in or his favorite chocolate cake that Mama made yesterday. I couldn't swallow the tiniest crumb because of the sudden emotion that paralyzed me from inside. Instead, I kept choking on my tears.

During the first week, I don't go out at all, wanting to forget the awful reality of the war. But one morning I decide to accompany Mama to the cemetery. It's time to go back to life.

The German part in me is dead right now; my loyalty belongs with my Polish roots. There is no confusion or sentiment—I want to be on the side of good, just like any decent German who despises Hitler's brainwashing.

But before the war, I considered myself to be more German than Polish thanks to my father's influence. He taught me to love German literature and music, and we visited Berlin often, where my grandparents still lived. But Mama was also persistent when it came to instilling her country's culture into me and she made sure that Kornel and I spoke fluent Polish.

The one thing my parents cultivated from the very beginning was the habit of treating all people the same, regardless of their nationality or religion. My city is a port, and sometimes I thought this a practical response, too, to the multitudes of people on Gdańsk's cobbled streets. They also taught me to judge others based on the way they choose to treat people. Later, Papa sacrificed these values out of fear of losing everything, including our safety, though he couldn't force me to follow him into that Nazi ideology.

We enter a cemetery in Wrzeszcz, not far from our villa, and walk through the main alley with hornbeam rows along it. This cemetery is being expanded and it's not so silent here with German soldiers supervising men in shabby clothes digging new graves. I swallow hard and keep my head up like I'm not seeing a thing.

Flowers with little black swastikas flood Papa's grave causing my stomach to twist in disgust. I clench my hands; it takes my entire resolve not to jump forward and clean his grave of those awful flags. My nails dig into my skin, making me wince, but I must control my anger.

Mama must sense my distress because she puts her hand on my arm and whispers, "Stay calm. We're being watched."

In this very moment, it strikes me how wisely and carefully she behaves. Where is the fragile woman who hid under the safety of Papa's protective arms? His passing has transformed her but I'm still unable to grasp the severity of the changes. Maybe she's still in shock.

"Frau Hartmann, how good to see you."

At the sound of a rather weary voice, I lift my head and meet a set of deeply blue eyes peering at me even though the man's words are directed to my mother. This broad-shouldered and tall man is so handsome that I feel a surge of heat rushing to my cheeks.

"Sebastian, what a relief to meet you here," Mama says in perfect German.

At the realization that it's Papa's business partner, I want to escape and hide where no one can find me. He's changed a lot, so I didn't recognize him at first.

He smiles slowly and kisses the knuckles of Mama's right hand. "I'm coming back from my friend's funeral who was a devoted soldier of the Wehrmacht. But I see you aren't alone." His gaze is back on me and once more I'm unable to blink, lost in the intensity of his eyes.

"I trust you remember my daughter Katharina. She's back home now Dietrich has left us," my mother says and brings her hand to wipe a single tear from her cheek. She turns my way. "Darling, I'm sure you're happy to see Sebastian after all of these years."

I nod and say, "Hello."

"It's a pleasure seeing you, Fräulein Hartmann. Your father talked of you with pride." He smiles while a mischievous glint plays in his eyes.

How much of the truth did Papa tell him? My father was a wise man, so I don't see him sharing with anyone the details of our family affairs, but the man's demeanor suggests he knows more than he should. After all, he was one of the reasons why I left.

"That he did," Mama says, wiping another tear. "I was hoping to have you over soon for dinner."

"I hate adding extra tasks for you during this difficult time. Why don't I come over tomorrow at noon for a brief chat? Would that suit you?"

Mama doesn't oppose this plan, but graciously accepts his suggestion, and I don't blame her. Nazi skunk, I snarl under my breath as we walk away.

The following morning, I help Mama bake an apple strudel and set the dining table with our delicate rose china, which Mama uses only for special occasions. I miss the presence of Jadwiga in the kitchen, the elderly cook we used to hire, but according to Mama, she left when the war started. Jadwiga baked the most delicious treats for me, and I loved her like she was my grandmother. Her soft, round face always smiled when I stopped by the kitchen. I wonder what has happened to her now and why she really left.

Mama nearly drops the strudel as she puts it on a serving plate; I can sense her nervousness about this "chat" with the man she's convinced could be our savior, while being stricken with worry that he'll turn his back on us.

Once everything is ready for his visit, I go to my old room upstairs and put on a V-neck, black dress with short sleeves that I got from Mama. I didn't bring much of my wardrobe with me from Warsaw but it's not like I have much there anyway.

I brush my hair for a very long time. It's thick and wavy; Papa always said that I inherited it from Grandma Gertrud who passed away over a decade ago.

I'm hoping to be able to go to the beach after this meeting and listen to the sea. I must put my thoughts together and plan. But first, I will see what this man tells us. What if his intentions toward us are sinister? Kornel and I were born as German citizens and have the Nazi-approved Aryan looks, but Mama's situation is sensitive now Papa is gone, and that man knows it. He might still be holding a grudge against me.

When I hear the door ring, I pray for inner strength and walk down the stairs into the foyer just as Mama lets him in.

He laughs and says something to Mama but when his head lifts, his firm gaze takes me in while I freeze in the middle of the staircase.

I hold in a breath and fold my lips into a smile despite my better judgment. He seems even more masculine and robust in his black suit.

He lowers his voice. "You look stunning, Fräulein Hartmann," he says without taking his softening eyes from me.

I release my clenching hands. I have to keep a safe distance though, because I don't like the vulnerable way this man makes me feel. But I also must pretend. "It's a pleasure having you over, Herr…" I stammer, realizing that due to my distress I don't remember his family name.

"Richter," he says in a firm tone. "But please address me as Sebastian, just like back then."

"In this situation, I trust you can call me Katharina."

He nods with approval in his eyes and lifts my hand to place a kiss on it.

I make sure my fingers don't tremble like my betraying heart does at his touch on my skin.

Mama ushers us to take a seat at the table and serves coffee and strudel while Kornel chats with the man like they are good friends. I can't disregard his soft approach toward my brother because they genuinely seem to like each other. Normally, I would take it as a good sign but not in this situation.

"Kornel, darling, why don't you find Maciek and make sure he has enough water to drink?" Mama says.

My brother takes a hint and he's out of sight in no time. I appreciate Mama's attempts to get to the purpose of his visit right away. This tension in the room makes me feel uneasy, and I can only imagine its effect on my mother who's constantly distressed about the very real prospect of being evicted from our home.

"The strudel is exceptional, Frau Hartmann," our guest says, "even my own Mutti can't compete."

His words make my mother visibly relax her rigid posture.

"Thank you, Sebastian, but I'm afraid it's all my daughter's effort."

Mama tells the lie with such ease that it scares and stuns me at the same time. She has a clear agenda here for him hiring me. Never have I caught her being so sneaky. I want to laugh and hug her because finally, after all these years, she turns out to have flaws just like the rest of us. Before, it was constant perfection under the scrutiny of my father's watchful gaze.

Now he's gone, I sense that she lives in constant fear of being exposed before the German population for her Polish roots. Her family name might be German, but her heart is fully Polish, it's why Papa often reminded her to be careful when they socialized with others in his Danzig.

Sebastian's attention switches to me. "Then I can already see why your father thought you to be a non-replaceable asset to our chocolate business."

Maybe Papa told him good things about me for the sake of our family. Maybe the man doesn't know what exactly happened five years ago in the summer of 1938.

"Thank you for your kind words," I say and take a sip of coffee, preparing myself to hear the worst. I'm convinced now that he's come here to inform us of our fate, which has already been decided by his peers who oversee this city.

Nothing less, nothing more.

"Well, I'm sure you ladies know the purpose of my visit," he says and sighs. "Please rest assured that, most of all, I come here as your friend."

"I never doubted that, Sebastian. My husband valued you not only as an exceptional business partner, but also as someone he could trust," Mama says and bites at her lip, while straightening a vase of pink hydrangeas. It's not until now that I notice the smell of rich honey and vanilla hanging over this white-tableclothed scene.

I know how much it costs her to say this in such a calm way.

Like me, she doesn't trust this scoundrel one bit, but she knows it's wiser to have him on our side.

He clears his throat. "I'm glad to hear it. Though there're some things that I can't control." He pauses, fishes out a handkerchief from his pocket and wipes a sheen of sweat from his forehead. "Um... You see, Frau Hartmann, shortly after Dietrich's funeral, the authorities contacted me regarding our factory. They warned me that the Third Reich would legally seize the business if you were to become the owner of the second half. Of course, they were obliged to mention the fact that you are Polish-born." He pauses to add another slice of strudel to his plate, slicing into the pastry with his fork. "I have been informed, ladies, that I must immediately take over the company."

I've expected all of this but hearing him say it twists my stomach like a knot as tight as those tethering ships around the marine bollards down at the waterfront. I could dwell on how unfair all of this is, but it would just be a waste of my time. It's standard practice for the Nazis to steal. We all know it and there is nothing we can do, not until they lose this war. The ones who are brave enough to contradict them, are murdered in cold blood, their lives stolen along with their property.

I feel my pulse speeding, but I stay silent because I can't trust myself to speak now. Mama's pleading gaze rests on me for a moment, so I give her a reassuring look. She was clear before this meeting that I'm not to argue with him when comes to the sensitive subjects. I agree with her. We're in rather a vulnerable state right now, so angering the man may in fact strip us of the only person who could help us. But it's so hard...

I take another slice of strudel, attack the innocent pastry a little too viciously.

"My children were born as German citizens," Mama says, a visible tightness around her eyes. "As you know, my daughter is of age—" she doesn't finish the sentence but looks at him with expectancy in her hazel eyes. My mother's black hair strips her of any pretense of possessing the Aryan look, the one Kornel and I inherited after Papa. Right now, it's the best gift he could have given us.

"The concern of the authorities is that Katharina refused to follow her father's directions and has been under the influence of the Polish bandits in Warsaw for all these years. They were clear with their decision."

My mouth goes dry, and I nearly choke on a chunk of apple. So, Papa was open about what transpired between us. And their concerns about my stay in Warsaw...

"I understand." Mama's voice trembles. "I assume, Sebastian, that you've already taken over the factory then?"

He nods. "It was the only logical decision, or we would lose everything."

"This all seems very convenient for you, Herr Richter," I say unable to listen to this much longer, refusing to call him by his name as he asked me to and as my mother still does. "Is it *logical* for you to take this home over as well?" I make sure to instill a hard edge to my voice.

He cocks his head then shakes it. "If I was the way you imply, Fräulein, I would not be sitting here with you." His amused eyes stare at me for a moment longer. "But to answer your question: No, I'm not planning to seize your home. It's not what I do. I'm a simple chocolatier. Just like your father was."

"I'm assuming you expect us to thank you for letting us stay in our own home?" I take a deep breath and hold it in. I need to stop provoking him for the sake of my family.

"Katharina, enough of this," Mama snaps at me. "Please, forgive her. She's taking her father's death hard."

"That's understandable. Please know you're under my protection and if I could change the current situation with the factory's ownership, I wouldn't hesitate. But it must stay this way for now and once the war ends and things settle back to normal, Dietrich's children will receive what belongs to them as his rightful German heirs. You have my word on this. What's important now is to assure that the factory stays in safe hands."

My blood boils as I listen to his rubbish but my mother smiles graciously and says, "Thank you, Sebastian, I truly appreciate it."

He nods. "There is something else I must mention." He moves his gaze to me for a moment, then back to Mama. "Because of Katharina's past, I think the best approach for her is to start working at the factory. This way she can prove her devotion to the Reich and our Führer, and most of all—wash away all doubts the security services have. We want to ensure that the Gestapo agents don't disturb your peace."

"Of course," my mother says with the eagerness of a lost puppy, "she's ready to start immediately."

"When should I begin?" I ask, despising myself.

He gets up, brushing crumbs from his immaculate trousers. "I'm going to allow you some more time to settle but, Katharina, I would like to see you at the factory on the second day of August."

I only nod without meeting his eyes. The countdown on my freedom has begun. It's only a matter of days before I have to serve the people I hate.

THREE

FELEK: THE CHOCOLATE GIRL

August 1943, Gdańsk

"I apologize for interrupting your Sunday morning," I say to Pani Genowefa, an elderly Kashubian lady who busies herself with embroidery while I sip on some sort of herbal tea that tastes like the cod liver oil my mother made me drink when I was a boy. I'm here to meet with a key person from the Resistance, hoping to get the OK to go back to Warsaw.

"I'm glad to have you here. My husband is gone fishing at the Dead Vistula shore and I bet he won't be back until the evening."

"I like to fish too." This lady is easy going, and brave despite her casual demeanor. The Long Market is painfully swamped by Germans, and her tenement is in the midst of everything. Who would suspect this lady in her round spectacles and neckerchief, who doesn't hesitate to scream out her "love" for Hitler whenever she is out in the streets? I witnessed it firsthand. Though the fact that her husband, with whom she runs the amber jewelry store, is German is not without significance here.

At the sound of a ringing bell, she glances at her wristwatch and gets up. "Right on time."

When she's gone, I wonder if I should hide just in case it might be someone else. She seemed so sure that it's one of our people from *Armia Krajowa*, *AK*, the Polish Underground State and Home Army, but one cannot be sure about anything in this world of intrigue and collaboration. I walk into a tiny room with a wooden desk and bookshelves.

Soon she says, "You're clear, please come out, my boy."

To my astonishment, I'm greeted by a tall woman in her mid-thirties with curly brown hair; she's pretty but her face is somber.

"I will do some cleaning down there for tomorrow's opening," Pani Genowefa says and leaves.

"Let's get straight to the point as my time is valuable," the tall woman says in a dry voice and walks over to the sofa.

I follow suit and take a seat on the chair that I abandoned a few minutes earlier. "I expected someone from Warsaw," I say. After I recovered from being beaten by the German scumbags at the Gestapo Headquarters at Szucha Avenue in Warsaw, I received an order to come to Gdańsk for further instructions.

"I was just there and got orders." She leans back, her direct stare lacking warmth. "You're to stay here until we hear otherwise."

I curse under my breath. "There is so much to do there."

"It's too dangerous for you to go back, not after so many people risked their lives to get you out." Her monotonous voice is getting on my nerves.

I exhale long. "What's here for me?"

She narrows her eyes and tilts her head down before making eye contact. "What makes you think that Warsaw is the only place where the Resistance has its hands full?"

"I didn't mean it like that."

"Well, then going forward, be careful with your words."

"What about you? Can you relax a bit?"

She wiggles her eyebrows, and I swear her lips quirk for a second. "There is no time for relaxation, Felek. We've plenty to do here, so I can assure you that you will not be bored." Her tone isn't so coarse anymore.

"What's my assignment here?" I tell myself to stop being so critical of this woman; I must make the best out of the situation, here in Gdańsk. I must keep fighting for our freedom.

"You will be part of *Armia Krajowa*'s intelligence network here in the region of Pomerania. Of course, as we all know, *AK* is the dominant resistance movement in German-occupied Poland, but it needs to be open for help from other movements as well. So, here, we do cooperate with other groups, and the biggest of them is *Gryf Pomorski*. They've never united with *AK* but have proved to be useful when comes to collaborating against the Germans. I trust you will be, too, Felek." She waves a fly away and takes out a cigarette. "Do you smoke?"

I shake my head. I don't want to share anything of hers right now.

She lights the cigarette and takes a drag, before releasing clouds of smoke. "Don't get me wrong, intelligence will not be your only duty. We actively participate in different actions, whatever any given moment brings. Your first assignment is to contact Kasia. She's half Polish and half German but she's proved her devotion for us. She even had her part in saving your life."

"The chocolate courier from Warsaw?"

She nods. "Kasia recently moved from Warsaw because of her father's death. A German, he was respected by the Nazis here in Gdańsk, so she has opportunities to help us. We just need to start a collaboration with her."

She explains all the details and gives me Kasia's address. "Start immediately," she instructs. "See where she's at." She gets up. "Make sure to report tonight at the barn in Mirachowo village that I told you about. It's going to be your base now and I will meet you there." She reaches forward but before touching the door handle, she adds, "Felek, my code name is Zofia. You're to report to me just as you did to your leader in Warsaw."

After leaving Pani Genowefa's home, I head to Wrzeszcz's tidy streets of red-tiled houses, where Kasia lives. Not in a million years, did I expect to be seeing her again. There is something in her that brings on shyness in me, though I haven't exchanged a word with her so far. There was never an opportunity for it, as we always had separate assignments. But I do remember her well. She has a rare, independent beauty with those eyes and that mane of glossy hair: she isn't one to be easily forgotten.

Hidden behind a spruce, I watch a villa surrounded by a well-tended garden with bursts of colorful flowers, wondering if she will even emerge today. I will give her another hour before calling it a day as it's a long way to Mirachowo village. Before, I planned to spend the night in an abandoned shack not far from Motława River, but Zofia was clear on her instructions. She strikes me as someone who takes no nonsense.

A half an hour later, a blonde in a black dress leaves the villa and takes the tram to the city center. I follow her, tucking into a seat a few rows back from her.

I would recognize her anywhere from her gentle movements and the way she keeps her head up. Her long, wavy hair is loose, so different to the way other women keep their hairdos pinned into place or fashioned into some sort of a roll. She's natural and gorgeous, and just herself. I appreciate that quality in women very much.

The tram rattles to a stop, breaking my reverie. Kasia alights and I jump out the door before it shushes to a close behind me, afraid I'll lose her from my sight. For a second, I wonder how it would be to pull her into my embrace and feel her touch.

FOUR

KASIA: THE YELLOW STAR

August 1943, Gdańsk

I walk through cobblestone streets of the Long Lane, situated between the historical Golden Gate and the Green Gate in the city center. After entering the Long Market Square, the heart of Gdańsk, with ornate buildings like the Main Town Hall with its clock tower reaching the sky, I experience the strong sense of belonging to this city. If only this majestic place wasn't despoiled by swastikas...

The old tenements along the picturesque Motława now mostly serve as stores and cafés for German patrons. Since today is Sunday, the Nazi supporters are taking dinner, their laughter and loud conversations ringing out with all the look-at-me arrogance of the occupiers.

I've missed my city so much. I feel the thrill of being here, amid its warm bricks so full of history, but it pains me to see it this way, overrun by the Nazi ideology. This walk is forcing me to acknowledge my city's situation.

I enter Granary Island and eye the dirty-gray tenement called the Red Mouse granary. The Germans now use this old building as a ghetto for Gdańsk's Jewish population. That's all Mama told me, so I don't know any more details. Is there anyone still there, or was everyone already transported? I say a prayer in my mind and continue walking with soreness in my heart for the uncountable victims of Hitler's murderous regime. I can't begin to imagine the concentration camps they were sent to. Nothing makes sense in this world anymore.

As I cross the street and approach one of the side alleys, I pass a German soldier questioning a young, dark-haired woman in a chocolate-colored dress with a yellow star sewn into it, a little girl holding her hand.

"What the hell are you doing here?" the soldier shouts and sneers at her. "Today's order was to stay inside and wait for the transport. You might be on the list for deportation."

"I needed to get a few necessities for my daughter," the woman says in a shaky voice.

"I normally shoot parasites like you for treachery but I'm in a good mood today, so I will let you go back to your filthy quarters. Looks like we will get rid of you soon enough for once and for good." He spits horribly to the ground. "You don't deserve to live, Jewish slut."

The woman bites her lip, her eyes cast down.

It's obvious she dreads coming back to the ghetto. She must know she's on the list of people about to be transported to one of the German camps. My heart goes out to her, so without thinking, I turn back and approach the soldier.

"Hello, officer," I say in a crisp German and bat my lashes at him. "I'm so happy I found you." My mouth folds in a provocative smile. "I'm visiting my brother who works in the Gestapo Headquarters, and I seem to have got lost." I titter like a fool. "Would you be able to escort me back home? My brother will be generous when rewarding you." I treat him with a prolonged eye contact. "And so will I, as well." If I take his attention and walk away with him, then the woman will not have to go back to the ghetto. Though I will have to figure out what to do once he brings me to where I'm asking him to. And, to be honest, I don't know where she will go with her child, the yellow stars so incriminating on their shabby clothes.

He nods slightly while grinning and leaning forward. "Let me make sure these parasites go back to their quarters, and then I will be delighted to fulfill my duties and escort you, beautiful girl."

His eagerness and the odor of rotten eggs from his mouth cause nausea that grips my stomach muscles. What a vile piece of work.

But just when I'm about to think of another quirky response, the butt of a pistol appears as if from nowhere, gripped in a strong hand, and strikes the soldier on the back of his head with a sickening *crack*.

The woman gasps and the little girl cries, while my muscles go numb.

"Quick," the stranger shouts at us in Polish. "Let's continue along the alley before the *Szwaby* come here." He takes the little girl into his strong arms and urges the woman to follow him.

Not sure what else to do and not wanting to be found near the passed-out German soldier, I follow them as we all half-jog through a maze of narrow back streets, keeping close to the city's darker shadows.

In a quarter of an hour or so, the man draws our strange formation to a halt and ushers us into an almost derelict wooden shack at the less known, hidden part of the Motława shore. There is no one inside and we huddle together, catching our breath. Strong smells of mold and dust almost make me choke.

"Thank you for saving us. I knew we were assigned for today's transport, so I tried to run away when the soldier caught me," the woman says to him. She takes her daughter from his arms, then turns to me, "And to you too, my sweet friend."

"It's not much I did," I say feeling like I shouldn't even be here.

"Hello," the man says with a faint smile.

For the first time, I look up to his face and instinctively scold myself for not recognizing him right away. *Felek.*

"I didn't realize it was you," I say. "Everything happened so fast." But the truth is that we know each other only by sight. Back in Warsaw, we both belonged to the same resistance group, but we never had a chance to speak to each other. Not until now. "It's so good to see you're doing well."

His gray eyes take me in while he nods, a thick scar marks the left side of his forehead. "If not for you and others, I would be dead a long time now." His gaze is somber but also soft. "Thank you for what you did for me."

"I'm sorry you had to go through that hell." The faded bruises on his face tug on my heart.

I can still picture him lying motionless in a puddle of blood in one of the interrogation rooms of the Gestapo Headquarters in Warsaw. The image transports me back to that exact moment.

I'd been doing my deliveries of chocolate to that dreadful flat-fronted building with its rows of barred windows when I overheard what time the next lorry would take Felek to the terrifying Pawiak Prison, where so many were executed, tortured to death, or simply held in unimaginable conditions. I made a phone call and let the Resistance know, just as we agreed before. They waited for the lorry and ambushed it before it got to the Pawiak. And that was how Felek and others in the transport were freed. If he'd stayed in their clutches any longer, he wouldn't have survived without supplying Gestapo agents with the information that they wanted from him. I'd heard that he'd been sent out of Warsaw for recovery, but I had no idea he was here.

"Listen," he says, snapping me out of my memories. My

eyes meet his and I feel sure he's thinking of that day too. "It's best that you leave now and walk with your chin up, like all of this never happened. I will take this good lady and her little daughter to a safe house not far from here. I promise." For a moment longer, his eyes linger on my lips causing a fluttering in my stomach.

Feeling distracted by his open affection and softness, I manage to say, "Are you sure I can't help more?" I move my gaze to the girl with black eyes who now clings to her mother.

But his answer doesn't change, so I leave the broken-down shed and walk the streets back into the heart of the city, as he suggested, hoping he will indeed take them to safety. At the same time, I wonder at this unspoken connection between us that could be felt in the air.

Will I ever see him again? I shouldn't care. I'm glad I was able to help save his life. Now he helps others in return. That's all that matters.

FIVE

KASIA: A SIGN IN GOLD LETTERING

August 1943, Gdańsk

When I report to Papa's former factory, I can't believe my eyes. Engraved in gold lettering into the façade of the three-story tenement with its rectangular windows, the word shines in the sun as if there is no war. Papa renamed his factory shortly after I was born.

That sign, my name—"Katharina"—is still there.

It's hard to make sense of my feelings as I look at it: the German me, here on this old building in Gdańsk. How is it even possible that Papa didn't change it after our estrangement, or when the two factories merged? I almost smile at the irony of it all; no doubt Sebastian plans to take the sign down soon.

It's painful to set foot in this courtyard that once brimmed with life. Now, the Nazi emblems flutter in the wind while I lurch forward. Just when I'm about to enter the factory's main building, the door swings open revealing a man in the dungarees of a worker. He's carrying a large sack, probably filled with cocoa beans.

I instantly recognize Pan Alojzy, our faithful old watchman

whose duties were to clean the courtyard, transfer goods from the warehouse to dispatch, and carry coal in the winter.

"Hello, Pan Alojzy," I speak in a soft tone. When I was little and Mama took me for visits at the factory, this kind man often played with me and let me eat offcut or misshapen caramels when Mama wasn't around.

He gapes at me for a moment then chuckles, and after gazing around, he says, "Good to see you, young lady." He leans forward and whispers, "Be careful as you never know who'll turn to be a snake. Your father was a decent man, God rest his soul."

My brows knit, puzzled. Why would he say this? I'm sure he knows about Papa's connections with the Nazis. I don't have a chance to respond because the moment I open my mouth, Sebastian's warning voice sounds out from the back: "Alojzy, your assistance is needed in the warehouse."

While Pan Alojzy bolts away without another word, I get a strong desire to turn and flee, far from this intimidating man. But I brace myself to look up as he nears me. My skin prickles with alarm.

"I've been expecting you," he says, his eyes narrowing as he searches my face.

"Hello." I curse myself inwardly, unable to control my lower lip from quivering. It always happens when I'm nervous or distressed.

I'm sure he notices it because a thin smile edges his lips, but he steps aside and says, "Please, come in."

We walk through a corridor and turn left to Papa's offices, obviously now occupied by Sebastian. When we enter, a blonde secretary stops typing and jerks her head up, doing a double take at me. The air brims with the aroma of fresh coffee.

"Bertha, please make sure that no one disturbs us," Sebastian instructs and moves toward the room that adjoins my father's.

I get this sudden need to run into Papa's old office where he always sat at his polished, leather-topped desk and embrace him, breathe in the wool scent of his suit and listen to the ticking of the big clock on the wall, just like when I was a little girl. Except, Papa is not there now. My heart swells with pain but I follow the man into a tiny room where I used to play with my dolls while Mama helped Papa. Now the place smells of caramel, the burned sweetness mixing with that of fruits and flowers. He must be experimenting with different cocoa beans just like Papa used to do.

I settle on a chair across from his desk while he takes a seat in a leather armchair. His desk is neat with only a black telephone handset and some documents neatly stacked to the side; Papa's desk was always a chaos with documents and samples of various cocoa beans strewn all over it. The wall frame holds Hitler's photograph, I realize with a shudder.

"It's good to have you here," he says, his face unreadable. "I think it's best that you use your father's office as your own now."

I feel like I have a heavy rope knot in my stomach. "I don't understand," I say and meet and hold his eyes. "My father's office doubles this one in size, so why wouldn't you take it for yourself?" Is he playing some sort of twisted games with me and checking my reaction?

"I got used to this room, besides I didn't want to touch Dietrich's things. Everything you find there, it's how he left it. You see, I respected your father very much. He taught me a lot about the chocolate business."

"Well, I don't know what to say." This man surprises me more every minute.

He smiles. "A simple thank you will do."

"Thank you then," I say and sigh. "It's going to be strange being back in his office when he's not there. As a girl I always liked the smell in there..." I pause and take my surroundings in. "Just like the one that is now in this room."

He nods in understanding. "Right to the end, he was busy testing different beans and discovering new flavors. He always said that if you don't like how a new type of chocolate tastes, you shouldn't be selling it to customers."

"True. He enjoyed his work," I say, realizing how inadequate that sounded, but also how important.

"When the war started, we were faced with many changes, many challenges. We were forbidden from selling chocolate to civilians, instead we had to focus on manufacturing our products for the use of the Wehrmacht and Luftwaffe. So that's what we do here now. We also perform small deliveries to the Gestapo and SS headquarters." He gives me a meaningful look. "Now you will take over that department. The two girls your father employed will report directly to you. You may want to consider making some deliveries yourself, especially as you have experience of doing it for the chocolate factory in Warsaw. Getting around like this should help you to build your reputation as Dietrich's daughter and as a worthy server of the Third Reich."

I nod, holding his gaze. "I will be happy to do so." I keep my face neutral, but inside I'm excited. This role will create perfect opportunities for me to access information for the Polish Resistance, just like in Warsaw. So, I must convince Sebastian that I'm a perfect German woman, a perfect chocolate delivery girl.

I detect a hint of approval in his eyes. "We must keep good relationships with the right people as those connections will assure that we stay up and running. Businesses are being shut down daily because the focus is on the shipyards." For a minute longer he remains silent while turning over a pen in his hands, like his mind has escaped to a different world. "There is no one more suited for this task than Dietrich's daughter."

I almost flinch in disgust at how he envisions me. The fact that he chooses to please these criminals, to indulge their sweet tooth just to stay in business, appalls me. Shame threatens to engulf me as I realize that Papa did the same, however complicated his motivations might have been.

"Do you remember the three rules your father cultivated?" Sebastian says, jolting me away from my thoughts.

"Cleanliness, discipline, diplomacy," I recite.

A ghost of a smile brushes his mouth. "Precisely. These are the most important commands we exercise here."

"So, do the same rules apply in your own factory?" I ask, unable to remove the irritation from my voice. He keeps boasting about my father and now about his rules, but what if I don't want to hear about it? Can't he come up with something that is his own?

He wrinkles his nose with obvious disapproval at my tone. "I believe in learning from the ones who are most experienced and take the best from them, it's why you will see your father's touch in here. But I also go strongly by my own judgment and implement my own innovations. When I take you on the walk around the factory, you will see lots of new machines and the production process organized in a different order than before. Once we merged in 1938, I sold my business and invested in new machinery for this factory."

"I'm sorry, I didn't mean to question your decisions," I say, avoiding his gaze now. His mind is sharper than I thought.

He stands up. "Let me show you around."

On the way out of his office, I spot a little electric oven for roasting grains, just like the one my father always kept in his office. Not far from it, there is a table with small batches of cocoa beans. He must be working on his own recipes.

"Do you still have a large choice of cocoa beans?" I ask and turn back to face him.

"Because of the war, we only have a few at our disposal right now."

"Arriba?" Papa especially valued this type of cocoa bean for its intense flavor.

"Yes. The other two are Accra and Jawa. Hopefully once the war ends, we will be back to more choices."

I nod, screwing up my courage. "And what's the actual name of the business now?" I ask. "I see the old sign is still there."

The moment I say it, I feel his eyes searching my face. "What makes you think that the name has changed?"

"But why wouldn't it?"

He gives me a meaningful look that causes my heart to lurch. "Because," he smiles, lifting a cocoa bean to his aquiline nose and inhaling its scent, "it's already quite perfect, my Katharina."

SIX

FELEK: THE LITTLE SABOTAGE

August 1943, Mirachowskie Forest

Shortly before midnight Zofia points out a bunker amid a dense forest dominated by spruce and birch. We'd met as planned in the barn in Mirachowo, then scrambled our way here through the darkness of the countryside.

The smell inside the tiny fortification consists of dry wood and smoke, with dense whiffs of earth. Zofia turns on an oil lamp that hangs from the ceiling. The walls are made of wooden beams and one half of the space is taken up by two rough bunk beds fashioned from planks. A table with a typewriter occupies the other half, while a detailed map of Pomerania covers one of the walls.

"Cozy here," I say and lie down on a lower bed, the straw mattress crackling beneath me.

"That bed is already taken. The top one is yours," she says and without another glance my way, she starts typing.

I clamber up onto the top bunk, my body close to the uneven ceiling. I eye the other wall. There's a small metal cross and the Polish national emblem: an outspread white eagle on a red background. My father's words come to my mind: *Bóg—Honor—Ojczyzna—Rodzina.* God—Honor—Homeland—Family. The four values that mean everything to my Ojciec. He raised me to believe in those too. Polishness means our national pride and great love for traditions. Polishness is a force of survival even in the worst of times. My Matka always supported Ojciec in his views, but when I joined the *AK*, she couldn't stop her tears for days.

At the thought of Matka, my mind drifts back to my carefree childhood years. My family wasn't rich, but still we always had enough food on our table. While Ojciec was always reluctant to show his feelings, Matka was generous with kisses, hugs, and kind-hearted words. Through my childhood she loved singing me lullabies or telling me bedtime stories, even though I'd ask her to scare me witless with Baba Yaga again and again. I was spoiled rotten by my three older sisters who delighted in taking me on their adventures into the city. I grew to love Warsaw and often took it for granted, until the sound of German boots woke me from my idyllic life.

"Don't get so comfortable," Zofia says and shakes her head at my daydreamy expression. "Get ready as I have a mission for you."

"It's the middle of the night," I say, unable to hide my disbelief.

"There is no better time for action than now." She smirks and in the dim light of the lamp she looks wickedly mysterious.

And so, an hour later I'm on my way, walking through the forest and along deserted pathways, to a local train station to collect materials gathered by a railway worker who belongs to the Resistance. Before I set off, Zofia explained that railroaders help by providing information regarding rail transport, so the partisans' actions to destroy tracks or derail trains are more powerful. They also transfer our emissaries, reports, orders and even underground gazettes, like the *Głos Serca Polskiego*: *The Voice of the Polish Heart*.

The small station is bathed in darkness and silence when I get there; for a moment I wonder if there is even anyone here. I'm walking around with my flashlight on when I detect rustling noises near a resting train.

I turn off the flashlight and slip toward it. In the light of moon, a man in dark clothing and a railman's hat sets down a canvas bag filled with something, then unties a string on top of it.

I clear my throat and quickly say the coded password that Zofia gave me: "Bats enjoy eating termites at nighttime."

He straightens and for a short moment remains still, but soon says, "They also favor birds and lizards, but only sometimes."

"Zofia sends me," I say, when he turns my way.

"I've been waiting for you." He reaches under his thin jacket and fishes out a small bundle of paper.

I take it and hide it in the inner pocket of my blazer. "*Serwus*," I say. "Bye." I'm about to walk away when his voice stops me.

"Are you in a rush? Because if not, I could use a hand here."

I turn back to face him and motion to the bag on the ground. "Sure. What are you up to, good man?"

"Call me Piotr, will you?" Without waiting for my answer, he whispers, "This train is scheduled to depart in the morning, but I'm about to spoil it by pouring sand into the oil near the wheels."

We get busy with this task in the silence of the night, working alongside each other in that agreeable atmosphere of shared purpose, and when we're done, we move to changing the address stickers on wagons. It's such satisfaction knowing that our prank will cause confusion for the Germans. My fingers and knees are aching as the last one is swapped over. Piotr shakes my hand, his grip strong and a little tacky from the glue, then he pats me on the back as I stumble off toward the forest.

By the time I'm back in the bunker, it's almost three o clock. It's still dark, the dead of the night. Zofia appears to be asleep, so I climb to the upper bunk in hopes of getting some shut eye too.

"How was it?" her sluggish voice sounds out.

I yawn, unable to keep my eyes open, slowly drifting away. "I got the documents."

"It's impressive how well you navigate in these woods."

"I have good orientation in the wild," I tell her, my voice blurring. "I guess thanks to scouting that I did as a boy." I don't tell her I got lost on the way to the rail station and on the way back.

"Excellent. You are courageous, but for the sake of your family, you must be careful."

"We all balance with our safety every day, but these are the rules of the war," I say bluntly, for it's the truth. "Someone has to fight, so that we gain our freedom back."

She sighs. "You remind me of my husband. He was murdered in Stutthof camp. We were married only for two years."

"I'm sorry," I say.

"I've already cried away all my tears. Now I only fight this senseless regime that took my Jerzy away from me."

"I'm sure he's proud of you." Since the start of this damn occupation, I've faced death almost daily. My exhaustion seems to vanish, or perhaps it's what makes me want to talk. "I thought that my time came to an end when I was tortured by the Gestapo. I lay in a puddle of my own blood, and this girl Kasia stood in the adjoining room convincing my torturers to buy chocolate. The door between the rooms was open, so for one short moment her eyes found mine and within seconds she challenged me to be stronger. It's when I got hope, and I thought that even if I die, I'm thankful for what she managed to give me so briefly. She was like a ray of sun in the hell."

"The way you're talking about her is touching."

"What I'm trying to say is that life is unpredictable, and, in a blink, everything might change. Maybe there is a deeper meaning in your husband's passing, maybe God needs him over there, while you aren't still done here."

Zofia sighs and I wonder if I've stepped too far into her personal territory. "You see," she says, "the thing is that I don't want to go on living without my husband anymore. My life isn't important because I want to join him wherever he is, though I don't have enough bravery to end my misery."

We both lie in the silence of the bunker for a moment, the rhythm of our breath evening out in sync with each other.

"I will never forget what my grandma told my aunt when my uncle died," I say at last. "The Germans took him into Palmiry Forest and shot him just because he was a professor at the University of Warsaw. The message of her words stuck with me to this day, even though it was four years ago."

"I'm sorry to hear about your uncle," she says and after another minute passes, she adds, "I'm curious to hear what your grandma said."

"I may not remember her exact words, but it was like this: The pain in your heart is the proof of your love for him. You must trust that your souls will reunite when you meet again. Love doesn't cease to exist, unlike material things or everything else. True love shines through eternity. In the end, it's all that counts."

I hear a sob catch in Zofia's throat and some instinct makes me lean my arm over the edge of the bunk, where my hand meets hers. Our fingers brush, curl round each other for a moment and then pull apart.

SEVEN

KASIA: TWO SISTERS

August 1943, Gdańsk

The familiar chocolate smell, warm and rich, mixed with vanilla and oils fills the air. I close my eyes for a few seconds and inhale deeply, transported to a different time. Only for a moment.

I'm in a large hall with machinery where women and some miserable-looking men are moving swiftly in their white aprons. For a moment longer, I watch workers grinding chocolate beans into a smooth paste, which then will go through other processes like rolling. Many chocolate-making steps, while requiring the attention of human hands, benefit from the use of special machines.

"Here is the kingdom of our chocolate bar," Sebastian says, ushering me forward. "We've had to drop hard candy and production of other confectionary as we have a demand from the Wehrmacht and Luftwaffe specifically for chocolate bars."

"Do you still make a stuffed chocolate?"

"Not at the moment," he says, "though I'm planning to go back to caramel stuffed soon."

The atmosphere in this room is so different than the one

from before the war. I remember people chatting and laughing, but now they are serious and don't glance our way, like we are invisible. There are so many new machines here, unknown to me—probably the ones that he bought after selling his own factory.

"I don't see any familiar faces," I say.

"Many people left the city at the start of the war, so we had to hire new staff."

Left or were forced to leave, dragged from their homes and sent to the camps, or driven into the forest and murdered? I want to shout this in his placid face, but it would be a fatal mistake to do, so I only nod.

He takes me to the next floor where the cocoa roasting process has its place after the sorting step when things like little sticks, stones or insects are removed from chocolate beans.

The roasting here is performed in a rotating drum known as a Sirocco-type batch roaster. The hot air is being blown through the beans for around two hours. Papa favored this way over a different method of oven roasting, though the other one is often used as well. I basically spent my childhood in this factory, so every aspect here is very familiar to me.

When the roasting is done right, it brings out the distinctive chocolate aroma in cocoa beans. Lighter roasted beans taste more fruity, even citrusy, while darker ones have a more bitter flavor. In fact, the strong smell from the raw cacao beans has been always my favorite.

"In this room," he tells me, matter-of-factly, "we employ some of the French prisoners from the camp in Bischofsberg hill who were assigned to work at our factory."

Of course, Sebastian takes advantage of and "employs" the POWs from that camp as free labor. I would not expect anything better from him. At the same time, I reason, it's better for these men to work here than in murderous labor camps like the one in Stutthof out east, in marshy woodland where conditions are at best primitive.

The wrapping room is situated on the third floor where women in white head coverings work, cowed, at the long tables. Once more, they are all very serious and don't even peek at us when we walk around. They used to be so chatty and full of good humor. Are they afraid of Sebastian? Is he very strict? I guess time will show; for now, I need to focus on my own tasks here.

When Sebastian is done showing me the factory, I head back to my father's office. The air is stagnant, so I open the window facing the courtyard where Pan Alojzy is busy sweeping dirt from the walkway.

I slip into Papa's chair and eye the clutter on his desk. Old and new recipes written in his inky scrawl in his notebook, samples of cocoa beans... I close my eyes and picture my father chewing on roasted beans or preparing new types of chocolate mixtures. He always said that I have a good palate, so he would bring home new samples for tasting and I would give him my opinion on their flavors and textures.

I would give everything to go back to those times, when we were a normal family. Just like in the photo that is displayed on Papa's desk where the four of us stand at the beach. I remember the day well; it was before I learned my father's sinister plan regarding my future.

A knock on the door brings me back to reality. "Please, come in," I say and sit straight in Papa's chair.

Sebastian escorts two young, pretty girls in white aprons and headscarves into the room. They keep their gazes down. "I would like to introduce Malina and Alina to you," he says. "Both are experienced workers in Dietrich's delivery department and are available for your instructions. I will leave you ladies alone."

As he marches out of the office, I say, "It's nice to meet you."

I point to the two chairs in front of Papa's desk. "Please take a seat."

They obey and quietly settle in the chairs. It strikes me how skinny they both are.

"Are you sisters?" I continue speaking in German even though the girls are Polish. A few minutes ago, I was able to hear Sebastian's phone conversation while he was in his office, so I'm aware that the walls are very thin here.

"Yes, only a year apart," Malina, the taller girl with freckles says, still without meeting my eyes.

"But people think we are twins," Alina chats on, "though Malina is taller and already eighteen."

Malina elbows her sister. "Shush, Alina. The lady doesn't need to know all of this."

I chuckle. "That's okay, you're safe to talk freely here. And please call me Katharina." I can see why Papa chose these two girls for deliveries to German officers. They speak perfect German, have Aryan looks and are bold.

Alina jumps up. "You see, I told you she's nice."

But Malina wrinkles her nose. "Please forgive my sister as she's a scatterbrain sometimes." In this very moment our eyes meet, and I detect a trace of warmth in there. I know I will grow to like both girls, I just sense it.

"Well, I hope that our work together will go smoothly. Have you made any deliveries since..." I find it difficult to utter the words, but I clear my throat and continue, "Since my father's passing?"

Malina treats me with a sympathetic look. "As per Herr Richter, we were to wait for instructions."

I nod. "Did my father have a certain schedule for deliveries?"

"Yes, he kept it in his drawer," Alina says with such energy that it earns her another nudge from her sister.

I have a hard time suppressing my laughter but when I open

the drawer, I fish out a folder with schedules. It seems like both girls had specific days and locations assigned. Since they are Polish, I allow myself to think, maybe at some point they will cooperate with me in gaining important information for the Resistance on their delivery runs. But first I must get to know them well enough to determine if I can trust them. Some people are excellent actors, and as far as I know these girls might be working for Abwehr or Gestapo. Though I don't think that's the case.

"Very well then. I will look through it and write up a new schedule and share it with you tomorrow," I say, leaning back in my chair. "What departments do you work in when you don't do deliveries?"

"We work in the wrapping room," Malina says but she can't elaborate any more as a heavy knock on the door makes both girls jump in their seats while I drop a pen from my grasp.

A middle-aged man in a gray-green SS uniform and with a pencil mustache charges in and spreads his arms with ostentatious drama. "Katharina, I couldn't wait any longer to finally meet you."

My skin tingles with discomfort. Who's this man? I don't even know him. I gain my composure quickly and realize how fortunate it is that the girls still face me because their eyes reflect pure terror.

"You can leave," I say softly to them and stand up to greet the intruder, while the two sisters slip away without a word or another glance.

"Hello, sir. It's a pleasure to be meeting such a grand officer in this modest office."

He chuckles then proceeds to kiss my hand. It's all I can do not to wipe it on the handkerchief in my pocket. "It's all my pleasure. I'm Bruno, your father's faithful friend."

"I see you've already met Dietrich's daughter," Sebastian's voice rings out from the back, making me swallow with relief.

At least I will not have to deal with that man on my own. I don't have a good feeling about him.

"Yes, yes, and she's as beautiful and sweet as you had told me, my friend."

Heat rushes to my cheeks and I avoid Sebastian's gaze. I wonder if he truly thinks that about me. After what happened all those years back, I would assume otherwise. At least when it comes to me being "sweet".

"Slow down, my friend," Sebastian says and claps at Bruno's shoulder in an extravagant gesture of bonhomie, "before I tell Ilse that you have hot eyes for this lovely young woman." They both chuckle.

"Well, I'm glad I finally met you. Please accept my deepest condolences on the passing of your father. He was one of us and we are here for you whenever you need us."

"Thank you," I say with a gentle smile, but I wish I could throw something at this fake man.

Sebastian declares he has a business matter to discuss, and the two leave Papa's office. I try listening to their conversation through the wall, but they speak in such low voices that I can't make out much. But after pressing my ear against a wall, I do catch on words like the "chocolate bombs" or "sabotage". I make a mental note to mention it to the Polish Resistance.

After working on a new calendar for deliveries, I decide to call it a day at five o'clock.

Just as I leave the office and enter the corridor, I bump into Sebastian who must be returning from the factory.

"I'm sorry," I say, "I didn't see you coming."

"It's all my fault as I should have slowed down," he says, displaying his perfect teeth. "I was actually going to ask you to an early dinner at the nearby café, so we can discuss all the details in regard to your employment at the factory."

I bite my lip, wondering how to get out of this. "I'm not sure if I should. Mutti will worry."

He takes my hand in his and brings it to his lips, his blue eyes sparkling with admiration. "I've already sent word to her, so we're all good, of course, if that's fine with you."

His touch sends tingles up my hand, making me shiver from tantalizing pleasure.

"Yes, that's fine," I say, avoiding his gaze, afraid he could realize the effect his touch has on me. At the same time, I feel myself turn pale as dread hurtles back toward me, enveloping me.

"Please be assured that you have nothing to worry about. I will give you a ride home once we are done," he says, briskly, as if sensing my unease. "There are topics that we should discuss, and the quicker we do it, the better. Plus, I promise that you will enjoy the café and excellent food."

"I look forward to it," I say returning his smile as we walk out of the factory, beneath the sign with my German name in gold and through the tall gates. There is something irresistible about his gentle approach and his good looks.

EIGHT

KASIA: A SQUARE OF PAPER

August 1943, Gdańsk

True to his words, Sebastian drives me home straight after dinner. I feel a little disappointed as I hoped he would take me for a walk at the beach. I crave the sound of the sea and waves crashing on the shore.

After today and our dinner together, I find myself more comfortable near him. It makes me wonder how my life would have turned out if I'd stayed all these years back and married him. Could I have impacted his beliefs, his values, now so deeply invested into the Nazi ideology?

Through the whole conversation he focused on my employment at the factory. In addition to running the delivery department, he wants me to work on new recipes. He admitted to simply not enjoying that aspect of his duties and is pleased to leave it in my hands, since it was always Papa's thing. His reason is that once the war ends, we need to be prepared to take the market over with new products. Right now, the factory manufactures the simplest chocolate possible due to the war, the limitations on ingredients and the fact that our main consumers are soldiers, whose tastes seem to be no more sophisticated than those of children.

Now, I sit beside him as he drives his black Mercedes through the roads of Gdańsk.

"How does it feel to be back in Danzig again?" he asks without a hint of the formality he used when explaining my duties.

I take another whiff of air rich with leather scent. "Lonely," I say without thinking. I shouldn't be so honest with him. But that's the truth—I feel lonely to be back in my childhood city, which is now transformed into the fortress of evil. Just a glimpse of their uniforms brings a surge of anger in me. But I don't say as much to him because he's one of them.

For a moment longer he doesn't react, but then his voice is so quiet that something in me freezes. "You're not alone."

I don't know how to interpret his words, so I change the subject. "I think we will be under the blackout hours soon. Will you be okay driving back home?" After dark, it's extremely hard to navigate in the city as the streets are not lit. Streetlamps are painted blue or covered, and the windows of the houses and trams are darkened with newspapers or curtains, bands are placed on car headlights. The only glimpse of brightness comes from the fact that the streetlight poles and curbs are painted in white, so they are more visible. Because of the shroud of darkness crime has increased, and shop lootings happen daily. Accidents are more common as well, so most people stay in the safety of their homes.

"I live right next door from you," he says in a quiet voice, his gaze on the road.

My mouth falls open at this revelation. "No, you don't. I've never seen you there." Then I recall a black Mercedes parked beside the old property that used to belong to the Borinsky family.

He chuckles. "If you need a pair of glasses, I know just the place to get it."

I nudge his arm but can't suppress my laughter, while still in shock at this news.

∾

"Are you hungry, darling?" Mama says when I walk into the family room. She takes her glasses off while Kornel runs into my arms.

"Please don't get up, Mama," I say. "I ate enough at the café." She knows full well I went there with Sebastian.

"I will make some tea then and you will tell me all about your day." She shuffles toward the kitchen.

"I have something for you," my brother says and winks at me. "I hid it in my room, so it's safe."

"Hmm... What that can be?" I say and narrow my eyes like I'm deep in thought. Kornel loves to collect shells from the Baltic shore, so he probably found something special while out with Mama today.

He gives me a mischievous grin. "You will see."

I drop to the chair, arms cradling my head on table. I dream of nothing more than to wash myself and curl up on my bed. It's been a draining day. But I know Mama wants to hear about it.

Soon she walks over with two steaming cups and sets one before me. "How was it, sweetie?" Her gaze takes me in.

"It was fine. Sebastian explained my duties to me and showed me the factory."

She sighs. "It's not the same place anymore, I know, but once the war ends, we will get it back on track. People will look forward again to our special launches each Christmas and Easter. They will feel safe and protected, and we will all live in the normal world..." Her voice drifts away while despair settles in her features. I can tell she struggles to believe in her own words.

"Now its only role is to serve our oppressors," I say, feeling weakness in my muscles, the sensation so familiar to me whenever I'm overwhelmed.

"It's not like we can do anything about it." She stares down at her hands. "But it will all pass one day."

I admire her optimism, especially since the Mama I remember was almost always somber, seeking out the negative aspects of things. Now she tells me daily that the war must end one day, and our lives will get back to normal. I guess it's her way of coping with what's happening around us. Though she doesn't realize how peaceful her life is here, where she is able to tend her garden and look after Kornel. Every day she tries to block out any horror stories, just to give my brother at least a sliver of normalcy.

If my mother lived in the reality of Warsaw and the daily *łapanki*, rounding up anyone the Germans find in the streets, then she would truly understand how dangerous the capital is. She never had Ciocia Lucyna's strength or resilience, so maybe it's better that she's here, after all.

"I'm finding hard to understand why Sebastian decided to stay in the tiny office while he wants me to take Papa's."

Mama's fingers touch her parted lips. "That's a surprise, indeed. And humble of him." She thinks for a moment. "Your father was very generous and taught him all his secrets when it comes to the running of a successful chocolate factory. Sebastian only managed his business for a few years before merging with ours. Maybe it's his way of showing thankfulness to our family. It's not like he can do more for us."

"That's possible." Why, then, don't I fully trust him? Maybe because he makes no secret of the fact that he stands strong with his Führer. *And,* a voice murmurs in my head, *because of the past,* your *past, too.*

"He treated your father like his mentor," Mama continues and sighs. "It hasn't been easy for him. His parents and sister moved out of Gdańsk in '36 when his father took on another position in Berlin thanks to his brother's connections."

"Why didn't he go with them?" It's not like it's any of my business but Mama volunteers all this information on her own. Besides, since he's my employer now, it doesn't hurt to know more about him.

"Some people don't like big changes. Sebastian was born and raised in this city where he would like to start his own family one day." She gives me a meaningful look.

Does she expect me to get involved with him, just like Papa wanted me to all those years ago? Well, I will not be falling for the Nazi sympathizer, regardless of my obvious attraction or pull toward him.

"A couple of months after he merged his business with ours, he bought the house from the Borinsky family who moved to the Land of Israel, and he's lived there since. He's a good neighbor, but I'm sure you've already noticed that."

"I only found out today from Sebastian," I say, still in disbelief. It's where Ruth, my childhood friend, used to live. "How absurd that I've never seen him since I got back from Warsaw. I knew that Ruth and her family emigrated, but I didn't realize that Sebastian owns the house now."

"I'm sorry, I thought you were aware," she says and looks at me in an apologetic way. "Don't beat yourself up for it as we've been going through tough times."

"I must be more alert of our surroundings," I say more to myself than to Mama. At least he's not one of those that stole Jewish or Polish properties. He bought it before even the war started and that speaks volumes. If only he wasn't doing everything else in his power to please Hitler's followers.

After I answer all Mama's other questions about my day, I sip on my chamomile tea while she reads *Danzige von Posten*. I don't know why she keeps buying this propaganda gazette, but she says that it's better to get news from the enemy, than no news at all. According to her, it's mostly lies.

"Listen to this," she says not taking her eyes off the page. "The Polish man sentenced to death for listening to forbidden radio broadcasts."

"Poor man. Losing the privilege to live because of their stupid rules. They're cruel bastards." I grind my teeth.

She arches her brow. "Watch your words, young lady. But yes, you're right. Poor man."

I shudder to think of it, but everyone who lives in Gdańsk knows to avoid the *Sondergericht Danzig*, at all costs. Most of the time, the judges at this special court sentence Poles for the most trivial reasons, or even no reason at all. Besides listening to the forbidden radio broadcasts, there are other inoffensive acts that can doom Poles, like helping Jews or POWs, possession of a weapon even if it's an old blunderbuss from the past century, or meat production in the home or elsewhere, even if you have a smallholding and keep chickens.

Later, when I go to say good night to my brother, he whispers, "Do you remember that I have something for you?" He's already in his pajamas sitting on top of his comforter, a book in his hand.

I cup my elbow with one hand while tapping my lips with the other. "Hmm... What can that be?" I play along again, enjoying the game as much as him.

"I will give it to you now but make sure not to tell Mama because she's not going to like it," he whispers and reaches under his pillow. "The man gave this to me." There in his hand is a tiny scrap of paper folded into a square.

My stomach suddenly feels rock hard. "What man?"

"He was young and had a friendly face and knew that I'm your brother. I had to promise him that I would show it only to you."

I try to shake off the dreadful feeling that has crept into my stomach. I gently take the paper from him and read the coded note, which states a date, time and place for a meeting. The Resistance can't find a better way of contacting me than through my little brother?

"Let's keep this as our secret," I say and kiss his forehead. I will do everything to make sure he's safe. My involvement in the Resistance cannot affect my family. I will make that clear as soon as I meet the man.

"I know. It's why I didn't show it to Mama. She would be worrying." His blue eyes twinkle. "That man was Polish. I think he is from *AK*. Are you an underground fighter for Poland too?"

I go completely still. How does my little brother know about *Armia Krajowa*? "Of course not. He's just my friend from Warsaw."

He rolls his eyes. "I know more than you think, big sis. And I hate Adolf Hitler for what he did to my friends. They can't go to school with us anymore. Romek lives in a cellar with his family, and I don't know what happened to Ira."

"I know it's hard to understand it," I say, trying to find the right words. "Let's just hope that it all will change soon, and your friends will be back at school with you again." I hate myself for sounding like my mother.

He leans forward and whispers, "Romek's dad is a Resistance fighter and lives in the forest. But this is a secret too. A big one. I swore to Romek not to tell anyone beside you."

"Why beside me?" My brother surprises me more and more.

"Because I told him that you were fighting Nazis in Warsaw, and he respects you for it. And don't worry, he swore not to tell anyone."

"You both need to not talk about it anymore," I say and wink at him. "Remember that even walls have ears."

He winks back. "But you can tell me my story now?"

"I'd love to, sunshine." Since my arrival here, I've got into the habit of telling my brother a bedtime tale. It's good to have my family back, but most of all, it's heartwarming to see that my little brother hasn't been entirely brainwashed by the propaganda that they serve in schools. Whatever Mama has been doing, works.

When I'm back in my room, I can't help but look through my window, which faces the Borinskys' old home, and now Sebastian's. So, he is the one that plays piano in the evenings.

Tonight is no exception and soon I listen to Beethoven's "Moonlight Sonata". His skillful fingers bring me into a fantasy world of romance, to beauty and depth. Every time I listen to it, I think of Beethoven's unrequited love to Giulietta. The composition aches with loneliness, sadness and anguish, thanks to Sebastian's superb performance.

Does he think of me when he plays it, just like I think of him as I listen? I can't help but like him more each day.

NINE

FELEK: BREAD AND LARD

August 1943, Mirachowskie Forest

As days go by, Zofia's words about the amount of work here prove to be correct. And as a newcomer figuring out the area and locations is still at times confusing, an extra layer of work. We cooperate with other organizations here, like *Gryf Pomorski* whose members seem to be spread all over Pomerania.

There are railway men like Piotr; farmers; laborers like the watchman at Kasia's factory; post office and office workers who steal denunciation notices, eavesdrop on conversations on the telephone in offices and on street corners, issue false documents, certificates or passes. They are everywhere, camouflaged in ways that make it impossible for the Gestapo to discover them.

"*Niech będzie pochwalony Jezus Chrystus*," Zofia says. Praise be Jesus Christ.

When we enter one of the wooden cottages in the village of Mirachowo, the smell of grain coffee greets us. We are here to see a man called Zbigniew, who belongs to another unit of the *AK* intelligence network.

"Zofia, how good to see you," a bald and round man in his

fifties says while getting up from a table set with black bread, garlic-infused *smalec*, lard, and steaming mugs filled with coffee. He leaps to Zofia and kisses her hand, then he ushers us to the adjoining room. "Adka, please bring us through some coffee and bread," he says, addressing a pretty brunette in a floral dress.

"Yes, Papa," she says and before walking away, she bats her lashes at me.

At first, the conversation is about a man who was caught while being smuggled on a ship from Gdynia Harbor to Sweden.

When Adka closes the door behind her after setting three coffee mugs and some chunks of bread caked with the garlicky lard on the white-clothed table around which we sit, Zofia says, "What's new?"

Zbigniew grins and rubs his hands. "Last week RAF bombers raided the German missile and scientific research center in Peenemünde."

I look between the two of them, unsure of the significance of this. As Zbigniew demolishes another hunk of bread scraped with the last of the *smalec*, Zofia explains how the intelligence network discovered the Peenemünde center. Located on a Baltic island called Uznam, it's a rocket aircraft construction and testing center—and the Third Reich's most secret place.

It appears that the Germans have accomplished the first, structurally successful, ballistic missile, one that can even enter space. Their other invention is an unmanned missile aircraft which uses new pulsation motors. If Germans use both designs toward their war efforts, the damage will be catastrophic. This is the information that Polish intelligence has been reporting to London.

Zofia takes a deep breath, sips on her coffee. "That's all I can tell you, Felek. So many people have already lost their lives, I can only imagine," she adds quietly.

"That's true, but don't forget we're at war." Zbigniew gestures, spreading out the palms of his shovel-sized hands. "What's most important here is that the German plan got delayed. So many more innocent people will die if or when they use this new powerful missile they've developed. Besides, *Szkopy* started all of this. How many of us Poles have they murdered? Do you want to speak about all the Polish Jews that they've slaughtered in their camps?" White foam froths on his mouth.

"I'm the last person you need to tell this to," Zofia says.

He sighs. "I'm sorry, I let myself get carried away with my rage sometimes." Then he glances at me, then back at Zofia. "I do have some more matters to discuss, but this must be only between us two."

"I will wait outside," I say and get up.

"Go to Adka, boy." He nods at the door. "She'll keep you company."

It's not wise to be sitting outside as unwanted eyes might get curious, so I listen to the man's instructions and stay in the kitchen.

The girl sits at a bench near a white-tiled wood stove and peels potatoes deftly into a growing pile. "You must come from a big city," she says.

I smile. "I'm from Warsaw."

Her gaze is dreamy now. "Papa took me once to Gdańsk and to the Long Market. He even bought me a soft scarf, of lambswool."

"You're young, you will get to visit more places," I say, liking her honesty.

"I don't think so. Knowing Papa, he will marry me to one of the farmers who care only about pigs and wheat, and I will never get to see the world." She sighs. "But maybe that's for the best. There are bad things happening out there, worse than here."

I drop to a chair and watch her at her task. "One has got to be positive."

She finishes her peeling job and rinses the potatoes of their starch in a tin bowl filled halfway with water. "Here, things are simple and old school."

"I like simplicity," I say, meeting her gaze. "It's where true beauty comes from."

She seems to appreciate my remark because she smiles shyly. "And I like pleasant men." After transferring the clean potatoes to a pot, she wipes her hands with a cloth, then takes my hand and urges me to follow her.

"I should wait for Zofia," I say, wondering where she wants to take me.

"They will be there for a while, trust me. It's how it usually is with them. Let me show you something."

She leads me down to a cellar that smells of sprouting potatoes and damp, then sets aside a lamp and for a moment longer she digs into a pile of greenish potatoes revealing a Mauser pistol. "I found it when blueberry picking in our forest."

"Picking berries during war isn't a wise choice," I say and playfully nudge her arm.

She laughs. "But sometimes it turns out to be fruitful. Besides, I'm not afraid of *Szkopy*."

"They should be afraid of you," I tease her. She pushes back her hair as she smiles at me and the sight of her swan-like neck makes my hands ache with the sudden need to touch her.

She must sense it because her face grows serious as she tilts her chin more gently this time.

In this moment, I know exactly what to do. I cover her mouth with mine and kiss her. Pleasure floods my body and I appreciate how excited she seems too.

She unbuttons her dress and drives my hand to rest over her breast, and that's when I lose my restraint and pull her closer.

I've not been this intimate with a woman for so long, I've forgotten how great it feels.

But her father's voice comes from above. "Daughter, where are you?"

Guilt runs over me as she hurriedly dresses.

"Are you alright?" I ask, touching her arm.

She chuckles. "I'm more than alright." Her face gains some color.

I caress her cheek, which is flushed and beautiful. "Good. I hope you enjoyed this as much as I did," I say softly, and hold her chin as I look into her eyes.

TEN

KASIA: THE OLD WOMAN OF KASHUBIA

August 1943, Gdańsk

The next morning, I am poring over the new delivery schedule.

It is peaceful in Papa's office, and I'm relieved that the calm atmosphere isn't spoiled by a glowering portrait of Hitler like the one on the walls in Sebastian's office.

After analyzing Papa's old routine, I realize that he sent both girls together to every location. It would be so much more efficient for them to do it separately, but I guess he thought it would be safer for the girls. Despite all his faults my father always tried to accommodate everyone. It's why he rarely fired anyone, instead, he sought out solutions.

I am looking for solutions, too, but I can't shake off my nervousness at the prospect of today's meeting with the man who left the note with Kornel. I'm supposed to be in the chosen location at noon. I only have one hour for my lunch break, so I will have to hurry to be back in time. Even though Sebastian hasn't been in today so far, I'm sure his secretary reports everything to him. She watches me like a vulture and judging by the way she stared at me when I walked toward Papa's office this morning, I sense that she doesn't like me much. Well, too bad.

By eleven, I'm done with the schedule. At last, I think, as I wipe the ink from my fingers. The first delivery will take place tomorrow morning. I'll go myself every day and one of the girls will always accompany me. Tuesdays and Thursdays are Alina's and Wednesdays and Fridays are Malina's. Weekends and Mondays are off from dispatching.

Sebastian must first approve this schedule, but I don't see why he wouldn't when he was the one instructing me to make deliveries only four days a week and spend Mondays working on recipes.

He was clear that those small distributions to Gestapo and SS Headquarters are being done precisely to maintain good relationship with the key people in Gdańsk. It's a blessing that he picked me for it. The real deliveries to the Wehrmacht or Luftwaffe are being done in big trucks, and I have nothing to do with those. I'm assuming Sebastian supervises them.

Closer to noon, I stuff a leather bag, the factory's logo of *Katharina* in gold lettering on it, with tiny boxes of chocolate. I make sure to carefully tuck a folded slip of paper with coded messages for the Resistance under the delicate chocolates. If for some reason I get halted by the German patrol, I can always say that I was on the way to deliver our goods.

I keep a rigid posture and my head up when I leave the office. The Long Market in the city center is only ten minutes' walk from here.

With my heart pounding beneath my rib cage, I approach the arch of the Golden Gate decorated with sculpted figures representing peace, freedom, fortune, fame, concord, justice, piety and wisdom. I glance at the so familiar inscription in Latin: *Concord makes small states grow; discord makes large states fall.*

I stride through the cobblestones of the Long Market, made

oppressive by the red and black of the Nazi Germany flags, toward Neptune's Fountain in front of the Artus Court. I face it and wait, tuning in to its splashing sound as the Neptune's raised trident and the sprinkling water glitter in the sun. The fountain stands as a symbol of city's connection to the sea. I wonder if it will survive this destructive war...

This is the assigned location for the meeting, right in the lion's mouth. How, I wonder, can anyone communicate in such a spot, surrounded by uniformed German officers and soldiers.

Soon an older lady in a patterned headscarf with shopping bags in her hands, stops beside me and throws a coin into the water. "For the victory of the Third Reich," she yells in German.

Nausea grips the muscles of my stomach. There is nothing else I can expect from the primitive lovers of Hitler than to ruin peace of everyone else.

"Mushrooms dislike birch trees," she whispers in Kashubian without looking my way.

It takes all my self-control to stop my jaw from dropping. It's the password that I got from the Resistance chief in Warsaw before moving to this city. "But birch trees love mushrooms," I utter in Polish.

"Wait five minutes and come to the amber store. I will be waiting upstairs," she whispers, again in Kashubian, and walks away. Her words sound so familiar, and I am glad to know a little of this native language, thanks to summers spent on the farm of Mama's good friend.

I watch her out of the corner of my eye, noticing which store she enters, and I follow five minutes later. The door sign states that only Germans are allowed to enter. As a *ding ding* sound of a bell announces my arrival, an elderly man with a white, curly mustache snatches off his half-moon glasses and smiles at me.

"Welcome to our amber kingdom," he says in pure German.

"Hello." I smile back and can't resist gazing around. Display cases crowd the small room, the glow of the amber making it warm and pleasant. When I was little, I liked to look for pieces on the Baltic shores; the collection still adorns a shelf in my room.

The man is German and since the authorities still allow him to run his business here, he must be a devoted supporter. Why then did the Kashubian lady point out this store to me? Am I being played here into something dangerous? Maybe that note wasn't from the Resistance, I think, my heart pounding with anxiety, but then I quieten my paranoia: the old woman knew the password.

She said that she'd be waiting upstairs, but how can I get there with the man here? Not sure what to do, I rove around pretending to admire the jewelry pieces.

"Are you looking for something specific?" he asks.

Before I have a chance to think of an answer, the lady appears and waves at me. "Please, follow me."

As I pass the man, he only nods, returns his glasses to his nose and continues reading his newspaper. I climb the stairs after the woman and reach a stylish decorated family room with a Persian rug covering wood floor panels, velvet sofa and chairs in shades of amber-yellow. The air smells of coffee and brims with scents of something sweet and vanilla extract. Chocolate, I think.

"Please, take a seat. Your contact is running late but he should be here soon."

I perch on the sofa while she settles in the armchair, picks up a shirt and begins embroidering. "I made some *brejka* and *kuch*. Please, help yourself, honey."

I swallow hard. "That German gentleman downstairs—"

She interrupts me. "You don't need to worry about him. I've been married to him for the last forty years and can assure you that he knows what's right and what's wrong. It's all pretend, my dear. We despise Nazis and their awful propaganda but make them think we love them." She smirks at me. "The fact that Hans is German serves us well. What's your name?"

"Kasia," I say my Polish version of the name, wondering what I'm doing here but I have a good feeling when it comes to this lady, so I stay put and reach for a porcelain cup filled with the *brejka* cold coffee and inhale the soothing aroma of roasted rye and chicory, with delicate hint of chocolate. "It's heaven," I say.

She laughs. "I'm glad you like it as I added some chocolate and milk. By the way, I'm Genowefa, and I'm also glad to have you here," she says and focuses again on her embroidery task.

"My pleasure, Pani Genowefa," I say and glance at my wristwatch, realizing that I only have thirty minutes left before I must return to the factory. "Are you sure that the contact will arrive today?" I take another sip, now tasting also almonds. She must have used the famous Gdańsk milk, which consists of whipped cream with almonds.

"He will be here any minute now. Why don't you try my homemade *kuch*?"

I do as she suggests and try the yeast cake with crumble. "This is so delicious," I say honestly. It's plain but tasty.

I watch Pani Genowefa embroidering flowers into a shirt. It's not like I have anything else to do.

"I've noticed that there are always the same color flowers used in Kashubian embroidery," I say, genuinely curious about it. "My mother likes to embroider but she uses darker threads."

"I use seven colors," she says and gives a knowing grin. "Each color has its own meaning and connects with nature and the old legend."

"The old legend?" I ask, sensing that she enjoys telling stories.

"Yes." She lifts her chin and begins the tale. "One day a little girl had to bring a meal to her grandmother. During the long walk, her crisp white apron got soiled with dirt. It made her so sad that her grandmother decided to take the apron to the meadows where she picked seven flowers and, using her threads, she embroidered them into the girl's apron." She places the palm of her hand over her heart. "That's how Kashubian embroidery began."

"Interesting," I say, touched by the emotion in her voice. "But what about the meaning of the colors?"

"Light blue—the sky; dark blue—the Baltic Sea; medium blue—the Kashubian lakes; black—the earth; yellow—the sand and wheat; green—the forests and meadows," she recites and takes another sip of coffee. "Your color is red," she says and winks at me, her needle still working expertly on the shirt.

I tilt my head to the side. "Why red?"

She sighs. "Because it represents the blood given in efforts to fight for our homeland."

"If that's what needs to be done," I say, unable to ignore the heaviness in my heart. Since losing Papa and so many of my *AK* friends from Warsaw, I can't help but often think of death and how I'm always on brink of it, for as long as I work for the Resistance. In the comfort of this woman's busy, homely room, the awareness that one day I will cease to exist, that there will be nothing left of me, almost overwhelms me. Is that what has happened to Papa? Has he left nothing behind him? And this day of my own non-existence might arrive sooner than later because of my determination to stand against the evil that is everywhere now. Still, these feelings don't change my decision to fight. It's something I must do.

Pani Genowefa puts her work aside and stares at me for a moment longer, both of us reflective. "Red also symbolizes love," she says in a quiet voice, "and true love is eternal."

"Eternal..." I whisper, unable to fully grasp at the meaning of the word. "My aunt often says that only eternity matters but I wonder if it even exists."

"It's more real than what's here," she says with a chuckle,

like it's something unquestionable, something we all should know.

"I hope you're right, Pani Genowefa. I truly do, because I feel that I don't have much longer left on this earth." I crinkle a smile to sound more lighthearted than my words suggest.

Her gaze now drills into mine, making me feel uncomfortable. "You, my dear, will taste the greatest love, which may become spoiled by never-ending pain. Remember my words and choose wisely."

The knock on the door jerks me away from the reverie this old woman's stories and strange wisdoms has captured me in, as if I'm a bee caught mid-flight in amber.

"Come in," she says in perfect German.

At the sight of the man who enters the room, my heart gives a leap.

What is *he* doing here?

ELEVEN

KASIA: WORKING FOR THE RESISTANCE

August 1943, Gdańsk

"*Serwus*, Pani Genowefa," the lanky man with his dirty-blond hair and familiar boyish face says in greeting as he shuts the door closed.

"*Witôj, knyp*," Pani Genowefa says in her native Kashubian and tilts her head cutely at him.

The man takes his seat across from me and says, "Hello again, Kasia."

Pani Genowefa turns my way and smiles for a moment longer. "I enjoyed our conversation, honey, but now let me go help my husband."

I assure her of the same. I genuinely like this lady.

When she's gone, I finally give the man my attention. "Hello, Felek. Looks like fate keeps crossing our paths."

He looks at me through narrowed eyes and when he speaks his tone is brusque. "When I recovered, I got an order to stay here with the partisans. I'm going to be your contact going forward. How are things so far?"

I give him an easy nod. "Today I started employment at my

father's former factory. I'm in charge of small deliveries being made to places like the SS or Gestapo Headquarters." I look him directly in the eye. "Hopefully I will be able to pass on a lot of useful information."

His gray eyes brighten. "Perfect. That's what we're hoping for."

It's hard to read him as his face betrays no emotion. I recall the softness the other day when he was thanking me for helping to save his life.

Now, it seems as if he's a different person, not the hyperactive kid from the streets of Warsaw. He's composed and careful, I can sense that. I guess the arrest and tortures were a tremendous lesson for him. A lesson that no one should have to endure.

"Will I be meeting you here?" I ask, keeping my demeanor serious too.

"For now, yes. We'll see how things go."

I nod and get up. "I have to go back as my break is almost over."

He rises to his feet too. "Kasia, I need to apologize for contacting you through your brother. But I was able to get to our other contact here in Gdańsk and now I will be passing messages to you through the watchman in your factory. I think it's safer this way."

For a moment I'm speechless. Pan Alojzy works for the Resistance... "What a small world," I say and allow my lips to quirk. "I see you've been busy already."

Once more, his face betrays no reaction. "I admit to watching you for a while, but you need not be afraid; we trust you. I just needed to gain some understanding of the situation here, now your father isn't here anymore. Please accept my deepest condolences."

"Thank you." I'm not surprised by his confession about spying on me; after all, it is normal practice for the Resistance. Something in him, in the intensity of this situation, emboldens me. "As you know my father collaborated with the Nazis," I say, not caring to protect his reputation.

After he nods, I pull a box of chocolate out of my bag, making sure it's the one with the hidden message for the Resistance. "Here, I got you some chocolate," I say and wink at him. "Don't forget to share with others." Last night I jotted down the most vital info I've gathered since my arrival in Gdańsk and at the factory, like the mention of the "chocolate bombs" by Sebastian and Bruno.

Then I turn and walk back down the stairs, through the golden glow of the amber store and away toward the factory that once belonged to my father. I'm so ready for this, to make a difference in this world. I will give all my heart and strength to helping the Polish Resistance. When this war ends, I want to look in the mirror without shame, I want to pass on the right values to my children. I don't want to be like my father...

As I stride through the cobbled streets of the city center, I admire a cascade of sunlight reflected on the old tenements. I take it as a sign from God, a prophecy that one day this city will be reborn again and freed from evil. To me, light relates to spiritual freedom, true happiness, true love.

Felek entered my life in the same unexpected way as this cascade of sunlight into this city. While those sunrays bring hope to my heart, he injected the overwhelming feeling of disappointment into it. I know I shouldn't feel like this. We are united in the mission of fighting for freedom and justice, there is no place for sentiment.

Still, his aloofness and matter-of-fact attitude today confirmed that for him I'm just another girl trying to do the right thing, and the gentleness he showed in the shack the other day was only his way of thanking me for playing my part in saving his life. Now he's down to business and I'm just one of his contacts.

But I can't help having a heart that feels...

TWELVE

KASIA: THE CASINO IN SOPOT

October 1943, Gdańsk

The leaves on the trees have turned golden, and my first two months at the factory have gone by fast. I've made small deliveries with the sisters and whatever information I'm able to gather, I carefully tuck under the chocolate and pass on to Felek.

At first, I failed to hear much due to my fear of being watched, which paralyzed me from the inside, especially in the Gestapo Headquarters on Neugarten. Slowly, though, I've eased into it.

Now, I don't miss a single word, just like back then in Warsaw when my senses were alert to my surroundings. It feels good to be back in my old skin, to be sure of myself, while displaying my acting skills in front of those criminals.

I spoke more openly to Pan Alojzy, as he swept fallen leaves that had blown into the courtyard, and he confessed that his only son was killed on the first day of the war while defending the Polish Post Office on Hevelius Platz. The Poles who survived it and were taken into custody, later were shot anyway, so his son had no chance...

My heart goes out to Pan Alojzy. He and his warm-hearted wife, Jadwiga, who my parents employed before the war and who I was so fond of, were evicted from their flat and, like so many others, are now forced to live in a dank cellar, so different from their old place with its tall windows and view of the park.

As I leave our villa in the Wrzeszcz district, a rattling sound from the sky makes me freeze. Then there is an explosion in the far distance and soon sirens howl. I turn and head back into the house, so we can all go down to the shelter.

"Katharina!" Sebastian runs from his property toward me. "Are you okay?" His calm gaze runs me up and down.

"Yes, I was just leaving for work." My head is spinning, I don't want to talk to him: the only thing I yearn to do right now is to get to my family.

He takes my hand. "Let's all go to the shelter before the next drop." We jog into the house together and quickly usher Mama and Kornel to the basement.

As we sit underground, we listen in silence to more and more explosions.

"Let's stay here for a little longer, just to make sure that the bombing is over," Sebastian says, once the commotion quiets down and we breathe with relief.

So, we do. Through the whole time, Kornel stays close to Sebastian as if sensing that he is safer with him.

Air raids have not been common in Gdańsk so far, but maybe things will change now. The rule is that sirens go on after the first bomb hits the city.

"Were these the Soviets?" I ask.

"No, I recognized Boeing B-17 F Flying Fortresses, so definitely Americans."

It's so different living in Gdańsk, after my time in Warsaw where I belonged to the Polish community with constant hope of help from the Allies. In this city, where almost the entire population is German under Nazi rule, I must act like the Americans are my enemy, which is so absurd. Seeing those aircrafts brought a sliver of hope while also fear for our lives.

When we are outside, everything appears to be just as we left it before we hurried into the shelter. The air feels a little dusty and tastes as if scorched, but that is all. Sebastian offers me a ride to work, and I accept. But a few streets later, we see that one of the Dutch-style houses on Birkenallee is on fire.

People are working hard to put out the fire, running with water buckets and shovels filled with sand.

"We should help," I say and touch his arm.

But he shakes his head in dismissal. "The situation is clearly under control and I'm sure the fire engine is on the way; besides, we have more urgent matters to take care of."

As we drive away, I can't stop contemplating on his lack of empathy for others. I'm sure two more pairs of hands would be helpful, but I swallow my thoughts, lacking the strength to oppose his decision.

The fire and our late start to work mean that I cancel our delivery job for today and tell Malina and Alina to focus on their wrapping duties while I work on the schedule for the following weeks and test new chocolate mixtures, especially prepared for wartime needs. The recipes must be less extravagant now; still, my job is to make it tasty and compelling.

As I consider the differences between two types of hazelnut chocolate, I remember that last week Sebastian asked me to accompany him on an outing with Bruno and his wife to the casino in Sopot, a glamorous spa and seaside town north of Gdańsk. I love its vast expanse of beach and promenade stretching out into the Baltic. But that's not why I accepted his invite. I didn't refuse because going to a place like this one could be a source of new information for the Resistance.

~

Thanks to its famous casino, before the war Sopot was known as "the Monte Carlo of the North". Now the resort's main clients are German officers or soldiers who revel in their time here as if we aren't in the middle of the war.

We spot Bruno and his wife at one of the long green roulette tables. He's deep into a gamble while Ilse stands by his side in her silky dress that drapes in soft dusty rose folds over her figure, complemented by a string of matching sequins along her neckline.

After polite greetings, Sebastian joins Bruno and a cluster of other men at the roulette table while I stand near him, sipping champagne and keeping my ears alert. The air brims with cigarette smoke and sweat, mixed with various whiffs of perfumes. I imagine that all the patrons here are Nazi supporters enjoying their lives while regular people struggle to survive day after day of this brutal war; certainly, the ordinary people of Gdańsk and Gdynia aren't here like they once were. The buzz of German conversation and laughter makes me feel so lonely, but I make sure to fold my lips into a constant smile.

I cease my melancholy thoughts and focus on the current situation at the table. It seems both men have no luck at roulette today, so soon they decide to play baccarat in the other hall. Ilse and I perch on an antique, upholstered sofa in a small ante room while enjoying some more champagne. She seems to be much younger than Bruno: no more than in her mid-twenties.

"I'm so pleased to finally meet you in person," she says, her carmine lips curled like flames, her voluminous, blonde hair styled into a sausage-shaped roll on the top of her head. Compared to her I must look like a gauche schoolgirl with my loose pin curls that I only quickly brushed before coming here. "Bruno can't stop raving about what a great asset you are to Sebastian's factory," she continues.

I bristle. It's also my family's factory, not only Sebastian's, but I don't voice my thoughts. "It's all my pleasure," I say and crinkle the fake smile back at her. "Do you come to the casino often?"

"I would say no more than once a month. Bruno has been extremely busy since we've moved to Danzig. First, he worked so hard to rid the city of the Jewish outcasts, then he took responsibility for putting the stinking Poles back into their rightful place. So, as you see, life here isn't easy or pleasant. The casino is a small respite. I worry for dear Bruno's safety on a daily basis."

I nod while my skin tightens at her words. I have to sit on my hands to stop myself giving into the strong urge to slap her. She's a model product of the Nazi ideology, that's for sure.

She goes on with her inane, hateful thoughts, then her speech turns to racial purity and how the German nation has been chosen to rule the world, while I pretend to agree with her by constantly nodding my head.

"Do you have children?" I ask at the point when her words are starting to make me feel physically ill, just to change the subject.

She leans forward and says, "We don't." Then she licks her lips and smiles. "But we're working on it."

"Good luck then," I say. "I'm sure you'll succeed soon."

"Succeed in what?" Bruno says as he approaches us, finger-curling his mustache. Both men are in expansive moods now, full of bravado and, no doubt, brandy.

"I was just telling Katharina about our plans to start a family," Ilse says and blushes in an irritatingly coy way. "I didn't expect that you would be finished gambling so early, gentlemen," she adds.

"We've no luck today." Bruno shrugs and taps out a cigarette, then holds it out to Ilse as she pouts prettily at him. I watch her blonde hair shimmer as the flame flares between them.

THIRTEEN
KASIA: MORE CHAMPAGNE

October 1943, Gdańsk

On the way back home from Sopot, Sebastian and I don't talk much. I'm just happy to be free from Ilse's company. I couldn't listen to or even look at her or Bruno anymore.

I can't help but think that going to the casino was a waste of my time. I learned nothing new or crucial to the Resistance, instead I had to listen to Ilse raving how great her Führer is and how Germans are the true rulers of the world. Not to mention her hideous flirting with Bruno about their baby plans.

Sebastian parks in front of his villa and shuts down the rumbling engine. "Would you like to come over for a glass of wine?" His inquisitive but also pleading gaze stays on me.

At first, I want to reject his offer due to the late hour but I'm curious to see Ruth's old home again. "I'd love to."

As we cross the threshold, the pungent beeswax smell of furniture polish greets us, and my nostrils also detect a whiff of lavender oil. He points to a leather sofa, so I take a hint and sit on it.

"Do you prefer white or red wine?' he asks and walks

toward a wood bar cabinet with a tray of bottles and glasses positioned atop.

"White. Thank you." I can't shake off the feeling that everything here is perfect but cold. Items are stacked neatly in the right places, not a speck of dust on the furniture or a particle of dirt on the floor. But I've already observed in the office that he likes to be meticulous and precise.

"Your house is beautiful," I say thinking how it's different from when Ruth lived here with her parents and her younger brothers. It was always chaotic and untidy, but homey and warm with children running around while Ruth's mother cooked or baked, releasing savory or sweet aromas. Her home often smelled of cinnamon with the waxy smell of candles on Shabbat afternoons. I wonder, as I often do, how they're doing now; I know that leaving Gdańsk before the war was the best decision they probably have ever made. It most likely saved their lives.

"Thank you, my housekeeper does a great cleaning job." He hands me a glass of wine and takes a seat on a small sofa across from me. "I'm afraid it's way too quiet and empty here though. You see, I bought the house in hopes of finding a worthy woman and starting my own family." Sadness passes through his face.

"It seems like a good plan to me." I don't question why he's still alone because it's not any of my business. I noticed the way women in the casino looked at him tonight, as if hoping he would show them any interest. He's a handsome, cultured man, so it doesn't surprise me that their attention snagged on him.

His pale blue eyes freeze on my face. "That's not what you thought all those years back."

I meet his gaze and say, "I hope you never took it personally as we only met once back then. I had other reasons to leave Danzig." My father had invited Sebastian for dinner and then we all went for a walk along the Baltic shore. It was a pleasant evening, and I liked Sebastian right away. From what I recall, we all talked at the dinner about various topics from the vagaries of the chocolate business to recent classical music concerts we had attended; not once did it cross my mind that my father already had plans for us to get married.

I notice that his jaw is set. "Well, I'm not going to lie when I tell you that I felt disappointed by your departure because I hoped to get to know you better." For a moment longer, he presses his lips tight into a grimace. "You chose to study business at the University of Warsaw, correct?"

"Commercial law and statistics," I say and cross my arms. He obviously does have a grudge about the past. That day at Stogi Beach, shortly after we began our walk, Mama started complaining of a bad headache, so Papa decided that he would take her and Kornel home to let her rest. He insisted on me staying with Sebastian and continuing with the walk, to which we both agreed.

"How did that go?" His voice is soft now, just like all those years back during our walk on the Baltic shore. I'd enjoyed every second with him as he told me old stories about Gdańsk and kept a respectful distance the whole time. When we were parting, he asked if I would like to go to dinner with him, and of course, I was excited about it. The truth is that from the moment I saw him, I felt a tremendous pull of attraction toward him. If I'm honest with myself, I felt the same magnetic force at the cemetery even before I realized it was him.

I shrug. "I finished one year of my studies, but once the war started, I couldn't continue." We never went to dinner together because the day after our walk on the beach, Papa told me I was to marry Sebastian, stating that he was a perfect candidate for my husband and that I should start preparing for the wedding. He didn't ask my approval or how I felt about it, he'd made his decision and that was that. It was so unlike him. All my life, he'd been this compassionate, hardworking man with a gentle spirit and sense of pleasure in life. But I knew that had changed since he joined the NSDAP party; he'd started to have less and less time for his family and his attitude hardened into something inflexible and authoritarian, as if he was mirroring Hitler's own stance. Certainly, my father had changed for the worse.

"If I can speak frankly," Sebastian begins, twirling the wine in his delicate glass, "I just want you to know that if you had stayed in Danzig and married me, I wouldn't have stopped you from going to the university. I was going to encourage you to do so as in the long run it would benefit our business." He sighs and drills his eyes into the wine glass in front of him. "But I thought you ran because you didn't want to be with me. I wish you took your time to first get to know me before making such a decision."

I take a sip of wine for courage, to numb all the words that I would love to throw at him. How dare he expected all this of the eighteen-year-old girl who only yearned to taste the wonder of the world, bask in her youth, grow her knowledge? I have a feeling he wouldn't understand my argument anyway as he seems to be as narrow-minded as Papa became. But I leave these thoughts to myself to avoid further conflict. Instead, I try to smooth things out.

"I can see now that I made a huge mistake," I say, so he thinks that I regret not marrying him back then. I need to have him on our side, so Kornel and Mama are safe. I gulp the rest of the wine, savoring the blissful warmth spreading down my body.

"We can't change what already happened, but the future is ours." With an amused expression on his face, he picks up the bottle from a bucket with ice and fills our glasses. "Despite the war, you decided to stay in Warsaw instead of coming back to your family. Would you mind telling me why?" he asks.

"I knew my father was angry at me." I pause, remembering that time, but unwilling to share it with Sebastian.

When I refused to obey, he countered my refusal, reasoning

that my duties as a future owner were to do what was best for the family factory, and with Sebastian by my side our business would flourish and cement success once and for all. I begged him with tears to let me go to the university, insisting that I didn't want to marry when I was only eighteen. Our dramatic exchange ended with Papa slamming his hand down on the table and looking at me with such venom in his eyes I felt he no longer cared to recognize me.

"If you do not obey me in this, Katharina, you stop being my daughter from this moment on."

I met his glare with one of my own, then I threw some dresses and books, my winter boots and best coat into a suitcase. Packed, I marched myself to the train station heedless of the near-horizontal rain and left for Warsaw the very same day. There I knocked on my aunt's door and collapsed, still drenched and shivering, into her generous arms. There was no question about it: I was to live with her in her tiny flat. Papa never contacted me, but this was something I expected. When I didn't hear from Mama, that was the worst punch to my heart. Thankfully, I had my sweetest Ciocia Lucyna.

"He wasn't," Sebastian says, bringing me back to the present as he tilts his head to the side. "In fact, he worried about you to the point that he hired a private detective to get updates regularly about your well-being." He leans back, his eyes focused intently on my face.

A rush of panic storms through my body. If my father spied on me the whole time I was in Warsaw, then surely, he knew about my involvement with the Polish Resistance. Did he share that information with Sebastian? No, I'm confident he didn't, or I would be in prison right now—or worse, dead. Deep inside, I know Papa loved me despite his harsh words.

"Really?" I say, with a shrug. "I was so busy working and trying to stay away from trouble, there won't have been much for the detective to report to my father." I make sure to keep a neutral tone.

He raises his eyebrows. "Yes, we were proud to hear about your employment at the chocolate factory over there. It's good that you kept learning new things. But what concerned both of us were the reports describing your connections with certain... shady people in Warsaw."

It seems as if my heart just came to my throat, but I manage to clear it and say, "All Poles in Warsaw look shady to the good citizens of Danzig." I meet his eyes and give a nervous laugh.

He answers with an indulgent smile. "You have nothing to worry about. We decided to keep that information to ourselves, trusting your good judgment. And now, I would never say anything to anyone. I'm here to protect Dietrich's family."

It all terrifies me. After all, he's a Nazi sympathizer and I can't trust him a bit.

He continues in a frank, intimate tone that astonishes me. Has the wine loosened his tongue? "I know you've already judged Dietrich and me, but life can't be split into black and white. Your father and I did what we had to do to keep our business afloat, even if it meant accepting the demands of the Nazi party. These are the tough, terrible decisions we're compelled to make, and believe me, it's not comfortable. I must continue this way until the war ends, but I ask you to remember that I'm only a chocolatier." He looks at me, as if he knows what I think of him. "I don't belong to SS or Gestapo. I keep my enemy close to me, that is all, and thanks to that the prisoners employed in our factory have easier jobs than many others; they are not behind the barbed wire fences and watchtowers of that inhuman camp at Stutthof." His eyes close for a moment as if imagining the rows of soulless wooden barracks. "Katharina, I even have a secret bakery in the basement of the factory where we bake bread for the poorest of this city. I try to help as much I can. Everything that has happened to Poles and Jews, and others too, at the hands of the Nazis is a terrible sin and I, as a good God-fearing German, condemn those atrocities. Though if my factory closed, I would have no means of helping others in need. Sometimes, I have realized, even in war the most effective way to fight isn't on the open battlefield."

My eyes widen and I catch myself from letting my mouth hang open. I can't believe the things he's sharing with me. I guess he isn't afraid to be honest with me because he knows I wouldn't give him away, not only because of my past in Warsaw, but also, he is our only protection right now when Papa is gone, and the factory is lost to us.

"You're a good man, Sebastian," I say, while reminding myself that all of this might be merely a way to manipulate information out of me. I curl up in my chair, feeling rather vulnerable right now, aware that my judgment is skewed after all the champagne in the casino and wine now.

"I'm doing what every decent German should." He leans forward and for a moment I think he's going to put his hand on my leg. "In fact, I would like to do more, if only I could get in touch with the Polish Resistance." He wets his lips and his eyes flash to meet mine.

FOURTEEN
KASIA: CHOPIN'S WALTZ

October 1943, Gdańsk

I make a puzzled face, as if I can't think why he is even telling me this. "Polish Resistance in Danzig?" I say, the question clear in my voice. "Does such a thing even exist?"

"I assure you it does."

"You know, Sebastian, I'm staying away from trouble of any kind, so I'm not aware of such things. My priority is to keep my mother and Kornel safe and to bring success to the factory my father loved so much." My mind is whirring like the painted carousel horses on the beach front at Sopot. Is this charming man trying to use me to gain access to the Resistance? As far as I know, he might be in the employ of the Abwehr, though I can't imagine that's the case. Still, I must be wary because the lives of so many people are on the line here. I have no right to give him any information even if I believe him, which I'm not sure I do. It's all so overwhelming.

He nods. "If something ever changes, don't forget that I want to help."

I don't react in any way to his words but change the subject. "I enjoy listening to your piano concerts in the evenings."

His face brightens. "I'm pleased to hear it. Do you play?"

"Mama tried to teach me," I say, smiling at the memory of her hands over mine across the keys, "but I wasn't good at it, and to be truthful, I always preferred listening to other people playing, though most of the time I can't ever guess what's being played." I chuckle and spread my hands as if in defeat at my own lack of musicality.

"Everyone likes different things and there's nothing wrong with that. Do you have favorite composers?"

"I can't tell," I confess. "It's either I like the music or no." But I'm lying; there's one composer whose romantic, poetic music I'd always recognize.

"Then I bet you will enjoy what I will play for you now." He gives me a mischievous grin, shifting the mood between us to something much more relaxed, and puts his glass on a table. Then he walks to the baby grand in the corner with all the swagger and flourish of a concert pianist.

As music fills the room, I swallow hard at the reality of what he has chosen to play. The one composer whose work I know as if by instinct. The forbidden Chopin. When I was little that's all Mama played, and Chopin's nocturnes and polonaises will always remind me of my childhood. I lose myself in the exquisite flow of the music. Maybe everything he's told me is the truth and he's a decent man; surely one of those Nazi heretics wouldn't play Chopin's "Waltz Op. 69, No. 2 in B Minor", the piece closest to my heart.

Is this a coincidence or does he simply know? My mind drifts with the melancholic chords, and for a moment I don't have to focus on being alert to everything said or happening around me. This music is on the darker side, maybe why it feels even more emotional now. The times my family were together are lost for good, my mother's homeland bleeds from the knife of the oppressor, my loneliness soars more than ever. This music brings me much needed consolation, though it intensifies the aches within my heart.

When he's done, he turns my way, his gaze filled with traces of emotion and nostalgia as he takes me in.

I forgot to wipe my tears and now I'm afraid to do it, hoping he would simply not notice it.

But he leaps forward, kneels before me and takes my hands in his. "I knew you would appreciate this one."

I clear my throat. "How?"

"Before the war, after you already left, your mother liked to play this piece by Chopin saying it's your favorite. So, I learned it."

I wipe my tears away. "Thank you. I hope you won't get in trouble because of it. You never know who might have been listening."

He traces my cheek with his palms, while his eyes stay on my lips. "It was worth it," he whispers. Then he kisses me and there is no softness in his touch as his tongue probes mine. His mouth possesses mine with such determination that confusion runs down my spine. Soon though I catch up to his rhythm and take pleasure from it.

When he cups my breast with one hand and travels to my thigh with the other, I gasp for control and part my lips from his.

I quieten down my shallow breathing and say, "I should go back."

"Stay," he whispers while caressing my hair. "I dreamed of you for so long."

As tempting as his offer sounds, I hold onto a shred of rationality: I can't allow myself to get swept up in the intensity of his desire—which, I confess, is matched by my own. I don't want things to progress with such speed between us, not when I don't know his true intentions. But his elegant hands dancing so fluently over the keys of the piano, his words about Chopin, my mother and our past, have left every nerve ending in my body trembling. Perhaps that's why I let him kiss me tonight, I think, surprised by the surge of feelings within me.

"Let's take things more slowly," I say with as much dignity as I can. If he touches me again, I feel sure I'll be unable to resist. I must leave before I let this man take me to his bed. "Thank you for the most charming evening."

Back at home in my own bed, I can't stop reflecting on what just happened. Images from the evening flash through my mind as I struggle to order them. His kiss was nice, I must admit, even though it was demanding, with an element of pressure and expectation—as if he believed it long overdue, or even that I'm his rightful possession. He didn't hesitate to test my reaction, before moving on in hope of more.

I must be honest with myself; I'm not sure what to think. No, I must be really honest and admit something I've never told anyone. That was my first kiss. Yes, it's true. I've not been kissed by a man before. Through my years in Gdańsk, I simply wasn't interested in boys, preferring to run to the factory after school to help Papa because it was something I enjoyed. Then in Warsaw, while I liked when men paid me attention, I was way too busy with my work and the Resistance to take any of their flattery seriously. I could see, too, how they liked to flirt with any pretty girl, and I didn't want to fall victim to their charms. Deep in my heart though, I kept waiting for my prince, that's how naïve I was.

Based on the romance novels I've read, I might have expected his kiss to be gentler, I might have expected sparkles to run up and down my spine and flatter my heart. That's not what I experienced this evening. Though, I admit, once I got used to the briskness, I enjoyed it; my body couldn't help but react to the touch of his hands on my breasts, my thighs.

Maybe it's how men kiss in real life. Maybe that's what seduction is. Perhaps I need to stop being a fool and cease to believe what those enticing romance writers tell me. Life is not a fairy tale. In fact, I tell myself sharply, the war has proved it to be a pure, inescapable nightmare of death and loss and out-of-control inhumanity. There is no time for romance during the war—this is going to be one of the most important rules until this terrible war ends. I must give all of myself to fight the evil.

Tonight, though, I changed the way I look at Sebastian. He trusted me and confessed things that made him vulnerable in front of me. Still, I must pretend like I have no contact with the Resistance, though I will tell Felek about Sebastian's declarations. Maybe the decision will be taken to trust him.

FIFTEEN
FELEK: AIRPORT ACTION

November 1943, Mirachowskie Forest

Why does it bother me so much that Kasia let that German creep kiss her? Since I saw them together, I can't find my place. But it makes no sense at all. After all, I've kissed Adka too, more than once, while lacking deeper feelings for her.

I'm rattled and I don't understand why. Occasionally, I go and check on her as it's what Zofia expects me to do, just to make sure that she's not under Gestapo or Abwehr observation. It seems as if the German takes her out to dinner usually on Saturdays, and to my relief she usually doesn't go to his house, though she sits in that Mercedes of his and engages in passionate kisses with him. Disgusting.

"Stop daydreaming, Felek," Zofia says and pokes my arm. "You must focus and not think of your Adka." She smirks.

"She's not mine," I say, ignoring the jittery feeling in my belly. I like Adka but I don't feel anything more for her. We share occasional kisses when we're alone, that's all. She suggested sneaking to the cellar again when Zofia and her father discussed things in private, but I said that we should take it easy, that we made a mistake that day among the potatoes in the cellar. She only laughs and shrugs, then gets generous with her sweet kisses.

I hope she isn't counting on something more between us because I can't give it to her. I must focus on my duties, and I told her so, making sure not to hurt her feelings. I had to be honest with her, after what had happened between us. For me it was a moment of weakness, a rare taste of physical pleasure amid this filthy war, and I feel terrible for giving her false hope.

"That's not what Adka says, but let's go back to our discussion." Zofia fixes a coarse blanket on her shoulders and takes a sip of warm water from her tin cup.

It's night now but an hour earlier we had a bonfire going not far away from here. It's so cold in this bunker that it was nice sitting close to a flame.

"So, you will be helping boys from *Gryf Pomorski* and some other groups to attack the German airport in the village of Strzebielin. It's where they train Luftwaffe pilots."

"When?" I like Zofia, as simple as it is. She might be rough around the edges, but deep inside she is a sensitive soul in unbearable pain. She refuses to move on and forget about her husband. This is the true definition of unconditional love.

"Not sure yet, but tomorrow you will attend a meeting, and they will fill you in. It's good that your German is fluent."

In the following days, I learn all about this mission and watch the airport along with other men to see how the checkpoints operate and the location of guards. We find, too, a route leading inside the airport.

Our preparations are meticulous, observing time and time again until we are sure of every detail, even recognizing the mannerisms of the different guards, like the short, barrel-chested one who has the walk of a penguin. Once we determine that it's time to proceed, we act with crystal precision, cutting the telephone lines and splitting into two groups. I'm among the boys who are dressed in German uniforms and who drive a truck that was *stolen* from Germans for this mission. We are to act as the relief crew and pretend to do an early change of shift.

When we approach the guard posted at the gate, the driver stops the truck. I'm sitting beside him, looking out through the windshield.

"Heil Hitler," the guard salutes. It's the Penguin, I realize.

"Heil Hitler," our driver salutes back. "I'm bringing the change crew."

"You're new," the guard says and settles his piercing eyes onto our leader.

"Yes, but an order is an order, and we were told to relieve you early today, so you can take a well-deserved rest. Is there anything we need to know before you leave?"

He presses his lips together in slight grimace, then says, "Password?"

My spine stiffens at this one word, and I try to keep my face steady, but the driver replies with a short remark that I don't even fully understand.

The guard nods and his rigid posture relaxes. "About time we got relieved. It's been a long day."

The leader smiles a little too wide, revealing his bony-white teeth, and the moment the guard gesticulates for us to move on, we pass the gate and halt again. Then, the driver shouts in his fluent German, "The crew assigned for this post must take their place now."

The boys take off, and the moment the guard turns away, one of ours strikes his head with butt of the pistol causing the man to drop motionless to the ground. Then the boys charge inside the guardhouse and swiftly, silently disarm the other Germans within.

I put aside my worries of getting caught and keep alert to surroundings. Now we drive toward the weapon magazines where we continue our pretense that we are the change for the guards' shift. With no real struggle we manage to disarm them and usher them briskly to their guardhouse where we tie them with heavy ropes and lock the door behind them.

Now time is of the essence. With no working telephones, the Germans are harmless, but only until the actual change of the shift arrives.

With adrenaline pumping through my veins, I systematically, ruthlessly work with the others to load our truck with weapons from the German warehouse.

After reuniting with the other group, who have succeeded in their mission to partially damage six German planes, we drive away thrilled, all of us bouncing in the truck with energy and exhilaration, pumped up with the spirit of resistance. Best of all, no one in our group got even slightly injured.

We immediately hide what we gained in one of the storage shelters in the forest. We obtained ten boxes of ammunition for long and short weapons, seventy rifles and pistols, forty grenades, ten mines, five kilos of trotyl, five-hundred meters of fuse, two typewriters and some German uniforms. I tick them all off on my fingers, like a shopkeeper counting his stock. It's a brilliant haul.

Of course, Zofia and others are thrilled with the results. She grasps my hands in hers and informs me that I've been assigned to a new action.

"I will fill you in on the details very soon," she says. "For now, all you need to know is that it's called 'Synthesis'."

SIXTEEN

KASIA: BIULETYN INFORMACYJNY

November 1943, Gdańsk

One day, when I'm on a tram back home after a whole day of working at the factory, I can't help but think how hard it is to figure out Sebastian's true nature. I toy with an amber bracelet that he gifted me today when he stopped by my office. His gesture touched me and assured that I'm often on his mind too, just like he's on mine. Still, I don't fully trust him.

Since our first kiss last month, Sebastian takes me once a week to a restaurant or theatre. He always finds something to do. We kiss afterwards in his car but I make sure that it stops at that, and I always find an excuse not to enter his house. I don't want to test my restraint and I have a feeling that one day after a few glasses of wine, I would not reject his eagerness to take me to his bed. I'm not ready for that, not yet anyway.

I find Mama sitting at our kitchen table which is now covered by white cloth embroidered with yellow tulips, a gift from Pani Genowefa.

"Hello, Mama," I say and drop into a chair. "Are you

reading that Nazi propaganda again?" I motion to the newspaper spread on the table before her.

"Hello, sweetie, how was your day?" she says without taking her eyes from the gazette.

"Decent," I say while she gets up and hustles at the stove.

I reach for a thick slice of black bread and apple marmalade. Mama brings over a ceramic mug filled with steaming grainy coffee that has the strong flavor of chicory in it. The sweet tobacco-smoke aroma reminds me of my Ciocia Lucyna and her flat in Warsaw with her stunning collection of various landscape paintings. I've always admired my aunt's artistic talents, and when I think of it, I miss her even more. Though I never liked when she smoked one cigarette after another. I will write a letter to her tonight as we received one recently from her in which she assures that she is fine. Her employment in the German sewing factory isn't her favorite but it helps her to survive the harsh realities of war.

"Thank you," I say and chew on the bread, my thoughts wandering. Maybe if I feel something deeper when Sebastian kisses me, it will be the indication that it's time to take the next step. That hasn't happened so far, though I remind myself daily that life is different from the one that authors create in their books. I resolved to not get involved seriously with anyone until the war ends. I guess that a kiss here and there isn't a big deal... or is it? I am not entirely naïve; I know Sebastian will be considering it at least something of a deal.

Mama nods and takes a seat back across from me. "Good." When she lifts the newspaper, a crumb blocks my throat, and I cough so hard that it makes her feverishly clap me on my back.

Once I can breathe again and she's back in her chair, I say, "Where did you take this from?" It seems I was wrong about her newspaper of choice. She is in fact reading one of the Polish Resistance papers.

"Kornel brought it over," she says cheerfully like it's full of nothing more dangerous than recipes and knitting patterns. "It's an old edition."

"Mama!" I almost scream. "It's an underground newspaper about Resistance activities. If the Gestapo finds it here, we will all be arrested." I pause, then gasp for breath. "Mama, if someone—"

"I know, I know, don't you worry. When I'm done reading it, I will hide it in the false bottom of my desk's drawer."

False bottom, I think, stunned. "How did Kornel get hold of it?"

"He visited Romek after school today." I know Kornel feels sad for Romek that he can't attend the school because of his Polish citizenship, so once a week he goes to study with him. Mama agreed to it on condition that he's very careful and no one finds out about it. Romek only lives in the basement two houses from us, so the walk isn't far.

"For once I'm able to read the truth and not some propaganda and lies," Mama says and smirks. "Listen to this: *On the second day of February 1943, the German army was defeated by the Soviets. So far, it's been the most brutal and deadliest battle of all time, claiming more than two million lives. From the accounts heard, the involved soldiers would have preferred hell itself. The Battle of Stalingrad has marked the turning of the tide of war for Poland and the Allies. It's the beginning of Nazi Germany's end.*"

"We'll never learn something like this from the German gazettes," I say and clap my hands together. "I only hope this is all the truth."

"It is, darling, it is. Hitler made the same mistake as Napoleon Bonaparte before him. You know, the Russian winters are extremely harsh, and Germans aren't used to temperatures like that. The conditions will have been intolerable. I'm sure the weather played a big role in this calamitous defeat."

"You're right, Mama," I tell her as my heart glows with something like hope, at last.

~

A couple of hours later, I'm getting ready to tell a story to Kornel while he's already tucked in his bed for the night, his brown teddy bear beside him, though he claims that he doesn't need it for comfort anymore. "Would you like a story about the brave Napoleon Bonaparte?" Kornel prefers true stories over legends.

"I would like that. You read it in books?"

"No, Papa told me this story when I was a little older than you are now. I think you will like it. Sometime after Napoleon Bonaparte won over Gdańsk in 1807, he decided to reward his marshal. He summoned him in the very early hours of the morning, which made the marshal worry the emperor is angry. He was already in conference with his generals, so the marshal was asked to wait as Bonaparte wanted to have breakfast with him in a quarter of an hour.

"The marshal took a seat on an armchair on which the emperor's sword was leaning and waited, convinced that Napoleon intended to use this weapon on him. In fifteen minutes, the marshal entered the emperor's quarters and was taken aback by the smiling Napoleon Bonaparte sitting with others at a table loaded with food and drinks. It was all so unexpected to him that he didn't even notice when the emperor addressed him as 'your Grace'.

"When they finished dining, Napoleon gifted him a package stating it's a block of Gdańsk chocolate to sweeten the hardship of war, while he called him again as 'your Grace'. The marshal thanked him and put it into his pocket thinking that his wife will be happy to see it. But when later he unwrapped the chocolate, he found a pile of banknotes and a beautifully calligraphed imperial decree awarding him the title of the Duke of Gdańsk.

"Later when the French soldiers needed money, they often asked if their colleagues happen to have any 'chocolate from Gdańsk' in their bags."

When I'm done telling the story, Kornel is already asleep, so I kiss his forehead and turn off the lamp. I love this boy to pieces; he fills me with tenderness. He has Papa's eyes and sometimes I feel like it's him looking at me from Kornel's face. I miss my father so much, despite everything. I sit with my sleeping brother in the quiet dark for a long moment, till I feel my own eyes start to close.

Almost in a slumber of my own, I turn the light switch on in my bedroom. The second I do so, my heart jumps to my throat.

There is a man sitting on my bed, as if waiting for me.

He touches his finger to his mouth while meeting my eyes calmly. "Shhh…"

"What are you doing in my bedroom?" I whisper and fold my arms across my chest. "You'd better have a good explanation because I'm very upset right now."

"Well, get over it." Felek's voice is full of sarcasm. "Since obviously I had no other way of getting in touch with you tonight."

"A simple apology would suffice instead of your bad attitude," I say and refuse to be the first to break eye contact.

He sighs with exaggeration. "Fine, I'm sorry. And now, madam, please get ready because Zofia needs to have a word with you."

Looks like someone has a hard time admitting to his faults. "First, I would like to know how you got into this villa." I could swear I locked the door and there is no way for anyone to break in through the windows.

"Part of my skillset," he bats back. "I'm good at unlocking any door without a key. Do I need to apologize for that too?"

I've never seen him so defiant and bolshy. Through the years in Warsaw, during the meetings, he always seemed easy going and even showed a good sense of humor while taking part in conversations. And within the last few months in Gdańsk, even though he hasn't talked much to me besides asking questions about the information I supply for the Resistance, he was always respectful. Today he's revealed his true face, I'm afraid.

I ignore his comment and say, "Who's Zofia and why does she want to see me?"

"Zofia is one of the leaders of the Resistance network here and she wants to meet you. I'm taking you to the Oliwa Forests, so please dress warm as we have to walk over there." He averts his gaze as I pull on some more clothes.

A few minutes later we slip downstairs, and I reach out to the rack for my coat. As I put it on while my back's turned to Felek, my brother's small but determined voice causes me to swirl around.

Kornel stands with a wooden slingshot in his hand. "Leave my sister alone if you want to stay alive," he sneers at Felek.

I expect him to get angry at my brother or even laugh at his childish naivety, but he obediently raises his both arms, his face motionless.

"Kornel," I say, "this man is a good friend of mine, so please put your *weapon* down and go to sleep. We must take care of something, but I will be back soon."

My brother takes a deep breath and pushes out his chest. "Then I'm going with you."

"We need you to stay and protect your mother, will you do that?" Felek says and winks at Kornel. "You are a brave boy, besides I promise to keep your sister safe."

In this very moment, I'm thankful that he managed not to hurt my brother's pride. Perhaps he's not such an arrogant pig as he seemed just a moment ago.

"Fine, but make sure she is back soon."

Felek salutes. "Yes, chief."

We navigate through the city's quiet and dark streets; still, due to the blackout hours, no streetlamps are on. I'm glad I put on a coat and knitted hat, which shield me from the wind. Once we enter the Oliwa Forests, set apart from the city by moraine hills, the wind is less noticeable. I inhale a musky, sweet scent, one of tall trees and monastic peacefulness that reminds me of my childhood.

Felek uses a flashlight but seems to know the area well because he doesn't stop at all. The whole time, he utters not a single word to me.

His aloofness makes me determined to hold it all together, to prove to him that I'm not just a city girl easily intimidated by brutes like him. I make sure to overcome the shaky feeling caused by being alone with him in these forests.

SEVENTEEN

KASIA: THE CHOCOLATE BOMB

November 1943, Gdańsk

As we continue deep into the eerie forest in the dead of the night, I become accustomed to the sound of chirping crickets and hooting owls, accompanied by crunching of dry leaves under our feet. I inhale crisp air, letting myself enjoy the freshness of nature.

Closer to midnight, we're approached by a voice from within birch trees asking us for a secret password. When Felek says it, the man ushers us toward a bonfire where a woman in a black beret sits with two men in shabby clothes, surrounded by smoke.

The men get up and walk into the forest, while the woman invites us to join her at the fire. Scents of burning wood and leaves calm me, despite my nervousness about meeting this woman for the first time. The only thing that Felek uttered to me on the way here is that she's an exceptional chief to this network.

She looks up and smiles. "Nice to meet you, Kasia," she says. "I've heard a lot of good things about you." There is something in her gaze and mannerisms that makes me instantly trust her. I sense there is not a single fiber of fakeness in her.

We take our seats and I feel comfort at the warmth enveloping my skin as I savor the aroma of ash-cooked potatoes. The temperatures must've dropped close to zero and the wind isn't helping either.

"You too. I didn't expect to be meeting you today." To be honest, I didn't even know of her existence. Whenever Felek mentioned his chief, I always pictured a man. I'm ashamed of my thinking because women are much stronger mentally than men and make exceptional leaders.

"Call me Zofia, please," she says allowing her mouth to fold into a warm smile. I do have an important assignment to discuss with you regarding a sneaky practice of German sabotage services."

"What?" I appreciate that she goes straight to the point without small talk.

"One of their ways to disguise explosives is in chocolate bars. It's something your father worked on."

Suddenly, I have difficulty breathing. "My father?" It's dark but I see her face glowing in the light from the bonfire. The wrinkles under her eyes are deep.

She takes out a cigarette and after offering one to me too, which I politely reject, she lights it and takes a drag, her eyes closed for a few seconds. Then, after exhaling bouts of smoke, she continues, "The German sabotage services are finding unusual ways to camouflage their explosive devices these days." She glances across at Felek who's holding his hands out toward the flames.

"In order to assassinate important political figures," Felek says in his arrogant tone without looking my way.

He's grating on my nerves today, but I ignore him, and look at Zofia when I say, "How do you know?"

Hands shaking, I grab a stick and poke the bonfire, making

the flames spark and crackle in the blackness of the night. Suddenly, I can't sit still, or I will go insane. There's more and more bad news about Papa. I wonder what else I don't know… and I wonder what Sebastian knows of it. Just how deeply was my father involved with the Nazis and their agenda?

"Alojzy managed to get hold of some documents from your father's office after his passing, and shortly before his partner ransacked the room," Felek says.

Sebastian's words that Papa was the last who touched anything in that room come to my mind. He lied.

"And," I manage to say, feeling the blood drain from my face, "what did those documents show?" My body braces; I need to be prepared to hear the worst.

"We learned that your father worked on a special assignment of preparing a batch of 'chocolate bar bombs' made of steel with a thin covering of rich—and real—chocolate. These are packaged in expensive black and gold paper," Zofia says. "Once a section of chocolate at the end is broken off, the detonator is pulled. Then the bomb explodes in seven seconds."

I recoil from her words, imagining such a device. "Have they used this already?"

After exhaling clouds of smoke, she says, "In May of this year they tried to place one of their chocolate bars in the War Cabinet's dining room in London. Thankfully, the British spies discovered the plot just in time to stop it."

"They planned to kill Winston Churchill?" I gasp. "They don't waste their time."

"Yes, indeed. We don't know when or where else they'll try to use these bombs, but the Brits are on the lookout, and so are we. Our priority now is to find out if your father's partner is still working on this mission, or if the factory has nothing to do with it anymore." She takes another drag from her cigarette, exhales the rough-smelling smoke. "His name is Sebastian Richter, correct?"

"Yes."

"If he's still working on this 'chocolate bomb' project, we must do everything to stop him. Especially, that a while ago you reported to us overhearing him talking about it."

She's right because I did hear Sebastian mentioning the "chocolate bombs" to Bruno, though I failed to hear the details of their conversation.

"I will see what I can sniff out." My throat muscles tighten and my voice sounds shaky even to my own ears. "I doubt that Sebastian continues with my father's *project*. He confessed to me that he only pretends to be on the Nazis' side, so they don't close the factory." I pause, wondering if I can share what I want to say next. "He asked me how to contact the Polish Resistance, so he can help."

Felek snorts loudly, then says with a hint of panic in his voice, "Please tell me you didn't give him any information."

I grind my teeth but manage to say, "I told him that I know nothing of a Polish Resistance in Gdańsk. I wanted to first run it past you."

Zofia tosses the cigarette butt into the fire. "Good. Let's keep it this way. If he turns out to be a worthy man, we'll consider his help. For now, let's be extremely careful."

"That might not be as easy as you think, Zofia," Felek says, a sly edge to his voice. "Kasia seems to be involved intimately with this man."

A dash of heat enters my cheeks as I glare at him. "My private life isn't any of your business." I glance at Zofia and say, "He needs to stop spying on me."

"Calm down, Kasia," she says. "He only does it to protect you. You're very important to us. And when it comes to Richter, please be careful. We don't know his true intentions, not yet anyway."

After we say our goodbyes to Zofia, we remain silent on our way to the city. I can't wait to be back in my bed, far away from

Felek, who seems today like the most primitive boor in all of Poland. Even now, with every step he takes, I can feel his anger. I just don't understand why, suddenly, he decides to be like this when before he showed decency.

"What the hell," he yells and stops without warning, just when I bump into his back. "What's this?"

I can't stop a bubble of laughter that bursts out of my throat. This simple act helps me to release some of tonight's tension.

If I was able to see his eyes in the darkness, I'm sure I would detect only fury.

"I'm glad I made you laugh," his voice is softer now. "Though I still don't know how on earth we ended up right at this giant rock. I thought I'd broken my foot." I giggle again as he says, "I think we're lost."

"Stop worrying and hand me the flashlight, so I can lead us to the city. I know this area as well as you know your Warsaw."

When he gives me the heavy torch, I run its light over the object we bumped into. There's nothing funny about it, I realize, as drops of ice run down my spine. I hope bumping into it won't bring bad luck to us.

"What is it?" Felek asks, his tone somber.

"It's a..." I take a breath, steadying my voice. "It's a devil stone."

"Excuse me?"

"It's the name of the stone, and the hill is called the Devil's Mountain. There is even a legend about it." We resume walking. After leaving Zofia, I felt drained of all my energy, but now when I must navigate through the woods and lead this antagonistic man, all my senses are awake and sharp.

"What's the legend about?" His voice is low now, nothing like the fuming one from before.

I sigh and decide to indulge him. "One day a poor man was on the way to work when he was approached by a stranger dressed all in black," my story begins. "When he asked the man about his well-being, the man confessed to not being able to feed his children or buy them clothes to wear. In response, the stranger offered to make him rich if the man gave him his soul in return. The poor man realized he was speaking to the devil. But he was desperate, so he signed the bond with his blood.

"After many years, they both met again, and the devil intended to take what was his, but the clever man offered another deal. They were to play cards and if the devil won, he would take not only the soul of the man, but also his wife and children. If the man won, the devil would take back the bond and never bother him or his family again.

"The devil was sure of winning, so he agreed to the new bargain. But the man came up with a card game with rules the devil didn't know. The man won, making the devil so angry that he hit a huge stone up the hill on which they stood. He hit it so hard that it split into two. And that's why the devil stone has this shape."

By the time I'm done with the legend, we're nearing the city. The curfew is still in effect, which means we'll need to slide through the streets of Gdańsk like we're invisible.

"What would have to happen to convince you to sell your soul to the devil?" he asks.

"I would like to think that there is nothing to convince me. What about you?"

"I would be like the man from your legend," he says and grins.

"I hope you don't ever have to prove it," I say and quicken my steps.

Soon we are navigating the avenues and alleyways of the city in silence, my ears fully alerted to faint dry sounds around. Are these the footsteps of ghosts passing over the deserted cobblestones? Why am I thinking like this right now, when normally I just move forward, ignoring the stillness of the night?

But since we entered the city, every sound makes me whip my head round so fast it almost hurts.

"Ssh, it's only rats and stray cats and dogs," Felek says. But he must have noticed my discomfort because he takes my hand in his, and a tiny shock runs between us. How did it get from him being so rude to me before to now holding my hand in this tender way?

Just as we slip from one street to another, a sudden clang of boots makes me pause while the blood in my veins freezes.

Felek pulls us both behind the ornate metal gateway of one of courtyards, then he holds me tight into his body as we wait. We make sure not to move or breathe because our spot could easily be seen from the street if someone intently looked this way.

My racing heartbeat causes pain in my chest but being held in his strong arms eases my shaking nerves as we remain in the gateway's shadows.

"So, Günter, how was it at the Alhambra last night? Have you found yourself a pretty girl to warm your bed on this cold evening?" a cheerful voice says with a hint of mockery.

As the steps get closer and closer, my nostrils detect a whiff of cigarette smoke that intensifies with every second. I pray as hard as I've ever prayed that they won't look our way.

"Nah. There was one cute waitress with nice tits though." The man whistles his lewd appreciation. "If only she wasn't a rotten Polish swine." The two men give a gruff laugh that dies out as they keep marching away, smoke trailing behind them.

After holding our breaths for a minute that seems like eternity, we both exhale with relief at the same time. Felek lightens his grip, and I expect him to spring away, but no such thing happens. We stay in this entangle of limbs as if frozen under some sort of spell.

The truth is that I don't want him to let go of me. I don't know if I've ever felt the way I do right now—so peaceful and warm inside, cozy like at home before Papa changed. I don't want to be free from his touch because it brings security to the very deepness of me, the illusion that there is no harsh world up there. So, I gently press the side of my head into his chest and listen to his chaotic heartbeat through the wool of his jacket. A button presses into the soft flesh of my arm, but I ignore it, lost in his human sturdiness.

His fingers slide down the back of my neck, leaving their warmth on my skin, making me feel a foreign emotion in every fiber of my body.

"Kasia," he whispers with a faint catch in his voice, fanning my ear with his warm breath. "I'm sorry."

I lift my face to his though I don't see his eyes in the darkness. I only feel his gaze, breathing in a woodsy scent mixed with a trace of sweat. It flashes through my mind how delicious his smell and his touch feel while I also scold myself for not jumping away from him. But still, I don't move, not understanding why I feel the way I feel, why my body reacts in such a way to this man with his rakish face, and arrogant curl to his lip.

"For what?" I whisper, unable to control my voice shaking.

"For being rude today. I just... I mean you shouldn't trust that German in the factory."

"I'm being careful," I whisper. "Please don't worry. You've more important things to think of than this."

"Seeing him kissing you, well, it made me angry because you shouldn't let him cloud your good judgment. But as you said before, it's not any of my business." His voice hardens on those last words, and I sense very clearly that he feels it is his business.

"We need some enjoyment in this life too," I say, a little primly. "Don't you think that the war has taken already enough from us?"

He doesn't answer but surprises me by finding my lips with his. The touch is soft and probing, as if he expects that I'll push him away. But how could I when my heart is bounding with such pleasure that it makes me breathless. I can't deny those sparks that run through me, in precisely the way my favorite romance novels describe. I almost laugh out loud as I realize I'm feeling the exact same bliss as the protagonists on those fictional pages, except, this is reality, a shadowy corner of wartime Gdańsk, but, yes, our reality.

I yearn for more and more as our lips touch and he deepens the kiss.

Our tongues entangle and play as if attuned to the music of our hearts.

I want more and more and more… and he gives it, reading me to perfection, fulfilling every particle in my soul.

∽

An hour later, as I lie in my bed, I can't stop thinking of him and our kiss. It was *our kiss* because I was a willing participant, without any hesitation. I succumbed to his touch with my whole heart, my body and soul in tune with him, just like he did when my lips tamed him to take my lead.

It didn't feel like this with Sebastian, not ever. He demanded and took, not making any room for my instincts. Maybe that's why I never felt those sparks when he touched me. I honestly don't understand, and feel my bedsheets tie themselves in knots around my legs as I try to make sense of all of this. Sebastian looks like a prince from my dreams with his handsome features and charm, with his charisma and the way he treats me like I'm his princess, driving me to the theatre, treating me to fine dinners and glasses of champagne. He's told me he hates the Nazis and even at work, he tries to help others by running the bakery. He should be the one my heart reacts to.

Why then does my heart seek that Polish lad with his hair always disheveled and his freckles like a farmer who's been out in the sun, with his stubborn personality and incredibly strong hands? Just the thought of him makes my body feel on fire. When he embraced me today and then kissed me in that night-time street, for a moment I forgot all about Papa's dark secrets, about the war itself. The world around us ceased to exist.

Still, I must be practical, stay focused on what counts. My future lies at Sebastian's side and with the factory, especially when now I should feel sure that his heart is with the good side, not the bad.

I know he is right when he says that if the factory was closed, there wouldn't be much he could do for others. And, by the same token, I would not be able to supply information for the Resistance. To fight the Nazi regime, both Sebastian and I need to maintain our investment in the chocolate factory.

EIGHTEEN

KASIA: THE CHOCOLATE GIRLS

November 1943, Gdańsk

Gold and red leaves dance in the gentle breeze of early November as we walk through the city center. There are not many days with such mild weather, so I embrace every touch of sun on my face as Malina and Alina stride along.

"I'm surprised that Herr Richter isn't going to be there," Alina says, a hint of relief settling in her face features. I've noticed on a few occasions that she simply doesn't like Sebastian, but she does well to hide it most of the time. I keep this observation to myself, so she doesn't get into trouble. I've grown to adore both girls for their simple approach to our deliveries; they focus on getting the job done as swiftly as possible.

"It's not any of our business," Malina scolds her sister.

"Well, he wasn't invited as this meeting is only for the SS officers," I say and go through an internal battle of not spitting on the street at the thought of the evil men. "Anyway, you girls seem a little on edge today. Is everything alright?"

Malina sighs. "It's just that…" Her voice fades away as if she's afraid to say it.

I gaze at Alina who bites her lip, but then, perhaps encouraged by the softness in my eyes, she blurts out, "We don't have the right clothes to go inside."

I look them up and down, and realize my mistake. I should have asked them before coming here if they need outfits. "We must make it work today," I say. "You both look fine thanks to your natural beauty."

We've received a special request to serve our chocolate at an event that Bruno organized for his work peers in the hall of the Artus Court, a monument located along the famous Royal Route of Gdańsk. This path consists of the Long Market near the historic port of the Motława River and the Długa Street.

I force myself to ignore the Nazi Germans parading in their uniforms and I refuse to acknowledge their swastikas and propaganda all over the streets. They suck out the real beauty of this old city and whatever they contribute is marked with blood and misery.

Soon we enter the Old Town Square and approach the Artus Court in the Dutch style, located opposite the Neptune fountain, and named after the legendary Celtic leader Arthur who was a model of knightly virtues, like courage, justice or mercy. The building is decorated with statues of antique heroes and the statue of Fortuna on the gable. Now it serves as a restaurant, bakery, and banquet venue for the local *elite*.

After we enter an enormous hall, I cringe at the whiff of warm air and cigarette smoke mixed with savory aromas of food. The place is crowded by uniformed men who sit at tables and listen to Bruno's speech about the Nazi party achievements in Danzig.

A lanky waiter in a black tuxedo leads us to a white-clothed table in the corner. "Please let me know if I can be of any help," he says in crisp German, but his eyes betray his reluctance when he glances at the girls.

In this very moment, I beat myself again for my selfishness

and self-absorption. I should've made sure that both girls had fancier pieces of wardrobe for today unlike the worn cardigans. They should be wearing something more suitable, like the black, elegant dress I have on. Still, their true beauty shines through it all. I make a mental note to go through Mama's old outfits. They also need better coats than the patched ones they currently have.

The hall shines with richly ornamented furniture, tapestries and paintings, like the one portraying Orpheus among animals, or one showing a siege. Another thing that always stands out for me when I'm here, is an extremely high furnace covered with hundreds of tiles.

Soon we are done setting all the chocolate samples on the table and I leave Alina and Malina to help the patrons. When Bruno is done with his speech and the men engage in separate conversations, I mingle in the crowd with a tray displaying our newest chocolate pieces. I walk from table to table and with a smile glued to my mouth, I offer the sweets to Bruno's guests.

Most are polite while greeting me with enthusiasm and some look at me with suspicion. I ignore it all and go with the flow. It's my punishment to do it myself for not making sure that the girls have appropriate clothes. I was so wrapped up around my own problems that I failed them. The least I could do is to let them stay at that table away from the commotion here.

"My Katharina, how good to see you." Bruno's dramatic voice makes me swirl around and bump into an officer passing by.

"Please forgive me," I say and plaster a smile onto my mouth.

The red-faced and heavy-set German smirks at me but then to my relief he walks away. What a grouchy man.

"Thank you for making it so special for me," Bruno says when he nears me. He looks me up and down, and picks up a chocolate piece from the tray. "You look stunning as always."

"My pleasure," I say and crinkle a smile. "It's what we are for, to serve the Third Reich.

He sighs with exaltations. "You're a doll. I fully understand Richter's infatuation with you, my dearest." He glances at his wristwatch. "Speaking of him, please remind him of the card game tonight when you are back, will you?"

"Of course, I will do."

"Very well, thank you, darling." He fingers his mustache and leans closer. "Some of the officers here are concerned about your workers."

I pretend to be surprised by his words. "What about them? From what I see both employees are fulfilling their duties with perfection."

He looks around before speaking. "In this world it's all about the right appearance. I think it's for the best if you ladies leave early." He takes my hand between his and places a kiss on it. "Before we get any unwanted attention."

He doesn't have to say it twice and soon I prompt the girls to pack the chocolate, and we exit while feeling many pairs of eyes on us. Damn Nazis, for them it's all about perfect looks and fancy outfits. If I could only tell them what I really think of them... I can't wait long enough for that day to arrive. For now, they can live in their illusions of the perfect race in their Aryan lands.

As we walk to catch the tram, Alina pulls my sleeve and leans closer. "Kasia, do you know that the German plan to build their Wehrmacht *castle* on the moraine hills?" she whispers. "On the border of Strzyża and Oliwa districts."

I slow down. "What castle?"

"They call it a *castle* but it's really a project of an enormous school for future Wehrmacht officers," she tells me. "They already have a model of the building that refers to the old Gothic castles built in the Middle Ages by the German Order."

"Stupid idea. I hope they will never get to do it."

"It's intended to remind everyone the presence of the German Order in Pomerania all those centuries ago and to highlight the traditions from which the Wehrmacht drew."

"How do you know all of this?" I say and quicken my footsteps. I don't know the girls well enough to trust them, so I must be wary. I made a terrible mistake by expressing my hate for the Nazis just a moment ago.

"I overheard a conversation between the two SS officers that rudely took the chocolate samples without even glancing my way. They probably thought me too stupid to realize what they conversed about." She rolls her eyes and chuckles.

"Well, thank you for sharing this with me," I say and gently squeeze her arm to show my appreciation. I will make sure to write about it in the next report for the Resistance, but they might be already aware of it, not like myself returning to the city only months ago after being absent for five years. "By the way, will you girls be home this Sunday afternoon?" I ask, knowing what precisely I need to do.

∽

The following Sunday I take a tram to the city center and navigate the streets in search of the tenement where Malina and Alina live with their grandmother. I carry a suitcase with outfits and coats for the girls, thanks to Mama's generosity. Her prewar wardrobe was so rich that through the years she made a habit of putting away anything that came out of fashion into the trunks in the attic.

"Mama, you should donate the rest that you don't wear anymore," I said to her this morning when we were shuffling through the old trunks.

She shrugged. "I never liked to part with my belongings but now with the war, I should do just that. But who would want these?" She motioned to the overflowing black chests.

"I will ask around. Since the war a lot of Poles can't afford to buy new fabrics. They will take it with delight."

"You're right." She sighed and suddenly, she seemed so fragile with deep wrinkles under her eyes and dull skin, as if all the life had slowly evaporated from her. I felt exactly how she looked in that very moment—so resigned, but the perspective of helping the girls after the humiliation yesterday because of my indifference, brought back the lacking energy to me.

I have too much to do and no time to be tired.

Now I march through the streets of my hurting city while black clouds hover above me. Even the weather is in tune with my mood today. I would give everything to run into Felek's embrace and stay in there for a very long time, but these are only empty wishes. Who knows when I will see Felek now...?

As promised, Alina is waiting for me outside. Despite my anxiety today, I nod at her and say, "I hope you haven't been waiting long."

Her contagious smile reaches her blue eyes. "No more than five minutes. You are very punctual."

The earnest look in her face restores the belief in me that it is never too late to fix our faults or mistakes. "I have some outfits for you," I say and wink at her.

The basement room is gray with the only light infiltrating through a tiny window. The cement walls and floor, along with sparse and bitten furniture, are at war with the sweet scents of apple marmalade that bring on a homey feeling about the place.

"Please, take a seat," Malina greets me and points out a small wooden table with three chairs, all painted in dark brown. "Babcia made an apple strudel before leaving for the church."

I feel awkward eating their food when I know how little they have but rejecting it would be like insulting them, so I take a tiny piece—and it tastes like heaven. "Your grandma could be a baker, that's how delicious this is,' I say and take a sip of a grain coffee.

"Babcia is wonderful. With only a few ingredients she can make the best treats in the world," Alina says with her mouth full.

"How are you doing here? Winters must be tough."

"It's not that bad," Malina says and picks up crumbs from the table. "Babcia cooks soups every day and the stove brings some warmth too. We truly can't complain as there are many who would give everything for this." Her face grows somber.

I nod and put my hand over hers. "You must believe that your dad will be back soon." The girls' father was brought to Stutthof after the Gestapo discovered his *bimber*, the illegal still with which he produced his yeasty, far-too-powerful moonshine. Now they live with their grandmother.

Alina clears her throat. "We usually gather some wood from the park for the stove, you know when the Germans don't see," she says with a mischievous grin. "When it gets dark and cold in the winter, the guards don't really pay much attention."

It strikes me how savvy and brave both girls are, but I also feel obliged to start helping them whenever I can.

"Kasia, we wanted to ask you something," Alina says and glances at Malina who wrinkles her forehead, but she nods to her sister.

"You know you can tell me anything." I take another sip of the steaming liquid and glance at my wristwatch. It's getting dangerously close to the curfew hour.

"When we do deliveries, we hear the German officers talk, so we were wondering if any of the information could be useful to the Resistance."

I struggle to find the right words, not sure what to do. Surely these sweet girls cannot be working for the Nazis, but what if they are trying to get information from me, so they can get a reward when they denounce me. I know this is far-fetched and deep in me I sense that I can trust them. Still, I decide to be cautious. "And why are you telling me this?"

"I overheard you whispering with Pan Alojzy in the supply room," Alina says, then she quickly adds, "Please, don't fret. We will never tell anyone. We hate Hitler and his brainwashed followers." She presses both hands to her chest. "You must trust us."

If she's noticed my communication with Pan Alojzy, then who else might have?

For a moment longer, they both watch me as if unsure of my reaction. I want to be skeptical and do as I always do in these situations: act like I don't know what they're talking about. No, I tell myself, these girls are wearing their hearts on their sleeves, trusting me even though they know well that I could doom them for what they just told me. One word to Bruno would be enough.

I look up. "Can anyone up there hear our conversation?" I whisper.

They both exhale with relief and relax their rigid shoulders.

Malina pours more of the grain coffee into our tin cups. "They aren't home, so we are safe."

"I will contact my chief to see if you can start helping us, but please know that working for the Resistance is extremely dangerous. I don't think your grandmother will like that."

"Babcia would give her own life for our country. She will understand." Alina's face shows contempt, like someone finally seeing a string of light in darkness. "We want to do something, to be helpful."

"Even at the cost of your lives?"

I expect Malina to scold her sister and deem the entire idea as irresponsible, but she only smiles faintly and says, "Even."

"Very well then. You must be extremely careful not to talk with anyone about this. There are so many lives at stake here."

NINETEEN

FELEK: OPERATION SYNTHESIS

November 1943, Mirachowskie Forest

"You must get some sleep, Felek," Zofia says while we sit at the bonfire, not far from our bunker and eat the last of the potatoes from the fire, burning our fingers on their hot flesh. "You will have to start your journey to Szczecin in the early morning."

I've just arrived from my last assignment and it's near midnight. "I will put out the bonfire, and we can leave." I do as I say and soon, we enter our shelter lighted by kerosine lamp.

I climb up to my bed and exhale with relief at the thought of resting for the night and dreaming of Kasia and her intoxicating touch. Since our kiss, I can't get her off my mind, regardless of my tasks, though I make sure to be careful. If I got caught, I'd never see her again.

"What's in Szczecin?" I ask, unable to stop myself from yawning. Even though we only spend some nights in this bunker and rarely see each other during the days, I've begun thinking of Zofia as one of my older sisters. I've grown to trust her, and most of all, I hold a tremendous respect for her.

"Felek," she says, "I've mentioned to you about Operation

Synthesis and now it's time I fill you in more. You will be helping with it for the next couple of weeks."

"Yes, indeed." It's like she never gets tired. I try to sober my mind: whatever she tells me now is very important. I've noticed how she bombards me with important information at night, right when I hope for peaceful sleep. Thankfully, villagers have supplied us with a pile of warm blankets.

"Listen carefully then, and as always, don't hold back any questions you may have."

"Yes, chief, my ears are all yours."

"You will hang close to the town where Germans run their synthetic petrol factory named as Hydrierwerke Pölitz. They use coal to produce fuel mainly for the Luftwaffe and Kriegsmarine, and a local shipyard that produces U-boats. Since the start of the war, the factory has expanded because they use forced Polish laborers, POWs, but also camp prisoners from Stutthof, Sachsenhausen and Ravensbrück."

"Is this information all new to the Resistance?" The need for sleep has abandoned me now as Zofia sparked my curiosity. I was always good at chemistry at school, so the topic of producing fuel from coal is up my alley. Back in Warsaw I'd heard that they have several factories like the one near Szczecin. Before the war, there was intense research on coal liquefaction. I don't remember any names of scientists, but I recall that there was a method developed to create hydrocarbons from a mixture of carbon monoxide and hydrogen. This synthesis enabled the production of liquid fuels, which are now being used by the Germans for their evil purposes.

"No. The Allies bombarded the factory already in 1940 but didn't succeed in destroying much. The factory never ceased functioning and Germans strengthened their anticraft batteries and set up a balloon barrier in the area to make it difficult for planes to fly over."

"They will do everything to destroy the entire world and without their gasoline they can't do much," I say.

"True. Anyway, to facilitate effective bombings, Allies need detailed plans of the factory. The Resistance began the intelligence work on gaining the needed information, but in 1942 several people from the network were detained due to betrayal, and because of that, Operation Synthesis was paused. Until last month."

"So," I say. "What's my assignment?"

"You'll be one of the agents responsible for observing the area and gathering information from locals and the Polish forced laborers. Safely. I can't afford for you to get caught by the Germans."

∾

The three-week stay around the factory turns out to be intense. Even though there are many agents who also work on this mission, I've been in contact only with a man whose code name is Jan. We've never exchanged our real names, only the password. It's better to know the least, so when someone gets arrested, they will not be able to tell the Gestapo any names, even if tortured. I like this way of operating. It suits me.

Now we both sit in Jan's room, which he occupies in his aunt's cottage, having our last conversation before my departure tomorrow.

"Have you found out anything important when you talked to locals yesterday?" I ask.

He rubs his black beard and wrinkles his forehead. "Not much."

Every account we listen to, we note down when possible, and thanks to that we've gathered some information. "The intelligence still has so much more to do," I say and take a sip of beer from the bottle.

"Actually, I should not be telling you this," he says and listens for a moment longer for any noises from outside. "One of the intelligence members pretends to be a worker of the military construction company called Todt. Tricky and dangerous, but I guess it offers the highest chance to get hold of the detailed plans of the factory."

"It's probably the best move in this situation since we can't really find out much."

"Though I had a nice conversation with one of the laborers the other day."

Polish forced laborers, unlike the camp prisoners, can move around the town relatively freely, though must adhere to rules. "Anything worth mentioning?"

"Oh, not really. But it was an interesting conversation where he described the process of producing the synthetic fuel. As per his words, the coal gets sent to ball mills where it is mixed with solvents, and then gets crushed. Enormous pressure is needed, and temperatures reach around five hundred Celsius."

"Makes sense," I say and recall reading the exact thing in one of the magazines in Warsaw. "I guess after that, the created liquid must go through further processing before the distillation process."

"Precisely. He claims that seven tons of coal produces a ton of excellent quality synthetic gasoline that ends up in tanks of German planes, ships and tanks."

"Basically, it brings them more and more power to fight."

When I'm back from my mission, I hand all the information to Zofia. She will pass it to Warsaw to the right people, and then it will go on its way to London. I'm not sure if what I got is any different from what the other agents have gathered. But at least it might be one puzzle piece in the whole picture. I keep my fingers crossed that our intelligence will somehow get a hold of the detailed plans of the factory. Those plans would be enough for the Allies to perform successful air raids and shut down production.

But I know, too, that every bomb will kill innocent people who work in the factory. Nothing is fair in war. Every life is equally important, but this cruel war brings destruction, death and pain. It's easier to consider it as an action, but when you start wondering about the fate of all the prisoners or forced laborers, your heart aches for them.

Through all these weeks there wasn't a day that I didn't miss Kasia. I can't wait to head to Gdańsk and see her again, but first I must stop at Adka's cottage to hand in some documents to her father.

I pass the wooden barn and walk through cackling white geese before pausing in front of Adka's grandmother who sits on a small bench.

"Good day," I say and take my hat off.

"Good day," she says and gets up, then gestures for me to follow. "My son has been waiting for you."

Just when we enter their home's low threshold, the elderly lady gasps. Right in front of us is Adka, and she's kissing a tall, blond man, a stranger to me.

"Fear God, girl," her grandmother says and moves forward as if to sweep them away. "We have a guest."

Adka jumps away from the man and when our eyes meet, hers reflect shame and her face turns scarlet.

I wear a friendly smile, while everything inside me dances. In truth, I feel nothing but relief that she's moved on and found another man of interest. "Please, Adka," I say, cheerfully, "don't bother yourself with me. I'm only dropping off something for your father."

When I leave their house after conversing with Zbigniew she comes running after me. "It's not what you think," she says after catching her breath. "You were gone for all these weeks, and I was sure you wouldn't come back."

"Adka," I reassure her, "I don't think anything negative but wish you happiness. You deserve someone who will appreciate you."

"Please, Felek, forget about what you saw," she pleads. "I want only you, truly."

I'm taken aback by her stark words. It's time to be bold, I decide, and to end this thing for once and for all. "I'm in love with someone else."

"Oh yes," she says, a question in her voice. "And who might she be, Felek?"

I open my mouth as if to speak, but the way she's looking at me stops the words in my throat. My blood freezes.

TWENTY
KASIA: BAD NEWS

December 1943, Gdańsk

I pick a cocoa bean from my small roaster, and I chew it, enjoying its intense taste of caramel and creaminess. Cinnamon, vanilla and sugar would go perfectly with this cocoa bean... All bags store different aromas and flavors and one of the keys is to add the right ingredients and seasonings in right amounts.

Sebastian uses some of my new mixtures in the factory. Because of the war, he wants simple but memorable, something other businesses don't offer.

Before the war, in addition to chocolate, Papa also produced biscuits, cakes, candy, caramels and cocoa powder. Now production is only limited, for the Wehrmacht and Luftwaffe.

My senses are so focused on my new chocolate mixture that someone knocks on the door twice before I snap back to reality.

"Do you have a moment?" Sebastian asks as he closes the door behind him.

"Yes, of course. I'm working on my newest recipe. I think you will like this one. Care to try it for yourself?"

His face beams as he tastes it. "I like it. You have this way of adding the perfect proportions of components."

"And you have a way of making everything sounding so professional." I laugh and playfully nudge his arm.

He chuckles. "It's good that we're so different. Fire and water create an interesting combination, don't you think."

"I'm not so sure, but if I was to choose, I would stay with water."

"So, you can tame the fire inside me every time I look at you." His husky voice alarms me, but I don't protest when he pulls me into his embrace. I don't know what to think of him anymore, or whose side he's on.

His kisses are passionate, and I enjoy his touch, but whatever I'm experiencing is so far from the way I felt when I was in Felek's arms. This can't compete; there are no sparks or tingling in my skin, or that undefined warmth around my heart.

But since my kiss with Felek, I only see him briefly while handing over information I've learned during my deliveries. And at those times we act like nothing ever happened between us; if anything, he seems colder toward me.

And this man before me now looks like a prince from my favorite romance, the one I always dreamed of meeting one day, so why don't I feel what I should? Is this because I'm still worried that despite what he keeps telling me, he might be on the Nazis' side?

Why did Felek's slightest brush cause my entire being to spin in bliss? Still, I'm afraid to reject Sebastian because in this world of wolves, he's our potential protector.

"Come back to me," he whispers in my ear. "Where is your mind taking you?"

"I'm with you," I say and tease his cheek with my hand.

"Remember that you can always trust me," he says, his breath hot against my neck as he kisses me there. "And, you know, I have some important information that I'd like to share with the Polish Resistance." He pauses, reaches out and takes a chocolate from my tasting tray, puts it in his mouth. "If you, my pretty chocolate girl, could only get me in touch with them."

He's doing this again. How can I believe him? Zofia's order was not to betray my involvement in the underground activities to him, not until I'm advised otherwise. "I already told you I know nothing of any resistance movement. I'm focusing on being a good German woman, that's all."

The amusement in his eyes tells me that he doesn't believe me, but I do not turn my gaze away first. There is too much at risk here, too many lives. The chance that he might be trying to use me to infiltrate the Polish Resistance is high even though I almost believe him. Almost.

"Good German woman?" Is that a sneer on his handsome face? "That's not who you were in Warsaw."

I detect a hint of anger in his tone and his laugh has an edge to it. "I was lost in Warsaw, far away from my parents and I didn't know whom to trust," I protest as mildly and innocently as I can. "People used me though I always made sure to stay away from trouble. I'm not naïve or stupid anymore, so please be assured that I interact only with people worth my time, like you or Bruno." I lower my voice to whisper. "Besides, you must remember that walls have ears." I tilt my head, as if listening to the walls myself. "As far as I know your secretary might be able to 'overhear' our conversation. And then she'd be obliged to report to the Gestapo that you are trying to get in touch with the Polish Resistance."

He steps away from me and cracks his knuckles. "Would you do that? I mean, report me?"

"You're our protector, so what would I do that for? I think you should focus on running this factory," I fix his tie, my hands flirtatiously close to his chest, "so after the war we can live happily ever after."

"You always know how to make me feel better." He smiles

down at me. "And yes, I will always protect you and your family. I promised that to Dietrich."

The moment he grows silent, the door swings open and Bruno charges in, as always without knocking. Of all people, I think, and now.

"I need to talk to both of you. It's extremely important," he says in a decisive tone of voice.

Once we're all sat in Sebastian's office, the mean eyes in Hitler's framed picture staring at us from the wall, I try to calm down. It's obvious that something bad has happened because the usually ebullient and cheerful Bruno is deflated, edgy.

"I was informed today that your factory will be shut down in one month and designated as a storage facility for documents," he announces and takes a performative drag from his cigarette.

"Are you sure?" Sebastian fishes out a handkerchief from his pants pocket and wipes his forehead. "Is this final?"

"Pretty much. We must focus more and more on shipyards, so we can win this war."

"I was under the impression that our chocolate helps the German war effort as it lifts our soldiers' morale, gives them more energy," I say, acting crestfallen. Though, in truth, I don't need to act. It's not good news at all. If the factory closes, I will not be able to keep helping the Resistance under the cover my work here provides.

"It does but the plan is to have other factories in Gdańsk provide more chocolate to the Wehrmacht and Luftwaffe."

"Why then, don't they close down another location and spare us?" Sebastian's gaze is hard.

"I suggested as such and await their response, but things look grim right now." Bruno grinds his cigarette out, with such finality it's as if he's shutting down the factory at the very same time.

"Thank you," Sebastian says. "I will contact my uncle and see if he can pull any strings."

"That's what I wanted to suggest, my friend. I will do what I can, but I wanted to make sure that you're aware of the situation." He smiles and I see the mood shift on his face. "By any chance, do you have any of that delicious chocolate of yours on hand?"

Sebastian nods and walks to a cabinet then returns with a few bars which he hands to Bruno. I've noticed on many occasions that he will do everything to please him. I guess everything has its price.

"Excellent," Bruno says and beams, then he unwraps one of the bars, breaks it into squares. "Please, share it with me, Katharina."

"Thank you." His face expression is so sincere that I feel I can't refuse, so I reach for it but at Sebastian's stern voice, I jerk my hand away, uncertain what to think.

"Keep her away from it." His glare is now on Bruno.

Bruno lifts his hands as if in capitulation. "Alright, my friend. I'm only trying to be nice here. You may need some valium, or something." He chuckles, rolls his eyes then pops a square of chocolate into his mouth.

∾

Once I'm left alone in Papa's office, I put away the mask of pretense and exhale with relief. At this point, maybe it's all for good that the factory closes. It's like a ticket to freedom for me, far away from all the effort to please the damn Nazis. But the war is still here, and it doesn't seem like it will end any time soon.

It's all like a chain, I realize. The factory supports the Germans by supplying their soldiers with chocolate that brings boats of energy to them. People who work here have at least a sliver of protection from much the worse fate of laboring in much worse places. Malina, Alina and I use deliveries to gain crucial information for the Resistance, which often saves lives. Mama is happy that the factory still functions, so when the war ends it will go back to our family. Her hopes will dwindle when she hears Bruno's news though…

I sigh in resignation. It's all like a board game, one that someone must win. For the sake of humanity, I pray that the murderers will get defeated very soon.

There is a knock at the door. Probably Sebastian wants to see me before leaving for the day. He acts like I'm that one person with whom he can share things. I don't know how to find myself in this or what I really want.

But Malina's head peeks in the door frame. "Can I take a minute of your time, Fräulein Hartmann?"

"Of course," I say loudly in German and usher her to take a seat in one of the chairs opposite my desk.

"Is everything alright? Shouldn't you girls be leaving now anyway?" I glance to the wall clock that indicates a quarter to four.

Sudden sobs emerge from her and a stream of tears runs down her cheeks. "Alina got arrested last night."

"What? How?" I say in disbelief. "And why are you telling me this now, and not this morning?"

"I wasn't allowed to leave my workstation earlier. We went to gather some wood in the park when the German patrol stopped us. They checked our papers and were going to let us go but Alina got into an argument with one of the guards who said that we have no right to the wood as it belongs to the Third Reich. I tried stopping her, but you know her. Her stupid bravery finally got her into trouble." She wipes her eyes with handkerchief and continues, "They said they were taking her for further questioning and if she is clean, they will release her the next day. I just ran home and she's still not there."

I sigh as dread builds in the pit of my stomach. "I will see what I can do to find out her whereabouts."

"Thank you. I'm afraid that she's giving them her attitude and that may lead to something terrible. I pray that she comes out of this and takes heed for future on controlling her temper."

"I'm sure she will. Please, go home now to your grandmother as I'm sure she's worrying as well. I will let you know as soon as I learn something."

The truth is that at this point Malina can't do anything to help her sister, but I will not stop until this girl is free and safe at her home.

A few minutes later I'm lucky enough to still catch Sebastian in his office before he leaves for the day.

"I was going to stop by to ask you where you would like to go out this Saturday, but I see you've already missed me," he says and pulls me into his lap.

I stay in there without protesting as he kisses my neck. "Actually, I'm coming with an urgent matter. One of our girls from the factory got arrested last night for picking a few pieces of wood from the park." I purposely don't tell him about Alina's attitude to the guards because I know it would strip him of all empathy for her.

He doesn't respond but continues kissing me.

I move away from him and say, "We must help her."

He sighs. "Why do you always have to act like you must save the entire world? She got arrested like many others and there is nothing we can do about it."

His words don't discourage me. He's only a little upset that I'm interrupting his pleasure, so I sit back on his lap and put my hands around his neck. "Please, it's one of the chocolate girls. I need her for deliveries."

His muscles visibly relax, and he engages in teasing my

cheek with his thumb. "Everyone is replaceable. Pick someone else for the job."

I keep running my hand through his blond hair while he closes his eyes. "Please," I whisper, "she's perfect for the job. Can you speak with Bruno to see if he can help? She really didn't do much harm by picking some wood."

"Alright. I have a better idea though. She was probably brought to the Gestapo Headquarters on Neugarten and one of the crucial people over there is a good friend of mine. Since this is so important to you, I will pay him a little visit. But on one condition..."

I feel a floating sensation all over my body: tremendous hope that it's not too late to help Alina before she gets herself into more trouble while in their clutches.

"What's the condition?"

"You go straight home now and wait there for me with a nice supper." A slow grin quirks his mouth.

"I will do just that then," I whisper, truly ready to do everything just to save the poor girl that I adore so much. "What would you like?"

"Something sweet, just like you."

As I promised, when back at my home I bake his favorite apple strudel and wait nervously, frequently gazing at the grandfather clock on the wall. Mama rests in her bedroom due to a migraine and Kornel volunteered to read to her.

When Sebastian arrives, we take our seats at the kitchen table, and I watch him eating the strudel while sipping on my mother's chamomile tea. I want so badly to ask him about Alina, but I restrain myself, knowing that he will tell me once he's done eating. Sebastian is a man of order, so I do not want to frustrate him, not now.

"I spoke to Hauptsturmführer Abt and he promised to release the girl."

I feel a sudden lightness. "Just like that? He didn't give you any trouble?" I find it hard to believe.

He brings a fork with a piece of strudel to his mouth and for a moment longer he chews it. "I told you he's a good friend of mine. But you should know, she was arrested for talking back to one of the guards. That girl is ridiculous. She must learn to keep her mouth shut. I've noticed too the looks she gives me when I inspect their work."

I sigh. "I will make sure that going forward she controls her outbursts. Thank you for doing this for me."

He nods. "Abt would like to meet you as he knew your father very well. I promised him that you will gift him a fancy box of chocolate on your next delivery trip at Neugarten. Hope that's fine with you."

"Of course," I say quickly. "My next delivery over there is on Monday."

A smile curls at the edge of his mouth. "Well, since Abt is getting paid so generously, what's my recompensation for all the effort?" He keeps his sparkling eyes on my lips.

"I thought the strudel would take care of that," I say, making sure to sound lighthearted and change the subject. "I was thinking that we may go out this Saturday to the gallery in the Old Town. I'm dying to see some new pieces by the excellent German artists."

"You always do that," he says and takes my hand in his, "you always change the subject when you're not comfortable with something. Are you afraid of getting more intimate with me?"

I avoid his gaze. "No, of course not, it's just that I don't want to rush things between us, not now when we're facing the war."

He leans back in his chair, not taking his intense gaze from my face. "There is nothing wrong with two people falling in love. It can help us survive worst of times."

Love? Why is he talking about love? "Love is a big word," I say gently.

He picks up a napkin and wipes his mouth. "Not for someone who already feels it." For a moment longer his eyes drill into mine as if he's trying to guess my thoughts.

But to my relief, Mama enters the room, freeing me from this awkward situation. What was I supposed to tell him?

My stomach sinks at the realization that, if he declares that he loves me, I will have to do the same...

TWENTY-ONE

KASIA: THE CHOCOLATE DELIVERY

December 1943, Gdańsk

As tomorrow is Christmas Eve, Mama has invited Sebastian for dinner, stating that he shouldn't be alone on a day like this.

I've still not been able to search Sebastian's office as he locks it for the night, and because of his guard-dog secretary it isn't possible to sneak in during the day. I must think of something, and soon. However many dinners we share, or Saturday evening theatre trips, I feel more and more that my heart could never belong to him—even though my mind keeps arguing that he's perfect for me, especially after the war ends. Sometimes there are so many conflicting emotions tumbling within me that I can't even understand myself. At moments like these, when I make no sense to myself, I am glad of the factory's creative, productive atmosphere; it has an energy which even the restrictions and uncertainties of the war can't quite cow.

I walk down the long corridor and climb the stairs to the third floor, enjoying the intense smell of chocolate in the air. Just as I enter the wrapping hall, Sebastian's raised voice stops me in my tracks. This is the first time I have heard him shouting at someone.

"You're ruining good material," he yells, as his face turns red, "you are not fit for the position in this factory." He pours the garbage out of the trash can and fishes out a scrap of wrapping paper, then he waves it at a girl who stands in front of him, her head down.

When I realize it's Alina, my heart sinks. This sweet girl doesn't deserve his ugly treatment, no one does. He's been this way with her since the incident with the arrest.

"Waste and bad work," he hisses. "Get out of my factory."

The girl's sobbing is the last straw; without another thought, I march forward and hug her.

Then, I lift my chin and stare into his blue eyes marked by fury. "Sebastian, please give her another chance. She does a magnificent job with deliveries, so it's imperative that she stays. Moving forward she will be more careful when it comes to handling any extra material, so it doesn't go to waste." In truth, I want to tell him that he's an asshole and if my father was here right now, Sebastian is the one who would be sent packing. Whatever scrap he took out of the garbage can is a joke. But I keep this sudden surge of hostility to myself. I must pretend to be on his side, to be supportive of him, almost as if I were already his good German wife.

His muscles slowly relax as he smiles at me. "You're right, I have failed to control my temper." He moves his gaze to Alina. "You can stay but remember that the most important rule in this building is to respect and spare everything, including wrapping paper. Now, go back to your station."

"Yes, Herr Richter," Alina says and flees before he can change his mind.

"Did you come here to find me?" I detect a hint of hopefulness in his teasing voice.

"Yes, I received a phone call with a request for delivery to Neugarten, so I wanted to see if that's fine with you."

"Of course, do as they expect from us."

"Great. I will need Malina and Alina to help me as it's getting late."

∞

We don't need to take a tram as the Gestapo Headquarters on Neugarten 27 is in the city center, not far from our factory. Because of the blackout there are no Christmas lights in the streets, but the squares are transformed into Christmas markets with stalls holding piping hot mugs of mulled wine, bratwurst and sugary confections. The Hitler Youth boys sell their handmade toys and other vendors offer hand-carved ornaments, like the *christkind* figure of an angelic girl with blonde hair and blue-eyes, made for Nazi propaganda.

Unfortunately, the Nazi party has transformed the deeply rooted tradition of Christmas into a nationalist affair of glorifying German heritage. It's why they imposed their imagery into Nativity scenes, ruined Advent calendars with their sick propaganda and rewrote Christmas carols to suit their agenda.

We stumble through white and icy streets carrying bags with the factory's logo of *Katharina* in gold lettering. I snuggle my face in a cashmere scarf that I dug out of my drawer. Both girls look adorable in Mama's wool coats. These are in perfect shape as my mother probably wore them for no more than a few seasons. Papa enjoyed spoiling her with new and fashionable clothes throughout their marriage.

"Thank you for standing up for me with Herr Richter," Alina says, squeezing my arm. "I would defend myself but after what happened when I was arrested and because of Malina's reprimanding gazes, I knew it was for the best to just act like I was sorry. Knowing him he would drag me to the Gestapo the moment I opened my mouth to say something."

"Shush, Alina." Malina's warning gaze settles on her sister. "You have caused enough trouble already."

I've been aware of Alina's dislike for Sebastian but the fact that she doesn't hide it anymore concerns me. "Don't forget that he saved you from the Gestapo prison. And your sister is right—you need to pretend to like him for your own good." I sigh and continue whispering, "I'm sorry but these are the times we live in."

Soon we approach a tall tenement with a gray-stoned façade that, before the war, housed the General Kommissariat of the Republic of Poland. Since I started working in the factory, I've been coming here once a week. This place is a source of important information, though not every eavesdrop brings something new.

It is a terrible, oppressive place. In the basement there are prison cells for people who go against the Nazi regime. The worst treatment is given to the Polish Resistance fighters. They are brought to the third floor for interrogations and torture.

Before we enter through a massive wooden door, I pause and say, "Malina, you will tackle the first floor, Alina you focus on the second, and I'll cover the third."

We make a few steps up and pass a concierge, but when we near the guard station, a red-faced German opens our bags for searching. "You're clear to go," he says, his eyes like steel.

Without a word we climb a staircase secured with a metal mesh. Malina stays on the first floor and heads to the office of SS-Obersturmbannführer Günther Venediger, the head of the Gestapo. She handles deliveries in a professional manner, so I know she will do just fine.

I leave Alina on the second floor where SS-Sturmbannführer Jakob Loellgen resides. He leads a department that deals with foreign intelligence and conspiratorial movements. Alina is back to herself after the encounter with Sebastian, so I trust she will be fine today as any other day.

The third level greets me with its floors covered in dark linoleum. The offices here are occupied by Loellgen's agents who work on infiltrating the Polish Resistance and fighting sabotage. I've overheard some important information here on my prior visits, and I sense that this time will be no different as I walk from door to door and offer chocolate for sale.

When I knock at the last door located near a tailor's workshop, a female voice prompts me to enter.

A moon-faced secretary in her thirties works at a typewriter making clacking sound. "Oh, it's you," she says and wrinkles her nose. "Hauptsturmführer Abt is occupied right now in a meeting, but he has advised me to let him know when you arrive. Will you be okay waiting here while I go fetch him?"

"Yes, I can do that," I say and allow my lips to quirk though I can't stand the woman. Of course, she's eager to run for Abt as last time he gave her a black eye after she failed to inform him of my visit. This deranged man is not only serious about his chocolate, but also about violence.

I make sure to use his weakness for chocolate to my advantage as much as possible. Since his encounter with Sebastian, I gift the man with nicely wrapped boxes filled with chocolate in exchange for his favor when one of our Polish workers at the factory gets arrested for trivial reasons. He helps get them out from the prison in the basement, just like he did for Alina.

"Please take a seat," she says while walking out with her chin up.

Abt claims that he was good friends with my father, so he keeps a friendly attitude toward me, though his reputation of having a heavy hand when interrogating the Resistance members is well known.

I take a seat and eye the barred windows then move my gaze to a pile of folders neatly stacked on top of walnut desk. The secretary might be back any second, so I try to chase the thought of looking through them away, but then an opportunity like this one might not happen ever again.

Feeling the rush of adrenaline, I leap forward and open the first file with my trembling hands while listening for any footsteps outside. I see a lot of information about *Gryf Pomorski*, the largest underground organization in Pomerania. I keep looking up to the brown door and listening for any noise, but I detect no commotion.

My eyes scan the pages frantically, as I try to memorize as much as I can, until I get to my office at the factory where I will jot down everything that I've managed to keep straight in my brain.

But at the sudden sound of a door screeching open, my heart jumps to my throat and my knees grow weak.

TWENTY-TWO
KASIA: DENUNCIATION

December 1943, Gdańsk

At the sight of a blonde head peeking through the door, I shake my head and let out a huge breath. I thought it was the secretary.

"Don't worry, Kasia, I have your back and will knock once when I hear someone walking," Alina says and retreats into the corridor.

I focus again on the documents before me and when I open the third folder, it is full to bursting with denunciations letters; these awful scripts are usually neighbors reporting on others, often wanting to stay in favor by an accusatory act of petty betrayal. But then I spot familiar names: those of Pani Genowefa and her husband. My skin tingles with discomfort.

Their neighbor reports that she suspects them to be hiding Jews in their basement, though can't guarantee it. Still, a scrawled note in black ink states that the location must be checked immediately.

A light tap from the door makes me jump up and quickly put all folders back into order. By the time the red-faced Abt with his vast beer belly leading the way charges into the room and settles his gaze first on me and then onto the stack of files on his desk, I manage to get control of my chaotic heartbeat and crinkle a smile at him.

His breathing is labored as he says, "Pleasure to see you, my dearest Katharina. I'm glad it's you and not one of the other girls. I know I can trust Dietrich's daughter." He turns back to the secretary who follows him. "Helga, next time please ensure that no one stays in my office alone," he scolds her. "Of course, for security reasons. This time I will let you get away with it as I trust Katharina."

"Yes, Hauptsturmführer Abt." Her voice slightly shakes as she takes her place at the typewriter. I feel a pang of pity for her; she is broken by working for this hideous man so ready with his fists and his threats.

He rubs his meaty hands and surveys my bag. "What do you have for me today, my dearest?"

∽

When we depart the Gestapo Headquarters, I exhale with relief but also with a sharp tug of fear. I know I must go to Pani Genowefa as soon as possible. I hope it's not too late.

Both girls take my arms, and we lurch toward the factory. "Alina," I whisper, "how did you know that I was in that office?"

"I was done with my assignment, so I wanted to give you a hand. I saw you going in and the surly secretary leaving. At first, I waited outside but then I wanted to check on you."

I nod. "Did they see you when they returned?"

"Nope, I stepped into the tailor's store after I tapped on the door to warn you." She squeezes my arm. "Don't worry, Kasia, we have your back."

"Shush, Alina," Malina whispers. "It's not the time or place to discuss things like this." She meets my eyes. "But she's right and we will do everything to help."

~

I leave my office promptly at three o'clock and head toward the Long Market. The whole time I have this feeling that someone is following me. I try to shake it off, but I get paranoid to the point that instead of going to Pani Genowefa's home, I stop at a coat boutique on Hundegasse. I try on different coats, but I soon walk out and try a few more stores, just to make sure no one spies on me.

When the street gets separated by a Hitler-Jugend parade, which happens frequently in this city, I hide in a narrow alley between two tenements. To my astonishment, I spot Sebastian walking in a crowd, glancing around like he's looking for someone.

So that's what it is. He couldn't get to the Resistance by treating me kindly and gaining my trust, so he decided to follow me. When I'm sure that he's gone, I edge toward the amber store.

Pani Genowefa's husband turns the sign to indicate that the business is closed for the day and is shutting the door when I run to him. "Hello, I need to speak to Frau Genowefa. It's rather an important matter."

His kind eyes take me in. "Hello, please get in, my wife is upstairs." He's a man of a few words, so I thank him quickly, knowing I don't have to bother engaging him in small talk while we climb to their flat.

The air brims with the aromas of boiled sauerkraut and fried onion. We follow the clanging sounds into the kitchen where Pani Genowefa is adding small cubes of fried bacon into a metal pot with kraut.

"Hello, Pani Genowefa," I say.

She swirls around, her warm smile reaching her eyes. "Kasia, sweetheart, good timing. I'm almost done making the *szmórowónô kapùsta*."

"That's my favorite," I say and smile back at her. "Kashubian food is so delicious, especially when you make your special stewed cabbage."

She chuckles. "You're a doll."

"I actually come with an urgent matter, and I hope you can be truthful with me." For a moment I consider which words to use. "I sold some chocolate today at Neugarten and for the first time I was alone for a few minutes in one of the offices, so I took advantage and snooped through some files."

"My girl," she says and claps her hands together. "I'm sure you want to get in touch with Felek then?"

"That too, but first I need to find out something from you. In one of the documents, it says that your neighbor suspects that you shelter Jews in your basement. Is that the truth?"

Her husband utters a curse under his breath while Pani Genowefa drops a wooden spoon to the tiled floor. "Only a young woman with her daughter. Felek brought them to us."

"I need to take them out of here, and now."

"So soon?" She presses her hand to her chest. "But where will you take them?"

"For now, to my home, and then once I get in touch with Felek, we will plan."

"It's my fault," she says. "Lately, I keep them here with us because the winter is so bone-chilling and there is no heat in that cellar. But I always make sure to cover all windows, so I don't know how someone could have seen them."

Her husband sighs. "It's not your fault, dear. I know you've been careful, but Kasia is right, and they should leave right now, before the Gestapo breaks in. If those brutes find them here, they will have no mercy on us or them."

Pani Genowefa nods but at the same time the door to the

adjacent room opens and a woman in a black wool dress and little girl with brown curls appear.

I recognize her right away. It's the lady that Felek saved near the Red Mouse granary, and her precious daughter.

"Sara, this is Kasia, and she will take you and Rebekah to a safer place," Pani Genowefa says with tears in her eyes. "My dear, our home has been compromised."

"I heard it all," she says in Polish, then she gazes at me. "Hello, good lady." Her sad eyes meet mine. "I'm sorry you're risking your life again helping us."

"Please, don't worry," I assure her. "I'm happy to take you from here to safety. Do you need to grab anything from the basement?" There is no time to waste; we must leave. I am terrified we will be too late any minute now.

"Let me handle that," Pani Genowefa's husband says. "I will meet you all downstairs."

After long hugs with Pani Genowefa, and a brief word with her husband in the gloom of the amber boutique as we collect the woman's small bundle of possessions, we slip into the darkness of the streets. My heart jolts every time we pass someone, and my head twitches on my neck in case Sebastian is still seeking me out.

But it turns out that luck is on our side today because we don't get stopped by any patrol.

∽

Once we are inside my villa, I experience an unexpected, blissful release of all tension. The house is warm, the savory smells wafting from the kitchen. Mama has probably made one of her soups. But just when we pad up the staircase, Mama's voice rings out, "Katharina, is that you, darling?" She only calls me like that when we have company.

"Yes, Mama," I say praying that she stays there, but she

comes out and stares at us while wiping her hands off her apron. If she's surprised, she doesn't show it but says out loud, "We have a guest." She motions toward the kitchen.

I touch my finger to my lips but say in an equally overloud voice. "I will be there soon, Mama. I just need to refresh myself."

I leave Sara and Rebekah in my room and instruct them to be completely silent until my return. I don't know who is downstairs, but I suspect that Sebastian has decided to pay us one of his unexpected visits, just to check on me.

"Kasia," my brother whispers when I walk down the hall, "who's in your room?"

"Shush," I whisper urgently, "you must shush. I promise I will tell you later but please do not mention it downstairs."

Sebastian roosts on our armchair in the family room while drinking Mama's chamomile tea, his face sour. It was my father's favorite spot for reading his newspaper and I am irrationally angered at his presumption.

"You're here," Mama says and gives me an encouraging smile.

"I worried when I didn't see you coming back home after work like you usually do," Sebastian says and holds my gaze as if I should feel guilty.

"Hello, Sebastian." I take a seat next to my mother on a sofa. "I went shopping for a new coat." I don't owe him any explanations but the quicker we get on with this, the faster he leaves, and I will be able to assist the girls upstairs. They must be hungry I realize with a pang of regret: Pani Genowefa didn't get a chance to serve her *szmórowónó kapùsta*.

"If you had told me, I would have given you a ride. There are plenty of bandits hiding out there."

I wonder who the bandits are in his opinion because the only criminals I can point to right now are the Nazis. "I didn't want to bother you. I know how busy you've been."

"I will always find time for you, you know that." He glances at his wristwatch. "It's getting late, but I'm here to share the good news that Bruno was able to save the factory from being shut down. I'm sure that my uncle's interventions helped as well."

Mama claps her hands together. "This is great news, indeed. I'm so happy for you."

"Thank you, Frau Hartmann. I thought you would appreciate knowing as soon as possible." He addresses his words to my mother, but his intense eyes scan my face. "You don't seem to be so thrilled about it, Katharina," he says.

"Oh, I'm very happy. I'm just so tired that I'm having a hard time thinking straight," I say with a theatrical yawn.

"Don't forget that the factory will be yours one day as well." He gives me a look as if to remind me of my duty toward him. "What's happening now is only temporary, and we must be patient."

"You're a good man, Sebastian. We're blessed to have you," Mama says and takes my hand in hers. "Katharina appreciates everything you do, it's just that she's still grieving her father. Please forgive her for being so quiet."

Why is she speaking for me? I try to snatch my hand from her grasp, but she simply tightens her fingers, and I relinquish. Surely, she understands why I keep my distance from him or don't show too much enthusiasm for his diktats, but still, I'm nice and respectful, though I'm no longer certain if he deserves even that. Nothing is black and white anymore. Sometimes I don't have enough energy to keep pretending, and it seems like that's all I do when I'm with him.

Sebastian gets up with a sigh and makes to leave.

But before he walks out the door, he turns and says, "She should show more appreciation for my efforts to keep the factory afloat. I'm doing all of this for her."

TWENTY-THREE
FELEK: NULKA

December 1943, Mirachowskie Forest

"My daddy will be back for Christmas," says a little girl with walnut hair and hazel eyes who sits on Zofia's lap.

I have a difficult time swallowing because of a lump in my throat. We've brought some potatoes and flour along with some herring to one of the Resistance member's wife and daughter. The man got arrested last month by the Gestapo after they got hold of the written lists of *Gryf Pomorski*'s members. We've received word that he's dead.

Zofia's tone is soft and within a blink of breaking. "Your daddy loves you, Nulka. You must always remember this, princess."

Nulka's mother asked us to watch her daughter before running outside. She fought hard to suppress her tears after we broke the devastating news to her. Her daughter was still napping, so she does not know the truth. But how do you tell an innocent three-year-old that her father will never come back?

Zofia assured Nulka's mother to take as much time as she

needs, that we will stay with her little girl until she gains her composure. It's the least we can do for her.

"Daddy said that I'm his princess."

Henryk's fate is the result of another man's arrest who broke under the tortures on Neugarten and began cooperating with the Germans; I say "cooperating", but not everyone can withstand the Gestapo's merciless torture. Still, I despise him for what he did, the consequences of his ultimate weakness. He gave away the arrangement of shelters where they discovered the organization's top-secret materials. The man knew the secret codes, so once the Gestapo knew those, too, they had the tools they needed to decode intercepted documents. And because of that, nearly five hundred members were arrested.

Now, this child has no father and her mother no husband.

While Zofia comforts the little girl, I work on preparing potato *placki*, using my mother's recipe. I heard the child's stomach growling just minutes ago, so I figure it's important that she eats, especially since we don't know what emotional shape her mother will be in upon her return.

I peel and grate potatoes, add some flour, salt and pepper, and chopped onion. Normally my Matka would include an egg, but I do not have one. I drop small circles of the mix into an iron skillet greased with lard. I cook each mini cake until golden brown on both sides. We eat.

The little girl's mother comes back an hour or two later, her red eyes and blotched face betraying her misery. Before we leave, we promise to come back in a few days with some more food.

After we split, I head to Pani Genowefa's home in Gdańsk, because I've received an urgent message to visit the amber store. I race, breathless, up the stairs, and the old lady informs me that Kasia has taken Sara and Rebekah. The good lady is afraid, expecting a Gestapo raid at any moment. I reassure her the best

I can, then rush through the silent, icy streets. I have been cold, indifferent even toward her, but right now I cannot allow myself to waste another second before my eyes rest on my beloved girl's face.

TWENTY-FOUR

KASIA: THE ONE-BUILDING GHETTO

December 1943, Gdańsk

"Why are you suddenly so cold toward him?" Mama asks when Sebastian is gone, her arms crossed at her chest.

The last thing I expected is for her to be talking about Sebastian. I was sure her first words would mention Sara and Rebekah. "I don't know what you're talking about."

"Before you blushed every time you saw him, and now you can't even stand the sight of him."

I sigh and drop into a chair. "I'm not sure what to tell you, Mama."

"So, you don't deny it," she whispers, resignation painted on her face. "Please don't be so harsh when making decisions. I think Sebastian is perfect for you, my daughter. He protects us now, and once the war ends, you can make a good life together while running the factory."

"I don't love him," I say.

Mama throws her hands up in despair. "You know nothing about love, so please don't confuse infatuation with the true and mature love that comes with time," she declares, as if I am a foolish schoolgirl. "Once people grow together and accept each other's flaws they have a support system in the worst of times."

"That's what you had with Papa?" I ask, unable to remove judgment from my voice.

"Yes, our love will last until we meet again." My heart aches at her words and I know that I should hug her, bring her some comfort, but I'm having a hard time taming my frustration.

"Too bad Papa made such stupid decisions," I snap, "and because of that now you have to go on without him."

For a second, I detect a flash of disappointment in her face at my coldness toward her, but she recovers quickly and says, "It doesn't look like the apple falls far from the tree. Who're those strangers at our home? You'd better have a solid explanation."

"It's just a woman with a child," I say, deciding to tell the truth. "They avoided a deportation to a camp, but their hideout got compromised, so I brought them here for a couple of days, until there is a better option."

"You know that for sheltering Jews there are fatal consequences." Her breathing is now quick and shallow. "You are putting Kornel at risk, never mind the rest of us."

"I do what's right, Mama. I listen to my heart which tells me not to leave a poor woman and her child in the clutches of those monsters." I stand up but before stepping away, I add, "Of all people, I thought you would understand. You taught me that it's a sin to walk away from those who are weaker and in need."

I don't wait for her response. It's not a time for lengthy conversations while Sara and Rebekah are waiting upstairs, probably distressed.

When I enter the room, Kornel is there already. He's engaging the little girl by building a tower of wooden blocks. She seems to be greatly engrossed in it while a shy smile tugs at her lips.

"Let's have supper downstairs," I say, making sure to sound cheerful. "I can make some jam sandwiches for us."

"We don't want to cause trouble; it's better we stay up here."

"Nonsense," Mama's voice from the back makes me flinch. Is she going to tell them to leave? "You all should try the sorrel soup that I made today," she says as she gazes warmly at Sara, "I know it's popular in the Jewish kitchen as well. Plus, I made sure to cover all windows with curtains, so no one from outside will be able to see you, though not that many people would risk going out in pitch darkness like this."

I squeeze Mama's hand and whisper, "Thank you, Mama."

Sara clears her throat. "Gestapo agents don't care about the dark."

"Please, trust me, you are safe tonight," I wave my hand dismissively and make sure to continue with even more confidence in my manner, "but if they come, we'll hide you in the cellar."

Her darting gaze tells me that she isn't convinced but she picks up her little daughter and follows us to the kitchen.

"This soup is delicious," she says, the steaming bowl in front of her. "I haven't had it for a very long time. Pani Genowefa spoiled us with her Kashubian delicacies."

"Thank you," Mama says while cutting some more black bread that goes so very fine with the soup.

"I'm sure you'll enjoy my mother's kitchen as much as I do," I say. The green and slightly sour soup is simple but tasty. "When I was little, Mama liked to add two halves of a hard-boiled egg to my bowl with her sorrel soup. It's why I called it *the eggy soup*."

Mama laughs. "Yes, you did, and it was your favorite."

"It still is, Mama," I say softly. Since I moved back from Warsaw, I've noticed that Mama, in addition to various soups, prefers now to make Polish meals. When Papa was alive, our cook Jadwiga mostly prepared German dishes, and only occasionally were there some elements of our Polish traditions. I think how glad I am to eat her food again.

"I like red borscht the best," Kornel says, making a giddy face and winking at Rebekah who chuckles, her eyes glued to him in delight.

When we're done eating, the kids go to play on the divan in the family room where my brother brings some of his old toys. Mama, on the other hand, makes her chamomile tea for all of us. I smile at her love for this herbal cure-all; Mama's chamomile plants return to her garden every spring, so she has supplies that should last us a long time.

She places a mug with steamy liquid in front of Sara and says, "Drink, honey, as it's good for your digestion and peaceful sleep."

"Thank you, Pani Hartmann," Sara says in fluent Polish. "I'm so sorry for ruining the peace of your home." She puts her fingers around the mug and stares into it. "I know how dangerous it is to shelter such outcasts as we are."

"Don't ever speak like this about yourself," I say and make a sharp chin thrust. "You deserve to live in this city as much as we do. We're all equal. I wish that one day the Nazis will pay for the cruelty of their stupid ideology."

"My daughter is right—what they're doing is terrible. We'll do everything to help you." Mama moves her sad gaze to the little Rebekah who's now laughing at Kornel's faces. "How old is your daughter?"

"She will be three in May." Sara's black eyes betray hidden layers of sorrow. "She was born eight months after her father's death."

"I'm so sorry," Mama says and touches her arm. "Was he Jewish too?"

"Mama, please let's not talk about it," I say, "it can't be easy for Sara, especially today when she was almost caught by the Gestapo."

"That's fine, Kasia. I never talked to anyone about it, not even Pani Genowefa, but taking it off my chest might help me in some way. Of course, if you're up to listening."

After we both nod, she takes a sip of her tea and stays silent for a longer moment, as if organizing her thoughts.

I swallow the hot liquid and savor its floral taste with a hint of sweetness.

"Marek died while defending the Polish post office on Heveliusplatz on the first day of the war." She wipes her tears and blows her nose into a handkerchief. "We weren't married and at the time I didn't know that I was expecting. When I found out, I went to visit his parents, but they didn't live in their home anymore, and the German lady who opened the door wasn't exactly friendly, so I had no way of finding them."

She takes another sip from her cup, and continues, "When we were told by the police to pack and leave within half an hour, our neighbors started moving into our flat, without even waiting for our departure. We were always on cordial and friendly terms and my father often gifted cakes or cookies to them. You see, we had our own bakery.

"I realized that war changes people and often awakens new instincts in them, though the pre-war years weren't easy for us either. But a betrayal from the neighbors who always acted friendly and got only kindness from my family, was extremely painful to face. It's easy to lose faith in another human when something like this happens.

"We were moved to a building on Milchkannengasse where Rebekah was born but soon, they transported us to the Red Mouse granary on Mausegasse, which they started calling it as the ghetto. It housed over six hundred of us, and we lived crammed into cubicles, though we were still able to go out to work or shop for necessities. But in 1941 they started deporting people." She shivers in remembered horror and I look across to her little daughter, glad that my brother has taken the child under his wing.

"We knew that we were waiting there for our turn to die because they were so clear with their agenda of killing all of us. One day, three Schupo policemen came to our cubicle and read the names of people for the next transport. My parents and my two younger sisters were on the list, along with some others, but Rebekah and I were left out. At first, I wanted to go with my family, but my father reasoned that it's better to stay in Gdańsk as long as possible."

She talks with her eyes closed now and her hand squeezes the handkerchief that she has pressed tight against her chest.

"Soon I received the first letter from my family, and it turned out that they were brought to the ghetto in Warsaw. They complained of starvation, so I kept sending them whatever I could get, like sugar cubes. At first, the rule was that we couldn't send more than half a pound of produce, but later we were forbidden from sending anything at all, at danger of severe punishments from the Gestapo.

"I felt alone without my family, but I was determined to be strong for Rebekah. There were more and more restrictions in place, like we couldn't take trams or buses or go to parks. They took away our stamps for milk, flour or meat, so our diet became meager. Thankfully, some bakeries still sold bread to us, and we learned quickly which ones had kind owners who treated us with respect. Others forbade us from buying from them at all or demanded that we waited at the end of lines till nothing but crumbs were left.

"We had to sew into our clothes the yellow star that couldn't be covered. Out in the streets, German children would call us names and spit at us."

Her face flinches as she stays silent for a moment longer.

I glance at my mother, who has tears silently running down her face.

"You don't have to continue, Sara," I say and put my hand gently on her shoulder.

"That's okay," she whispers. "But this was all nothing compared to what awaited. In April of last year, I learned that my parents and my sisters perished in the Treblinka extermination camp..." Her voice fades and her hands drop to her sides in a gesture of pure despair and sorrow.

"I'm so sorry," I say and pull her into a hug, while Mama embraces both of us from behind. In this very moment, only silence can adequately express the tragedy, so we let it take over. There are simply no words.

"That day when you and Felek helped us, I somehow knew that we were going to be on the next transport, so I walked out the ghetto though we were told to stay inside. There was one decent guard that let us out, but we didn't have much luck in the streets. If not for good people like you, we would share my family's fate and be separated or dead by now."

"Oh Sara," I say, my voice breaking with emotion. "We'll do everything to keep you safe. I will get the basement ready," I say. "It's the safest spot in the house."

"No," Mama says with authority in her voice, "Sebastian doesn't have a cellar in his house, so whenever the sirens go on, he joins us in ours." She moves her gaze from me to Sara. "I already made a bed for you in the guest room upstairs, as it has the hidden entrance to the attic, in which you can hide when needed."

"That's clever, Mama," I say.

TWENTY-FIVE
KASIA: TRUE LOVE

December 1943, Gdańsk

For Christmas Eve dinner Mama served zander, caught in Motława River by Herr Krause, our elderly neighbor, who agreed to sell some to us. Mama pan-fried it in flour and served it with mashed potatoes and sauerkraut salad. It went smoothly with a white wine that Sebastian brought over.

In the past, Mama liked to prepare the traditional Polish *Wigilia* of twelve dishes with expert help from Jadwiga, none of which included meat. We'd also share a blessed wafer while wishing each other health, peace and a good year.

Papa always respected Mama's traditions, even after he joined the Nazis, though he kept reminding her to keep it inside our home, as a family secret—and made sure that, for our everyday meals, German food dominated our dinner table. But because of the food shortages in the war and the fact that Sebastian attended, we skipped the tradition this year. It's perhaps a small thing, but when this war ends, I resolve that part of resuming our normal lives will be that I learn how to make all twelve of the *Wigilia* dishes.

I make sure to be overly nice to Sebastian as it's best to be on good terms, especially now we're sheltering Sara and Rebekah. I can't afford to give him any reasons to snoop around like he did the other day when I headed to Pani Genowefa.

Well, I reason, if Mama questioned my coldness toward him, he must have noticed it too and I'm suspecting it's why he decided to follow me. The fact that he might be doing it just to access the Polish Resistance isn't missed on me either. Since I caught him shouting at Alina, I doubt more and more his intentions, especially after all the lies he's fed me. I sense that he's hiding something sinister.

He is trying to flatter me, impress me with stories he thinks I want to hear, I'm sure of it. Even his story about running the underground bakery turned out to be false. Alojzy told me last week that since Papa's death, Sebastian hasn't allowed any baking in there. Before that, my father donated loaves of bread to the poorest people of Gdańsk—officially to Germans but in practice to Poles living in dreadful conditions in the city's cellars.

At night I twist and turn unable to sleep. I know I can't reject him completely, but now I feel disgusting for once more letting him kiss me. I just didn't want to intensify his suspicion that something has changed. He must continue thinking that I'm infatuated with him.

Just when I'm struggling to keep my eyes open, a sudden bang on the windowpane makes me sit upright. Maybe it was a bird bumping into the glass. Then, the same noise sounds out sending chills down my spine.

I edge toward the window and open it. Everything seems still and bathed in darkness, including Sebastian's house.

"Kasia," Felek's voice rises softly from below, "can I come in?"

I exhale with relief. "Yes, let me open the door for you."

"No need, just stay in your room and I will be there in a few moments," he says.

I listen for any sign of commotion from Sebastian's house, hoping that he's deep asleep. When there is nothing, I close the curtains over the window, and turn on a lamp. I put a bathrobe over my nightdress and run my fingers through my hair. It's weird to be seen by Felek while not being properly dressed but it is the middle of the night, after all.

When he arrives, I let him in and lock the room door from inside. The last thing I need is to have Kornel pop in like he has a habit of doing when least expected.

I turn to face Felek, trying to quiet down my hammering heart. Just minutes ago, I dreamed of seeing him again and now he stands right before me with his cheeks red from the frosty midnight outside, his daring gaze slowly taking me in and stopping on my lips.

I like when he looks at me like that. "Is everything okay?" I ask, enjoying the delicious and so familiar scent of the woods. But my nostrils detect something else, and when he removes a small package from his coat pocket, the spicy and warm fragrances of ginger, cinnamon and nutmeg intensify.

"Yes, all is fine," he extends his hand with a small bundle wrapped in brown paper, "Pani Genowefa sends some cookies with Merry Christmas wishes."

I step forward and reach for it but when our fingers touch, my skin tingles and warmth fills me from inside. "Thank you. That's so nice of her."

"She told me about Sara and Rebekah, so I wanted to check on you."

We're standing so close that I crave his touch more and more. "They're sleeping in the bedroom that has access to the attic, so they can hide in case of emergency."

"You are good to take them in, thank you." He nods. "I'm afraid we don't have another location available right now but as soon as I find something, I will come to get them. How did your mother take it?"

"She's a little afraid but fine."

"We can't meet at Pani Genowefa's anymore, not until we know for sure that it's safe. The Gestapo will probably search the basement soon, and they will almost certainly keep them under observation for a prolonged time. For the time being, I will communicate with you through Alojzy. It's safer this way for you too."

I know he's right, especially considering that I caught Sebastian following me, but my heart sinks at the reality that I will not see him any time soon.

As if knowing my thinking, he lifts his hand and runs his finger down my cheek. "I've missed you," he whispers and pauses for a moment, his fingers lingering on the soft skin of my face. Our eyes lock and I feel myself give a tiny nod as he pulls me into his arms, his lips crashing into mine. This time the kiss is so fervent and urgent that I'm immediately breathless, overwhelmed, but just like last time, I want more and more.

I feel this untamed euphoria and love. Yes, this must be love, I'm sure nothing else can feel like it. This is so new and so desired. With him I'm being myself while with Sebastian I constantly play or pretend.

A moment later he breaks off and buries his face in my hair. "I didn't know that I could feel about someone the way I do about you. You're in my every thought and there is nothing else but this yearning in me to call you mine."

I'm unable to stop myself from moaning as his hands press me against him. "I want the same," I whisper. "Stay for the night this one time." I smile up at him, and I know my eyes are sparkling. "It's Christmas, after all."

"Are you sure?" His gray eyes are now all the shades of a stormy ocean.

And of course, I say yes, I'm sure.

I spend every minute with him like it would be our last. This war takes and takes and changes everything in a blink of time.

He never stops holding me close. "Have you ever been in love?" he asks, his voice shaking a little.

"Not until now," I say and let the words sink in.

He pulls me even closer. "I love you too, Kasia. You're the one I want to wake up to every day."

We kiss some more, slower and gentler this time. I say, "Tell me something about you. All I know is that you're in the Resistance. I used to see you at those meetings, but you never paid me any attention."

He laughs lazily. "Oh, I saw you, my darling. I couldn't take my eyes off you."

I pat his shoulder. "No, you didn't. Every time I looked your way, your gaze was somewhere else, so don't you lie to me."

He kisses the top of my head as I press into his chest, his arms encircling me. "Well, Miss Observant, I looked when I knew that you'd not notice. My friend Mateusz kept convincing me to find ways to talk to you, but I didn't think that you would take any interest in someone like me—an average boy from Warsaw."

I reach up to brush the scar on his forehead with my finger. "I'm very proud of who you are, Felek. When I saw you in that interrogation room on Szucha and how they slaughtered you because you wouldn't tell them anything, I knew I'd respect you for the rest of my life in the same way I respect others who were tortured to death. My heart broke just at the thought that you'd share their fate." I go on kissing every little scar on his chest and abdomen. "But now I'm blessed to call you mine."

He kisses the tip of my nose. "I want you to know that there's not a day when I don't think of our friends who sacrificed their lives for the freedom. Do you remember Poldek?"

"I don't really know him that well, but I do remember him. Wasn't he assigned to your group?"

He nods. "He's the one who betrayed me to the Gestapo," he says through clenched teeth. "If I could only get him in my hands, but of course, he has disappeared."

"How do you know it was him?" Poldek, a skinny boy with face covered in acne, always seemed shy and absent-minded. He did not strike me like someone who could denounce one of us.

"Zofia learned from my friend Mateusz when she visited Warsaw."

"Please, darling, don't bend to his level, instead forgive him and move on. Karma will get him on its own."

He sighs heavily, then says, "I can't guarantee what I will do if he ever gets in my way."

"Forget about this deceiving man as he's not worth your time. Tell me more about yourself and your family."

"I grew up on Krucza Street in the city center."

"Do you have siblings?"

"I have three sisters but much older than me, they all are married and have their own children."

"Do they live in Warsaw?"

"Thankfully, no. Eleonora moved to England; Liliana and Justyna live in Katowice."

"I've never been to southern Poland," I say. "So only your parents live in Warsaw?"

"One day we will visit my sisters; you will love the mountains around Katowice, and we can explore London together too. And yes, only my parents and some distant relatives. My mother is a seamstress and my father an electrician." He sighs. "Now I'm not there anymore, my friend Mateusz visits them occasionally to make sure they are fine. I worried that Gestapo would retaliate and hurt them, but no such thing has happened."

"I'm glad to hear it. What were your plans before the war?"

"Not much. I always knew I would follow Tata's steps and one day become an electrician." He clears his throat. "My parents might be simple people, but they have noble values. Thanks to them, I am who I am, and when the time comes to give my life for my country, I will do it without hesitation."

His words touch and terrify me, because I don't want to lose him. I change the subject to a lighter topic. "What did you like to do in your free time?" He doesn't know me long enough to think of me as a reason to not die for his homeland. But I know in my heart that Poland will always come first for him; I saw that in the ferocity of his defiance against the Gestapo's brutality. I take a deep breath: we must go with the flow and make the best out of whatever the future has in store for us.

"Fishing. I did it a lot during my days in the Scouts, and have enjoyed it ever since," he says and runs his fingers across my lower lip. "And my favorite color is green," he teases me. "Now it is time you tell me about yourself."

"Well, you already know my brother," I say.

He chuckles. "You're lucky to have such a protector. What a relief he's not one of those kids brainwashed by Hitler's garbage."

"It's all Mama's doing. You will meet her one day too. She's a good woman, my mamusia.

"Were your childhood years happy?" he asks, his hand massaging my back.

"Very. Papa was a different person back then. Growing up in the Free City of Gdańsk and with parents from different cultures, that was true happiness."

"Considering that the majority of people living here were Germans, it's difficult to understand why you turned out to have all this devotion for Poland."

"Actually, before the war," I admit, feeling I can trust him with this, "I felt more German than Polish. Through my childhood I was very close with my father who gave me so much attention. I mean Mama did too, but from her it was more about material things while with Papa it was more about learning German culture and traditions. But Mama spoke Polish to me and taught me her prayers, folk tales and legends. It's hard to explain it but I felt a stronger pull to my father's heritage."

I sigh and continue, "Still, I chose the University of Warsaw instead of some German one, and Papa didn't accept it. He decided to marry me to Sebastian Richter, so our family business would bloom. I couldn't forgive him for making these sorts of decisions against my will and hopes for my future, so I left Gdańsk in defiance of him. I knew he wouldn't look for me, especially after he told me that I would no longer be his daughter if I left." My last words fade as pain soars through my heart. I wonder why I'm volunteering all this information to Felek. Normally, I don't talk of it to anyone, not even Mama, though I know that I should one day.

"I'm sorry that this happened to you. Why did your father change so rapidly?"

"The fear of losing everything he'd worked for, of his family's security lying in ruins, transformed him into a shell of himself. He was so worried that the Nazis would take everything away from him, that he joined them. And he wanted the union with Sebastian because he suspected the approaching war—and how it might play out for us. In the end, he did it all to protect us, however naïve that may sound."

Felek holds me closer as he speaks. "I saw war and that kind of terrible fear change people completely; it would often bring out in them their worst instincts. It drives them to commit things that in a normal world they would never do, which is sad."

"Very sad. Still, I miss my father every day, despite him choosing the path of evil. It feels like such a burden of shame."

"It isn't. He's your father and nothing will ever change that, and please, don't be afraid of your feelings. You love the man that raised you and gave you his love. Don't ever forget that." The gentle strokes of his fingers wipe my tears though he can't see my face in darkness.

My throat constricts. "Thank you for not judging me."

"I must say this, though," he says, and I sense his tone shifting.

"What?" I murmur, a little afraid.

"Please be careful when it comes to Richter. My instinct tells me that his intentions are far from honest."

I let out a long breath, glad to be able to speak of this. "I saw him following me the other day and he keeps approaching me about the Resistance. Of course, I always tell him that I know nothing of it, but I'm sure his gentle attitude right from the beginning was to gain my trust. Who knows his true intentions since his behavior is so conflicting."

"You're right to be wary. Also, I was going to talk to you about the 'chocolate bomb' mission, which Zofia assigned to you. There is no need for you to attempt it anymore; it's been recently determined that there are no longer any camouflaged explosives coming from your factory. It seems like Richter didn't continue your father's mission."

"That's good news." I almost giggle at the contrast between the warmth of our bodies fitted together so intimately and the secret missions of our conversation.

TWENTY-SIX

FELEK: I CAN'T LOSE HER

New Year's Eve 1943, Gdańsk

"Zofia was arrested by the Gestapo," Adka's father says and spits to the floor. He paces back and forth in the kitchen while Adka rinses plates and cups in a tin bowl filled with clean water.

I clear my throat as dread washes over me. "Was she denounced?" I was gone for a week on a mission in Bydgoszcz, another city in northern Poland, where Zofia sent me. Not in a million years had I expected to hear such awful news upon my arrival.

"I don't know," he says without elaborating. The rule is not to volunteer any additional information, unless necessary.

I drop to a chair and put my hands over my face. I grew to like Zofia, even love her like my own sisters. Her compassion for others despite her own loss has inspired me to be a better person. And now she is in the clutches of the Gestapo.

"The blood suckers know the exact role she's played in the Resistance, so they aren't showing her any mercy. In fact, my sources report that she's under unthinkable brutality. It's why I contacted Alojzy with orders for the German girl to try getting cyanide to her, though I doubt she will be able to complete such a mission. Still, we owe it to Zofia to try at least."

"Damn it!" I smash my fist into the table. It's not enough that Zofia's life is already in danger, now Kasia has been given an impossible mission that could be fatal for her. "How the hell do you expect her to accomplish this?" I say through clenched teeth.

"There isn't anyone else more skilled or fit for this. You know it." His warning gaze drills into mine. "Don't you want to do everything to help Zofia?"

"Of course I do but not at the cost of losing the woman I love." The moment I say it, I wish I could take my words back.

The sound of a plate crashing to the floor makes me look away. Adka stands frozen in place, hurt painted on her face.

I storm outside, unable to stand being near either of them. I must go to the city and make sure that Kasia doesn't listen to this idiotic, deadly order. I begin on foot but soon I'm lucky enough to get a ride with a local farmer who's taking flour to a bakery in Gdańsk on his horse-driven wagon.

When I manage to slip into the chocolate factory's courtyard, Alojzy stops his sweeping and whispers that Kasia has already left for the day. "She plans," he murmurs, moving the brush over the courtyard's cobbles again, "to visit the Gestapo Headquarters."

Fear and anger torment me while I navigate my way toward the Neugarten and hide behind a small kiosk marked with German propaganda. If something happens to Kasia, I will never forgive myself. Waiting, wretched and miserable, in hopes of seeing her leaving this death-gray place unharmed, is torture.

TWENTY-SEVEN
KASIA: A DEADLY CAPSULE

New Year's Eve 1943, Gdańsk

I'm leaving the factory at noon to get ready for a special banquet at the casino in Sopot. Sebastian asked me to join him in celebrating the turning of the New Year with Bruno and Ilse and I didn't know how to refuse without making a scene. It's better to sacrifice one evening than deal with his anger for days, especially that now my situation is rather sensitive as I'm responsible for Sara and Rebekah's continued safety.

Sebastian has been more on edge lately when approaching me, like something constantly bothers him. I'm so tired of the entire situation and if I only could, I would tell him that I don't love him and that he should find another woman. But right now, it would be irresponsible to do it, so I continue to fake an interest in him. I will do what needs to be done to protect my family and fight for Poland's freedom.

At least he's stopped asking me about the Resistance, though often I feel like I'm being followed. In this situation, I'm glad that I don't meet with Felek at Pani Genowefa's anymore. I also urged Pan Alojzy to be extremely careful when approaching me. I usually leave the information for the Resistance in Papa's office, under the floorboards.

Pan Alojzy departs the factory last as one of his duties is to close it for the night. He has a spare key for the office. So far, it's been working well, and I feel confident Sebastian doesn't suspect anything.

As I exit the factory building and walk through the courtyard, Alojzy's whisper comes from the small shed where he stores his cleaning supplies and repair tools. "Kasia, there is something."

I know Sebastian isn't watching me through his window because he already left for the day saying that he had some errands to do before tonight. So, I enter the tiny shed. "What is it?" I whisper.

"One of the key people from the Resistance got arrested and is being tortured on Neugarten. Your assignment is to smuggle the ampoule of cyanide." He quickly puts something into my coat pocket. "But only if you can do it without putting yourself in danger. They don't want you to take too big a risk."

"But why? Maybe he will survive."

"It's a woman. Zofia." His wrinkled face is drooping, his sad eyes glassy. "We know she's suffering inhuman pain, and it's too late for her to survive. She deserves to die with dignity, so we must stop the Germans from prolonging her suffering. If you get it to her, she will at least have that choice. The security over there is so high that attempting to free her would be madness, even suicide."

Zofia, the woman I met in the Oliwa Forest, Felek's boss. "I will try." This is an unusual request. But Zofia is very important, so it's why they ask this of me. And I will do everything I can to help her.

There is no way I can get into that basement with its prison cells. There are guards all over the ground floor and everything is treated as maximum security, or at least according to my observations. I realize that Abt is the only one that can help me with this, though I'm afraid to ask him.

I go back to the factory and fill my delivery bag with chocolate. If anyone questions me, I will say that I got an unexpected request from Neugarten. It will not be surprising for Sebastian as these requests from Abt come often. That criminal loves his chocolate. Though this time I know it won't be enough. I must offer something much more valuable, to stand a chance of success, like Papa's golden coins that I found under the floorboards behind his chair.

I made sure to look there the first day I started working in the factory because when I was little, I saw Papa putting something in that hideout while I played with my doll. We were alone in the office, and I was only three or four, but that memory stayed with me. I don't think even Mama knows of it.

I grab all five coins and wrap them like I would normally wrap my chocolate samples, then I put it with the rest of the chocolate in the bag.

I walk to the Gestapo Headquarters on Neugarten as quickly as I dare and make sure to keep my chin up when entering.

The same guard as always halts me, his face even more wrathful today. I don't know if there is a single fiber within him that isn't taut with loathing; he probably hates himself most of all.

"Fräulein Hartmann, I'm surprised to see you today as most of our staff have already left for the day to get ready for the New Year celebrations." His pinched little eyes glower at me.

"What, is Hauptsturmführer Abt gone too?" I make a substantial effort to calm my nerves. "I received a special request for chocolate for New Year's Eve from him," I say and place my steady gaze on his, like I have nothing to hide.

He picks up a telephone handset and a moment later, he

says, "Hauptsturmführer Abt, I have Fräulein Hartmann here stating that you requested her service. Is that correct?"

My mouth fills with a sour taste. I wish I could just turn and walk away but I stand still with my chin up. Abt didn't request anything and that must be what he's telling the guard, whose forehead creases more and more.

He puts the black handset down and barks at me, "Go on."

I nod and march forward without another word while a flush of adrenaline is still tingling through my body. Abt didn't send me back, but now he knows that I lied to the guard. I must be extremely careful what I say to him. I feel like I'm right in the hyena's mouth.

Bribing Abt was easy before, because I only approached him regarding our factory workers who got arrested for trivial reasons. He did warn me once to never ask him to free any of the Resistance fighters or he will arrest me too. And here I am, about to do it anyway.

Mama keeps telling me that I force problems into my life and that sometimes I need to say no to make my life easier and safer. Maybe she's right after all, but what else can I do when this woman is living hell on earth? She needs help and my job is to do everything to get it to her, though I still hope that she might not need the cyanide, that she will go on living.

"Come in," Abt's loud voice rings out after I knock.

"Hello, Hauptsturmführer Abt," I say and quickly add, "I'm sorry for interrupting but I've finished working on my new recipe and I couldn't wait to have you taste the first sample, before anyone else. I trust your opinion the most." I'm glad that I made it a habit of having him taste my newest samples every time I visit his office. He's the only one approachable here to me, most likely because he valued my father and often played cards with him.

The confused look on his face transforms into delight. "You're right. Something like this couldn't wait." He walks around the desk and rubs his hands together while eyeing my bag.

I take some wrapped pieces out and hand him the sample I made the other day. I was going to give it to Kornel and Rebekah but kept forgetting to bring it home. Thankfully, I grabbed it before coming here; it's unwise to be superstitious, but it's like someone is watching over me.

He unrolls the small chocolate bar and takes a bite, then chews it for a moment. "This is exquisite. I taste a bit of mint and coconut, yes definitely these two flavors." He opens his eyes. "Thank you for bringing this moment of happiness to me."

I don't argue with his words though this chocolate has nothing to do with mint or coconut. "You're welcome, Hauptsturmführer Abt. This is my last delivery for the year, so please help yourself to whatever is in my bag," I say. "Of course, at no charge."

He narrows his eyes, still chewing on the sweet-scented caramel. "Why do I have the feeling that you're not here simply because of this delicious chocolate?" he says and winks.

I'm glad his mood is still good. "You know me well, Hauptsturmführer Abt. I do come to you hoping you will do me a small favor."

He sifts through the chocolate bars and adds more and more onto his "tasting" pile. "Someone from your factory again?"

I clear my throat and fish out the golden coins from the bottom of the bag. "No, this time it's a personal matter. You see, my school friend was arrested, and I was wondering if you could help me."

"Name?" he asks without beating around the bush.

The moment I say Zofia's name, he drops the chocolate to his desk and glares at me with more cold fury in his eyes than I have ever seen. "If you want to leave here alive, never mention this name again. Out of respect for your departed father, I'm willing to pretend that I didn't hear you. But only that one time." His dangerous voice makes me feel as if I might faint. "That woman will not leave this prison alive."

I know there is no discussion with him and that this is the only time that he is willing to let me get away. But I can't turn back, not now. I can't save the woman's life, but I can still try fulfilling my mission. I unwrap the golden coins and hold them in my hands while Abt stares.

His eyes are shining now; I was right in my judgment that his greed would extend beyond chocolate. But he says, his tone softer now, "I can't help you, even if I wanted to. Besides, the woman is dying anyway."

I summon all my courage and say, "I only wanted to see her to take what's mine."

He walks around his desk, settles in his chair and leans back. "She's your close friend?"

"No, not anymore. I knew her when I was much younger. She still has my favorite polka-dot dress that I lent her before the war. She never gave it back to me." I make a face of a spoiled and dramatic girl to match the absurdity of my words.

He watches me with his eyes wide open as if wondering what to think of my confession, or me at all, and whether he was totally wrong on the many occasions he's praised me for being intelligent.

"I haven't seen her since before the war as I serve our Führer, so I couldn't go on with our friendship." My mouth is so dry that it's painful to speak. "But I really want to have that dress back." I pout and it's almost as if I have childish ribbons in my hair too. "You see, it belonged to my beloved grandmother. It's a family heirloom."

He keeps appraising the coins in my hands. "I would like to warn you that it might be shocking to you to see the condition she's in. You'd better question her family members about the dress. I'm not sure if she can even talk right now."

"I did, Hauptsturmführer Abt, but they don't know. Of

course, they are probably liars too. Please, help me. I will be happy to pay you." I look down coyly at the golden coins.

"If I agree, this must stay between us." He motions to the coins. "It might be possible today because almost everyone has already left, but still you will only have five minutes with her." He gives me a forbidding look as I lay the golden coins in a neat pile on his desk. "I'm doing this only because of my sentiment to Dietrich."

"Of course, I will keep it to myself." I know this is a dangerous game I'm playing but there is no coming back from it now.

∼

On the way to the ground floor, we encounter no living soul in our way.

"Everyone must be gone by now and it's time for me to leave too," he says before we near guards on the ground floor who salute to Abt. We walk to the far end of the building and halt at the entrance to the basement where two soldiers are on guard.

"Manfred, please escort Fräulein Hartmann for a brief visitation with the prisoner in the isolation cell. Please allow her privacy for five minutes." He takes my hand between his. "I wish you a prosperous New Year, my dearest Katharina."

I wish him the same and follow the guard on the cement stairs. The entire conversation with Abt is like a blur to me. I put aside all my worries and fears, and I bargained with him like with a merchant at a market. I refused to show panic, instead I acted like a calculating bitch that only cares to get her "heirloom" dress back and doesn't give a damn that the woman is dying alone in a sordid cell. He ate his chocolates, took his money, accepted it all as something normal. What cruel, avaricious world do we live in?

We walk through a narrow and dark corridor with cells. The guard opens the door to one and prompts me in, then he bangs the door shut and for a moment I listen to his heavy footsteps.

The pungent odor, heavy with urine and blood, hits my nostrils. The cage-like cell is dark, but not to the point that I can't see. I leap to Zofia who lies motionless on a filthy pallet.

I kneel before her and touch her arm. "Zofia, can you hear me?" I whisper. Her entire body is covered with wounds, visible through her ripped clothes and caked in dried blood. When I notice spots of fresh blood, I realize that those bastards still actively interrogate her.

When she moves her head up and moans in pain, I brush her hair gently away from her forehead. My heart goes still at the sight of her mutilated face.

If I've ever thought that my heart was broken, I was wrong. It was never shattered to pieces like at this very moment. Little particles of it dig into my soul, my skin, everything. How could one human do this to another?

I'm afraid to touch her, in case I cause her more pain. "It's me, Kasia, the chocolate girl," I whisper as soothingly as I can, aware that mine might be the last voice she hears. I'm here to see how you're doing," I say, reminding myself that I only have a few more minutes left.

She opens her mouth, exposing bloody and toothless gums. "They got nothing from me." I can see that each word gives her excruciating pain. "Nothing," she repeats, grimacing in a wrenching mix of agony and pride.

"Here, I have some water for you." I take out a small flask and gently hold it to her mouth, so she can drink. But she's not able to.

I wet my handkerchief with water and bring it to her mouth. After wetting her lips, she continues, "I will watch over all of you if God allows me. I'm a lucky woman to be dying for my country." She closes her eyes. "God bless Poland."

The guard's booted footsteps sound in the corridor. "I have cyanide. I will leave it with you." I reach for her hand only to realize that her fingers in both hands are torn. She will not be able to take cyanide even if she decides to.

She opens her eyes. "Give it to me now. I can't...this agony..."

The footsteps cease and a clinking comes from the door.

I swallow hard and flinch, unable to put my thoughts together. "Are you sure?"

"Have mercy." Her begging gaze tells me what I must do. "Please."

I fulfill her last wish and place the cyanide into her mouth the moment the guard enters.

She smiles faintly. "*Dziękuję.*" Thank you.

"God bless you, our angel," I say and smile, doing everything to suppress my tears. Then I leap to my feet and walk away, making sure that the guard can only see the face of a heartless woman who cares merely for her dress. I'm sure Abt will question him regarding my visit here.

Once outside in the streets, I inhale the crisp air of the year's last evening, while my head spins, unable to grasp what just happened. I helped the sweet Zofia end her misery. I helped take her life away. I know very well that she wouldn't survive this anyway, not in this condition. She was slowly dying, in the worst imaginable pain possible. This woman has been in agony in that cell that became her hell on the earth, while we go on with our lives. We eat, laugh, fight, live, kiss and drink tea... not realizing how lucky we are.

Whatever I did to get to that cell, was all worth it because I ended her torment. Now she will go to Heaven, I'm sure of that. I wipe my tears away and quicken my steps. I must come up with some excuse not to go to this stupid banquet with those goddamn self-satisfied Nazis. I don't care anymore; I'll pretend sickness. It's not going to be difficult because my entire body hurts, my soul hurts. Sebastian is the last person I want to see right now. I need to be alone, to think of Zofia, to pray for her soul.

After taking few steps, a man in black parka catches up to me. When I realize it's Felek, I exhale with relief and take his arm. Felek is the only one right now that I want to share all this heartache with. With him, I'm fully myself.

"I was waiting for you," he says. "When I found out what you were sent to do, I wanted to kill the man that gave you this order. I was too late to stop you." His voice is strained.

"I'm fine," I say. "Where can we talk?"

"I know just the place," he says and squeezes my hand. He leads me to the abandoned shack, the same one where he brought Sara and Rebekah before. On the outside it's in a terrible state but when we enter it, Felek starts a fire in the wood-burning stove.

"I sleep here when I'm in Gdańsk," he says as the flames light up his face. "It's kind of secluded by the small woods in this less known part of the shore of Motława."

There is no other furniture here, just a small pile of blankets. When we take a seat on the floor near the warmth of the stove, he puts his arm around me.

"I was able to see Zofia," I say, not recognizing my own voice.

He swallows loud. "How?"

I tell him in short what happened, but only to the point when I entered the cell, because I can't stop my sobbing.

He brings me close to him and smooths my hair with his hand. "The most important thing is that you are alive. You don't have to keep talking; you will tell me another day."

"No, you need to know, she was your chief." I tell him about her fragile condition and what she said, I tell him about the cyanide.

"You did right, Kasia," he says quietly. "You ended her misery. They would continue slaughtering her even though she's already dying. I heard that once someone is in the worst condition they bring them to their courtyard, so other prisoners see how the Resistance fighters are being treated. Zofia was a tough, good-hearted woman." His voice catches, and I realize his sorrow too. "She didn't deserve this, and thanks to you, she's already at peace."

"Then why do I feel like I killed her? The guard was already entering, and she begged me to give it to her."

"They killed her. You freed her from the pain after the agony that they purposely inflicted upon her and planned to continue until the very last breath she took. Bastards."

"She was so brave, so clear in her mind."

"She is and she will continue to be." There are tears in his eyes, but I say nothing, just squeeze his fingers with as much compassion as I can. "It all doesn't end with our lives here on earth. I believe in God and know that, right now, Zofia is no longer in that cell; she is safe in His arms."

"I want to believe in that too."

"You know, she told me once that when I'm very sad I need to laugh because crying is too easy." He wipes his tears. "But how can I laugh?"

"Oh, darling, let's stay here for the night," I say. We let our tears mingle while there are no more words, just tears and darkness.

TWENTY-EIGHT

KASIA: THE FIRST DAY OF THE YEAR...

New Year's Day 1944, Gdańsk

I near the dark villa at nearly five o'clock in the morning, after a night spent with Felek. We both yearned for each other's company after what happened to Zofia, who was like a sister to Felek. He cried himself to sleep in my arms and I made sure to be there for him. She wasn't just a stranger, she was his chief and friend, and the bravest woman we have ever known.

I watch Felek taking the corner and disappearing in the darkness of the streets. When will I see him now in this unpredictable world? What will the year of 1944 bring us all? Will we survive another year of the war that certainly will prove to be worse and worse? At this point, I have no hopes for it to end any time soon.

My thoughts are disturbed by the screeching of tires and the next second a black Mercedes Benz parks right before me beside the sidewalk and honks. Its blasting lights are against the city rules of the blackout hours.

I want to turn and run into the villa, but Bruno emerges

from the back seat and slurs, "Katt... a... rrr... ina. Whe... where have you b... ee... n?"

He's completely drunk but I plaster a smile on my face. "Hello, Bruno. I guess you had a rather pleasant time celebrating." But the smile dies on my lips the moment Sebastian comes out of the car, his hurt gaze on me. He doesn't look drunk at all, just angry.

He pauses in front of me as I swallow hard, all words from my mind erased by this terrible, overwhelming fear. For the first time I'm afraid of him, of his reaction to being stood up last night. Worse, I didn't even think once of him through the whole night spent with Felek.

Despite his intoxication, Bruno must sense the tension between us because without a single word he backs away and orders his chauffeur to drive him home.

The noise of the rumbling engine dies while this unnerving and silent darkness settles. Sebastian keeps standing and staring into my eyes as if trying to read me. In the moonlight, the haunted expression of a hurt animal in his gaze appears almost creepy.

No, this is nonsense. I shake off my awkward state and say, "I trust you had a great time at the banquet?" I make sure to sound lighthearted. After all, we are not a couple, so his anger against me cannot be so strong because of this. "I apologize for not showing up last night. I found out about the death of someone and had to console my friend, and by the time I wanted to go back, it was too late anyway, so I just decided to sleep over there."

"You broke the curfew rules," he says. His voice shakes with fury, though his teeth remain clenched; red lines cover his whites as he continues to glare at me.

I manage to say with my trembling voice, "I'm sorry." He's in a stupor, and regardless of what I say he will lash out at me. It's better to say the least possible to not provoke him.

When minutes pass and he doesn't reply, I clear my throat and say, "I will let you get some sleep. Good night." But when I turn away to walk home, he grabs my arm and swirls me back to face him.

His hold is so painful that I yelp in agony. "What are you doing?"

His face is only inches from mine. He breathes heavily but his muscles are rigid and tense. "You belong to me. If you ever forget this and abandon me again, I will not hesitate to kill you and your pathetic family. Try me." He lets go of me and marches away.

I walk toward the villa on my wooden feet, with my heart on my sleeve. The whole time I thought he was our protector, he's been our worst enemy, much worse than the Nazis.

~

The next day Mama hands me an enormous bouquet of red roses. "Someone sent this for you," she says and winks at me.

How was Felek able to get so many roses, now in the winter? I unfold the little paper attached to it: *I love you with all my heart, my sunshine. Sebastian*

"Who's it from?" Mama asks but when I don't answer, she snatches the paper from my hand, and after reading it, she beams at me. "I told you that he loves you."

I can't take this anymore, so I jump from my seat and run upstairs. This is all so unfair. But I know that the only place that I can show my true feelings and cry myself to no end is my bedroom; outside of it I must pretend to be in love with him and the Nazi regime.

So, I do it and as days, weeks and months go by, I pretend. I act like that encounter between us never happened. Sebastian does the same and keeps playing our protector. But it did happen, and he failed to control himself exposing his true self, his true intentions. I just hope that this war ends before he gets the opportunity to hurt my family. For now, I'm a victim of Sebastian Richter and his malicious blackmailing.

There are no more meetings at Pani Genowefa's, and Felek is nowhere to be found. I pass my information to Pan Alojzy whenever I can, praying that we don't get uncovered.

I miss Felek so much. I trust there must be a reason why he keeps away, probably for my good as well, but it's so hard without him. I focus on my job at the factory, while making sure that my family is safe by keeping Sebastian tamed.

While Mama can't stop raving about him, I can't bring myself to stop her, even though she's so wrong. It's better that way. If she knew his true nature, she would be devastated. Right now, he is a knight in armor in her eyes and she already treats him like her son-in-law.

TWENTY-NINE
KASIA: BRUNO'S DUTIES

June 1944, Gdańsk

I take a tram from the city center to my home in Wrzeszcz. Traveling by train from Warsaw exhausted me to the point that walking would be too much right now. Looking through the window, I reflect on the city transformation from flowery spring to the greenery of summer. It brings a surge of hopefulness into my heart despite the ongoing war. I ignore the Nazi symbols and uniforms, instead focusing on the beauty of my city entangled between the sun rays of the gorgeous day.

I visited Ciocia Lucyna in Warsaw for a week, just to get away from here and get the right perspective on my life. It's been tough, but I haven't seen Felek since New Year's Eve. Pan Alojzy advised me to keep away from Pani Genowefa's home because it's being monitored by the Gestapo. Still, night after night for all these long months, I've waited for Felek to show up, but he never did, nor has he sent a note or letter. It steals sleep away from me and makes me exhausted.

Sebastian on the other hand keeps his usual approach where he controls my every move. Just being away from him for that one week did me so much good. He keeps engaging us in kisses after our Saturday dinners and imploring for more, but thankfully he stops when I remind him that I want to wait for our wedding.

Sara and Rebekah don't go out at all but stay upstairs and come down only when safe. To be honest, it would be heartbreaking for all of us parting with them now, especially for Kornel who adores Rebekah and treats her like his younger sister. They are our family now and we will do everything to keep them safe until this madness does end.

My stay in Warsaw was heartwarming because of the time spent with my aunt. The situation in the city hasn't changed much as there are constant roundups and shootings of people in the ruins of the ghetto, or other places, arrests, shortage of food… The list goes on and on. But there is also more hope in people's hearts now.

"I heard of a planned uprising to push the Germans out of Warsaw, and then Poland," Ciocia Lucyna said to me one evening. Her dark curls, gathered into a neat hairdo, make her look much younger. "People talk with hope about Allies invading the European continent and that we're entering the last period of the war." In her early forties, she shows so much enthusiasm and always feels positively, despite the harshness of war.

"This brings hope into my heart," I said, taking my aunt's hand in mine. Though I'm worried about you being alone in this city."

She smiled gently while leaning back into the soft armchair, the forbidden novel of Stefan Żeromski entitled, *The Faithful River*, on her lap. "You don't need to, darling. Franciszek helps me a lot and when the time comes, we both will join the rest of the Resistance in the fight. I'm sure you have full hands over there in Gdańsk too." Franciszek is Ciocia's long-term friend, a shoemaker, but there are deeper feelings involved. "How's the situation there?"

"The German population in Gdańsk continues to live without being harmed, unlike the Poles here. Though recently, there are some changes taking place. Most of the stores or cafés are closing down while the arms industry blooms. The blackout hours are still in effect and streetlamps and windows are still covered. German civilians have more and more trouble getting enough food and there are restrictions now in place which decrease the amount of food per person; much less milk or potatoes; fish substitutes meat. Still, they are having rich lives compared to Poles."

"So even in your German-populated city people realize that things will be changing very soon. Hitler is losing this war, and it's now only a matter of time before Germany capitulates."

"Definitely but the Nazi propaganda keeps Germans in the dark when it comes to the real situation on the front, even though now civilians are being obliged to work in the streets on constructing fortifications. They expect to be attacked soon by the Soviets."

Now, before entering the villa, I close my eyes and listen to birds chirping in the apple tree branches, enjoying the sun brushing my skin. I inhale sweet fragrance from flowers and thank the Creator for bringing me back home again. This is the place where I belong.

The house is silent and greets me with a delicate and sweet smell of lavender.

"You're back." Kornel runs into my arms while Maciek rubs against my legs.

"I have something for you from Ciocia," I say and kiss his forehead. My sweetest boy.

"What's that?" His wide eyes betray his excitement.

A bubble of laughter rises in my throat, but I dig into my

small luggage and fish out a brown paper bag. "Do me a favor and share it with Rebekah, of course if it's fine with Pani Sara."

He peeks inside the bag and giggles. "Ciocia is the best."

I suspected that the collection of tiny, rare stones will bring happiness to him. My aunt has been collecting them for years, since I told her how much he likes to pick interesting stones and shells.

"Where is Mama?" I ask, shuffling toward the kitchen.

"She went to buy bread." He lowers his voice. "Sara and Rebekah stay upstairs in their room because Sebastian comes often now to check on us, and Mama doesn't want him to know because she's not sure what he would do."

"Yes, Mama is right. No one can know of them being here, if you want Rebekah to be fine."

"You don't need to tell me that. I'm her knight and I will do everything to protect her, even if it requires me to keep that big mouth of mine shut."

I giggle and playfully nudge his arm. "You and your silly voice."

"I forgot to tell you that our old watchman visited us yesterday asking when you will be back. Mama told him today, so he asked if you could come to the amber boutique at five."

"Did he say anything else?"

"No, just that. Mama made him chamomile tea and they talked about Papa," he winces but quickly continues, "and about Jadwiga's health."

Since I moved back home, we haven't been talking much about our father. It's just too painful for us but holding it all inside isn't good either, especially for someone young like Kornel. I know that Mama does speak to him about it occasionally. Maybe one day it will be easier for me to remember Papa too and it will not feel like stabbing the already bleeding wound.

And after what happened with Zofia, I realized that it's important to live in the moment because tomorrow isn't guaranteed. I cherish my family and pray daily that they remain safe from any harm. I also pray for Felek's safety, hoping that one day he will return to me, because despite all, I feel deep in my heart that he loves me, and whatever he's doing, he must have a reason. I choose to trust him unconditionally.

I glance to the cuckoo clock on the wall. "I must get going then. When Mama returns home, tell her that I will be back soon."

He nods. "Be careful, sister. Let me go and share some of these goodies with Rebekah." He smiles mischievously.

～

"I'm so happy to see you, sweetheart," Pani Genowefa says when I arrive in their house at a quarter to five. "Warsaw is so dangerous."

After a long hug, she makes some grain coffee and puts a few slices of her *kuch* on the table. I breathe in the homely smell of the yeast cake with its sweet sugar crumble.

"Alojzy left a word for me to come over today. Is everything okay, Pani Genowefa? Is the Gestapo still bothering you?"

"No, they last 'popped in' in February, I believe, so the Resistance have decided that it's time for us to start helping again."

"I hope that—" The knock on the door makes my words freeze. "Are you expecting anyone?" Her husband wouldn't tap on his own door.

"It must be Felek," she says making my heartbeats quicken.

Her words prove her right because she opens the door and Felek's voice vibrates along my nerves. "*Serwus*, Pani Genowefa."

"Hello, my boy, please come in," she says and adds, "Kasia, darling, Felek is here. I will be back soon."

"Okay, Pani," I say without turning to him, afraid to see

indifference in his eyes. What if he doesn't care for me the way I care for him? Maybe I took it all too seriously and the fact that he hasn't contacted me for the last six months is normal behavior for a man like him.

I listen to the sound of his footsteps on the wood floor and swallow the lump in my throat.

But then he steps right behind me. "You don't want to look at me?" he says in a voice laden with emotion. It's when I can't take it anymore. I leap to my feet and throw myself into his arms.

His trembling hand brushes my hair, his lips find mine, our tears mingle. "Why?" I whisper a moment later.

"For your safety. Richter was snooping around and kept following you, so I had to disappear. Please, believe me. You are my everything."

"You could've sent me a note that you're okay."

"I didn't want to risk it. Besides, I know Alojzy told you that I'm fine. I prayed every day that you trust me."

"I do trust you," I say and press the side of my face to his chest. His chaotic heartbeat confirms that he tells the truth and does care about me.

"What now?" I ask and lift my gaze to his beautiful eyes with shades of the sea on rainy days. It's always that dark when he kisses or caresses. Any other time his eyes are more grayish.

"Whenever your lower lip quivers," he says," I know that you still care, after all these months."

"Stop making fun of my weakness," I tease. "What are months when we have our whole lives ahead of us?"

He doesn't get a chance to answer because Pani Genowefa runs in, her breathing labored. "Gestapo just parked their trucks near our boutique." She points at Felek. "You must hide, and quick."

She moves the table with Felek's help, then snatches out a

rug from its place. The boards below lift easily, revealing a hideout in the floor. After Felek lies down, we put them back in place, cover them with the rug and stand a table on it with chairs.

We take our places at the table. "Act like we only drink coffee and chat, and please put a slice of *kuch* on your plate, but first take a generous bite from it," she whispers, her mouth folded in a reassuring smile.

I do as she says, unable to smile back. What if they discover Felek and bring him for interrogations to Neugarten? Maybe Sebastian followed me and called the Gestapo when he saw Felek coming in.

The moment the door opens, I quiet down my frantic mind and act like I'm surprised at their arrival.

Two uniformed SS men enter, their guns pointing at us, then to my astonishment, Bruno walks in from behind.

"For goodness' sake, Bruno, you almost gave me a heart attack. You gentlemen should knock first," I say and stare at him as if expecting explanations. "I nearly dropped this delicious slice of cake."

He curls his mustache with his finger, then smirks. "What are you doing here, my Katharina?" He seems genuinely surprised to see me, though it might be just a game he plays along with Sebastian.

"I'm visiting my friend." I take a sip of my coffee. "Is that a crime?"

His laughter rings out. "That's perfectly fine with me." He instructs the other two men to search the flat, then he takes a seat at the table. "I'm only doing my job." He moves his gaze to Pani Genowefa. "We received another information that you are engaging with lowlife," he says, glancing at me. "Please be sure I'm not implying you, my dearest."

She rolls her eyes. "I bet Frau Wolf contacted you again with her false accusations. You need to stop treating her seriously. She is a nut." Pani Genowefa gets up. "Can I offer you coffee, hun?"

"I would like that very much, thank you."

She talks to him like he's her good friend while he's a damn criminal. He might be laughing constantly and acting friendly, but he can't fool me. His air-headed wife Ilse told me what kind of man he is and how he actively helped eliminate the Jewish community of Gdańsk; how he collaborated to remove Poles from their homes and send Polish intelligence to Stutthof and other camps and murdered them. Of course, she's so proud of his *achievements*. He doesn't need a reason; there is no court to try us in front of. He can arrest us for nothing.

But Pani Genowefa's approach is correct, and we must act friendly and with confidence, so he doesn't suspect anything. I hope that Felek has enough room to breathe down there. The two SS men search every corner of the flat, then inform Bruno of moving to the basement.

He sips coffee and talks about the victories of the German army, like he doesn't realize that Hitler gets defeated more and more. But their propaganda feeds them what they want to hear.

"Sebastian will be happy to see you returned from Warsaw," he tells me as he puts nearly a whole piece of Pani Genowefa's cake in his mouth. "He's been moody lately and I suspect it's because he has missed you."

He's the last person I want to see now, but I say, "I've missed him too." Was it him who sent Bruno here, I wonder?

When the two soldiers come to report that they didn't find anything in the basement either, Bruno gets up and bows before us. "Ladies, please forgive me for interrupting your leisure, but I hope you understand that I'm only fulfilling my duties. Please, don't take it personally."

Just when he turns away and takes the first step as if to leave, the unmistakable sound of a suppressed sneeze comes from the floor below us.

My blood freezes as Bruno swirls back and reaches to his holster to take a pistol out.

I laugh nervously and look at Pani Genowefa. "My sweet lady, you sneeze like your husband. God bless you!"

His face grows serious, and for a moment longer he holds my gaze, then moves it to the rugged floor under the table.

"You're silly, Katharina." Pani Genowefa has missed her calling, I think. She could challenge Pola Negri as the Polish Queen of Hollywood. "It was my husband sneezing. I scolded him yesterday that whenever he sneezes while in the store downstairs, I'm thinking he's upstairs and I start talking to him." She chuckles and reaches over for her embroidery basket as if she has some important sewing to do.

But surely Bruno can't be fooled. He heard it just like we did. We are done. He's about to start ripping everything out to find Felek.

THIRTY
KASIA: PERVITIN

July 1944, Gdańsk

A couple of weeks after Bruno's raid on Pani Genowefa's home, I sit quietly in my office, waiting for the work shift to end, when I overhear Bertha talking to a new typist who was recently hired by Sebastian. With a violent look in her eyes and red cheeks, she looks like she just came in from torturing the prisoners and I've taken an immediate dislike to her.

"Have you heard what happened yesterday?" Bertha says. My door isn't fully closed because I can't stand the stagnant air, so I created a breeze between the open window and door.

"Is it about your Mutti?"

"No, Mutti is not doing well at all, I mean still very sick, but I hope for a miracle and that she will recover soon. I was talking about the failed attempt to assassinate our dearest Führer."

That's new. I had no idea that something like this had taken place. I wonder who finally decided to commit something so smart. Too bad it didn't work out though.

I just came back from my delivery to the SS Headquarters

in the Oliwa Manor and decided to take an easy before leaving for the day. Sebastian doesn't check my work schedule and if he pops in, I will pretend to be busy with a new recipe or delivery schedule, or some other task. I got my monthly today, so I'm just not feeling well. I'm sure the stress doesn't help either.

Every time I go to that manor, I think of all those criminals working there, the same feeling as when crossing the threshold of the Gestapo Headquarters on Neugarten. Those people run the machinery of destruction and the bureaucracy of the slaughter of innocent people. They make me want to slam their unthinking heads against the wall. I honestly feel like I can't take it anymore. All I do is pretend every day, pretend to be sympathizing with them, and I know I must do this, or my family and I would be doomed, and we wouldn't be able to help Sara and her precious daughter.

"You're still here?" Sebastian peeks through the door.

I look up from my desk and fold my lips into a smile. "Yes, I'm trying to finish some things. Are you leaving?"

"Yes, I have an appointment with Dr. Fischer, otherwise I would give you a ride home."

"I will be fine. Good luck with your appointment." It's not like I care anyway.

"It's just a routine check-up. Good night."

He must be late already since he didn't bother to come inside and attempt to kiss me, like he usually does at the end of the day, like we're a couple. Well, officially we are, but only officially. I can't help but sigh. I wish I could end this farce and tell him what he surely already knows: that I don't love him.

He closed the door, so I walk over and open it ajar again, just so the air flow isn't disturbed. I get so sweaty here, with the summer sun beating down on the bricks of the factory all day. As I do it, I overhear him saying to his secretary to wait for Bruno before leaving for the day, and once she receives the document that Bruno delivers, she needs to lock his office and take the key with her home.

He's always been very particular about making sure his office is locked when he isn't there. He's hiding something. He must be. Maybe he's working on new explosives camouflaged in chocolate bars. I decide to stay here longer, at least until Bruno comes. Since our encounter at Pani Genowefa, he acts the same as always.

Felek climbed out alive from the hideout under the kitchen table, after Bruno and his peers left. I couldn't believe that Bruno decided not to investigate that sneeze.

Soon the new typist leaves and Bruno arrives, but he quickly places documents on Bertha's desk and rushes out as if the building, or his pants, are on fire. I watch through the ajar door as she disappears into Sebastian's office and then walks back to her desk.

Now or never. "Bertha," I say in a cold voice and stride toward her, "I just received a phone call regarding your dear mother's condition."

Her forehead wrinkles. "Why would they call you?" She's still holding the key to Sebastian's office in her hand.

"Well, I guess they dialed the wrong number. Anyway, I was asked to tell you that your mother's condition has suddenly worsened, to such an extent they don't expect her to make it beyond another hour. They advised that you should go home to her immediately."

I feel terrible to tell such a lie to her, but I needed something to shock her, so she doesn't realize what's she's doing, and I can somehow get hold of that key. God, please, forgive me for this.

She gasps and drops the key to her desk.

Bingo! I restrain myself from grabbing it there and then.

"Are you sure?" Her voice is soft now, not her usual arrogant tone when she speaks to me. She will find out very soon that this is a lie, but I will tell her tomorrow that it was a call intended for someone else, that I misinterpreted, and I will apologize. I need to do what I need to do, even though I feel awful for saying something like this to her.

"I'm so sorry, sweetie," I say pretending to care. "Here," I touch her arm, "let me help you get your things together so you can leave right away." I pick up the few personal items from her desk and put it into her bag, while she stands still, her shoulders slumped.

I snatch the key and slip it into my pant pocket. "All ready, my dear, now please be careful when walking out."

She thanks me, scans her desk then leaves.

My pulse quickens as I wait, making sure that she's left the building. Praying she doesn't return, I scurry to Sebastian's office and lock the door from inside. I have no time to lose. What if Sebastian decides to stop by after his doctor's appointment, before heading home? What if Bertha realizes that she doesn't have the spare key that Sebastian gave to her?

After glancing at the document from Bruno, which indicates an order for more chocolate for SS Headquarters, I thoroughly search the rest of the office. I find nothing indicating that he continues my father's job working on camouflaged explosives, but I see something else that makes me so confused. There are some official orders directing Sebastian to produce chocolate laced with Pervitin, for Hitler's army.

I quickly leave the office, thankful that no one sees me. I wonder what to do with the key, then I see Bertha's suit jacket still hanging on the back of her chair, so I place the key in its pocket. This way she will think that she put it there while rushing out.

I go back to Papa's office and sit down at his desk, trying to slow down my spinning mind. Sebastian is adding Pervitin to our chocolate. Now I know why he reacted so angrily when Bruno offered a piece of his "special" chocolate to me—it contained Pervitin. Every written order that I found in his office indicates the specific amount of chocolate to be produced with Pervitin, so it's not like he adds it to all products. Still, I find it repulsive that something like this is even happening. I bet Felek will be surprised at Sebastian's activities. He must be making a vast amount of money by doing it.

The name Pervitin is very familiar. Before the war it was heavily advertised in Germany as a magical pill for those struck low with depression. Everyone could buy it, even though it's basically a methamphetamine that speeds up the body's system, filling you with fierce bursts of energy.

Once the war started, the German leaders decided to use it to create warriors who live up to Hitler's twisted fantasies. It turns soldiers into unstoppable battle machines and killers who are less susceptible to pain and can go without sleep or food for long periods of time. Hyped and overstimulated, they take extreme risks more willingly, even at the cost of their lives.

But Pervitin is highly addictive and can cause hallucinations, severe depression, heart problems and even death. When Herr Krause's son, who served in the Wehrmacht, shot himself in 1940, Frau Krause told my mother he was addicted to Pervitin, and it had driven him to insanity and aggression.

It might have been banned eventually by the Third Reich, but I'd read in the underground gazettes that German soldiers had relied on it during the invasion of the Soviet Union.

And, I think now, based on the orders that Sebastian regularly receives, Pervitin is still used for certain missions. But there were no details on the documents, only directives as to a certain production. I wonder if Bruno is addicted to it, too, since he asked Sebastian for his "special" chocolate bar but, at the same time, I must admit that Sebastian proved to genuinely care for my well-being when he stopped Bruno from sharing his chocolate with me. Thank goodness, as the last thing I need is a drug addiction.

But then that slightly absurd thought raises an unavoidable question that gnaws at my insides.

Were Papa's heart issues caused by a guilty secret? Was Papa another of this wartime stimulant's many addicts?

THIRTY-ONE
FELEK: OUR SONG

August 1944, Gdańsk

It's near midnight and the Stogi Beach is empty, so we perch on the soft sand, and my arms encircle her while she presses the side of her face to my arm. We managed to navigate through the city under the curfew without being noticed by German patrols. Above the calm sea, stars glow through the night sky and the full moon shines in the mirror of water surface.

She reaches into her pants pocket and retrieves a few seeds from it. "Can you chew on one of those cocoa beans and describe to me what is it exactly that you taste? I've been working on a new chocolate recipe and could use some inspiration here."

"I love inspiring you," I say and kiss her lips.

"Felek, please," she says trying to sound serious but her smile betrays her.

"Alright." I pop one of the seeds into my mouth and chew on it. "The flavor is sour and a little astringent, and it reminds me of coffee. How's that chocolate? It doesn't taste anything like it."

"Well, it's all about the right production and proportions of ingredients. But it all starts when the seeds are extracted from the cocoa berries. The seeds are fermented, so they can gain a brown color, to later go through drying. Then to make chocolate there are many steps, like the conching process when chocolate loses the cocoa bean flavor as it can't be sour or too bitter."

"What else is chocolate made of?"

"My job is to find the right proportions of cocoa mass, cocoa butter, sugar and powdered milk, or whatever ingredients I feel like the certain cocoa bean would be complimented by, like vanilla or cinnamon, to create unique flavor."

"Interesting. You taste the bean, so you can decide what ingredients to use?" I like listening to her words and how she shares her passion with me.

"Yes. Do you have any suggestions when it comes to the bean you just chewed on?"

I narrow my eyes like I'm thinking hard. "Well, definitely some vanilla and plenty of honey along with a pinch of love straight from your heart," I say and wink at her.

"Honey?" She arches her brow. "Not much help from you," she adds and playfully nudges my arm.

I can't resist, so I pull her closer for a scorching kiss. "I'm just an electrician, so what do I know," I say when our mouths part.

"Let's talk about electric matters then," she says and runs her fingers through my hair causing my entire body to shiver in excitement. I can't ever get enough of her.

"No, I have a better idea," I say and kiss her again, our lips in this exquisite dance of love and affection. In this very moment, I feel like I'm holding the rarest jewel in the world.

A moment later she says, "You taste like that cocoa bean." She chuckles. "I think I will add some honey to my new recipe, after all."

"That flavor from the bean is still lingering on my tongue."

"The grain contains a lot of essential oils, so it's why the flavor stays on for a long time."

"That explains it." I inhale the salty and fishy smell of sea that has grown on me strongly. "What's your favorite song?"

"'Over the Rainbow' from the film *The Wizard of Oz*," she says, her voice dreamy. "The actress Judy Garland has a beautiful voice, so perfect for this song."

"I've never heard it," I say.

The moment I say it, she goes on singing quietly but steadily about a land somewhere over the rainbow, where the skies are blue, and dreams come true. Then she sings about one day waking up within clouds where bluebirds fly, free of any troubles. The whole time she keeps her voice low, still, I feel captivated by it to the point that blissful feeling runs through me, the same one I experience every time I kiss her.

"This will be our song from now on," I say and kiss her forehead while caressing her back.

She laughs with a high dose of delight. "Then I must teach you the words, so you can join me singing."

"It's so catchy that I promise to learn it in no time. What do you feel when you sing it?" I'm genuinely curious to hear her insight about this nostalgic but optimistic song.

"I contemplate the power of imagination and its limits, and I get hope that despite all the ugliness we witness in this world and how fragile our mortality is during this terrible war, there is a better place, after all. Maybe it's where Zofia has gained her peace."

"Yes," I say, touched at the thought of my dear friend in this innocent place of Kasia's song. "I shall think of her there, reunited with her husband."

"I hope that's where she is, too. Do you ever get scared, Felek, that the next day might be your last one, just like it proved to be for way too many innocent and brave people?"

"I don't think of it," I insist. "I just go with the flow of every mission and get my job done. It's easier that way. In the end, what truly matters to me is that I love you. No one can ever take it away from me, not even death."

"I feel the same. I don't mind that we sometimes don't see each other for so many months. Our love can sustain absence, I'm sure of it. My life is meaningless without my love for you. It's why you must promise to be careful, to always come back to me."

I look out at the ink black sea. At first, I want to tell her that I can't promise such a thing. But I can't disappoint her. Not now. So, I say, "Kasia, I promise to do everything I can to always come back to you."

THIRTY-TWO

KASIA: NO, I WILL NOT...

August 1944, Gdańsk

I've been plagued by what I found out about Pervitin for the weeks since, pondering over and over the chance that my father was a victim. Part of me knows that a man with strong principles like Papa wouldn't even consider touching such a drug, but the other one keeps arguing that nothing in this world can surprise me anymore. Not after all the atrocities that the Nazis have committed, and all the different people they've recruited to carry out those atrocities.

"How did you manage during last night's bombardments? Looks like the Americans decided to visit us again," Sebastian asks and smirks at me as we walk on the soft sand. Today is Saturday, so after a fancy dinner at one of the Old Town bistros, he brought me to my favorite Stogi Beach on the Baltic shore. "Thankfully, no significant damages to the city."

I still don't know on whose side he truly is, though after I found out about the Pervitin, I realized that he's only a marionette in the hands of the Nazis.

Felek doesn't trust him, not an inch, and I never got an OK

from Zofia to start trusting him, so whatever Sebastian told me about his willingness to help the Polish Resistance was never explored. I'm sure our leaders have their own reasons to shun Sebastian, because normally they use any available outlet to fight the Germans. But I can't deny that he does care for me, and he's proved it so many times.

"We managed fine and made sure to stay in the basement until it was safe again. What about you?"

"I took a risk and stayed in bed," he winks at me, "but don't tell anyone."

Such a bold statement surprises me, especially as he always makes sure to achieve perfection in everything he does. "You probably sensed that it wasn't anything serious, though you never know." I tuck my lose hair behind my ears as the wind on this exposed stretch of sand has no mercy and blows it all over my face.

He turns his head and looks down at me. "I like when your hair is like this, so natural and beautiful." His pale blue eyes are soft now and my tormentor and the demanding and calculating owner of the factory is gone. In this very moment, he's once again the man that I began to be infatuated with, before that day when Felek kissed me, and my true feelings emerged.

"I forgot my straw hat," I say and listen to the crash of waves and fizz of foam as it sweeps ashore and spreads across the sand. "I always do when I come to the beach."

"It's not like you knew that we would stop here after dinner. I wanted to surprise you as you seem quiet lately and there is no better cure for apathy than sun."

"You know that I enjoy the beach, so your surprise is perfect." I inhale the briny sea air and remind myself to cherish every second here. "When I was little, I loved hunting for amber."

"I collected shells," he says and takes my hand in his.

I don't take it away because I must pretend, something I'm

more and more exhausted of lately. I wish the end of the war could put a stop to this farce.

Suddenly, he kneels and before I can say anything he snaps a small velvety box from his pocket.

"Katharina, I might have many flaws, but I will do everything to protect you and to love you for the rest of my life, if you only give me the chance. Will you marry me?"

I gasp at a round stone that sparkles in the sunshine. This is so unexpected that at first, I gape at him in disbelief, but the earnest look on his face pulls at every string of my heart. I know that he tells the truth and that he does care for me, to the point that he often forgets to control his jealousy. Just like that New Year's Day morning when he failed to tame his anger...

While the naïve me of the past would have been thrilled with his proposal, now I don't know what to do. The practical part of me reasons that marrying him would seal the deal, allowing the factory to stay in our family—something that Papa cared about so much. Sebastian would protect my family now and after the war. He's that type of person. But these are egoistical, pointless reasons because I simply don't love him. He deserves at least honesty from me, but he can't get even that, not now, because telling him that I'm in love with another man would put my family in extreme danger. While he cares, he can also be violent and act cruelly out of hatred.

I wipe tears from my eyes, tears for not being able to tell him the truth. "Sebastian, this is so unexpected. You see, I'm not ready for a serious relationship, not for marriage."

His face looks crestfallen. "You aren't ready, or you don't want me?"

"I think we should wait until the war ends before making that type of decision. It would not be fair of me to accept this ring now. War has changed all of us and it would be dishonorable of me to commit to anything right now."

He leaps to his feet, brushing sand from his tailored suit, and drops the box into his pocket. "Is there someone else?"

I hate myself for lying to him in a moment like this, but I'd do everything to keep my family safe. "No. I'm just not ready. Please, my dear, give me a little more time."

His hurt eyes betray that his pride is suffering right now. "Let's go back."

We only exchange a few words during the ride home, and he doesn't walk me to the door.

"Good night, Katharina," he says. Without looking into my eyes, he turns and marches away.

"How was the dinner with Sebastian?" Mama asks when I enter the kitchen. She is in the middle of wiping counters; a strong chamomile scent brimming in the air.

I sigh. "Oh, Mama. I just refused Sebastian's proposal."

She freezes for a moment longer, but when her gaze meets mine, the layers of understanding mix with worries. "What exactly have you told him?"

"I didn't want to risk yours and Kornel's safety, and now we must keep Sara and Rebekah safe, so I told him that I'm not ready for serious commitments and that it's best to wait until the war ends."

She exhales with relief. "Good girl," she whispers. "How did he take it?"

"He's upset. But I couldn't do it, Mama, because I don't love him."

She puts the wet cloth away and picks up the kettle from the white-tiled stove, then adds boiling water to the glass jar with its dried leaves of chamomile. "Darling, I told you what true love is about, and let me tell you, Sebastian does love you. I know because I see the way he looks at you with softness in his eyes when you don't realize it."

"I remember everything you told me about love, and trust me, I tried feeling something more toward him. But he isn't the one, Mama, I just know it." I wrap the wet cloth on the counter around my fingers. "I feel very sad, but not because I had to reject him—because I must wait to the end of this war to tell him the truth that I don't love him and will never marry him. He doesn't deserve this, despite his support for the Nazis. I feel like I'm playing with his feelings and that deeply upsets me."

"You love someone else." She doesn't ask, it's more of a statement. "I was like that once too. I thought I was in love with a boy from my village but when I visited Gdańsk with my friends to enjoy a week on the Baltic beaches, everything changed—I met your father. I knew deep inside my soul that he was the one for me and that before I had no idea how true love felt like."

Mama grew up in a small village in north-eastern Poland, not far from the city of Łomża. But when she met Papa, they soon married and began their life together in Gdańsk. Before the war, we visited my grandparents every few months. Later, when I lived in Warsaw, I accompanied Ciocia Lucyna on those trips to visit them and my uncle Roman who runs the family farm with his wife. They have a beautiful son Ignaś who now must be around Kornel's age.

"Thank you for sharing this with me," I say. Before, Mama never talked much about her feelings, so this is special. "And thank you for understanding me and not being angry that I didn't seal the safety of our family by agreeing to marry him. I feel selfish for not doing it." In truth, I'm so torn by the emotions that run through me. Sebastian exposed his deep feelings for me and watching the heartbreak reflected in his eyes after I didn't accept his proposal, was hard. This will ultimately change his approach toward me, I could already sense it in his vague and distant behavior on our way back home.

"We must be careful because his pride suffers right now, and we don't know what that will do to him. You know the saying that the hurt animal may attack with the ferocity of a monster."

"It's what I'm afraid of." I sigh. "I wanted to ask you about something else."

"What's that?"

"How did Papa spend his last day?" I never told her about my discovery of Sebastian fulfilling the Nazi orders to add Pervitin to chocolate for the Wehrmacht and Luftwaffe. It's better she doesn't know. I didn't confront Sebastian about it either, of course, because he would only question where I know this from. I was so sorry to hear that Bertha's mother did die that evening due to health complications. Ironic that my lie turned out to be true.

She sniffs and wipes at her nose. "Let's take a seat." She still struggles to talk about Papa without crying.

I take her arm as she seems to sway a bit, and we stagger to the family room and drop to the sofa. I bring us both a glass of chamomile tea; I think we might need it.

"It was Sunday, so we went to church in the morning and then for a walk on Stogi Beach. You know it was his favorite." For a few seconds she stares down at her hands and continues in a tearful voice, "When we were back, I went to kitchen to make dumplings and he went over to Sebastian's to play cards. It became their Sunday routine, and Bruno and Dr. Fischer often joined them too."

So, he did see Sebastian that day. "What time was he back home?"

She rubs at her chest. "He didn't come home," her voice cracks, "Sebastian ran over to let me know that he'd suffered of a heart attack and that Dr. Fischer wasn't able to help him."

I feel like a waterfall of ice is cascading down my spine. Did someone add a dose of Pervitin to Papa's drink, which caused him to have a fatal heart attack? Did they *kill* him? This thought has circled the most shadowy reaches of my mind since I found out about the presence of the drug in our factory's chocolate, but now the dreadful feeling intensifies, grows closer to the surface, where I can see it more clearly. If yes, was it Sebastian, or Bruno?

"Did Papa complain about his heart before?"

"Actually, he did complain a lot in the last year of his life. The factory brought on tremendous strain, and he felt such a weight of guilt for scaring you away from us."

I feel pain in the back of my throat, but I quickly remind myself that it was all Papa's doing. It seems that Mama doesn't really know much about Papa's Nazi party involvement, nor about the explosives he created in chocolate for them. I want to save her as much heartache as possible, so she'll never hear about it from me. She has enough on her plate, enough sorrow, and besides, it's better that she has only good memories of Papa. She thinks he pretended to be on their side for the sake of our family; she has no idea that he voluntarily contributed to camouflaging bombs in chocolate bars, which murdered innocent people.

"If I could only reverse time, I would have come home earlier," I whisper, unable to suppress my tears, but whether they are for the loss of my father or the loss of my dream of him as a good man, I can't be sure.

THIRTY-THREE
KASIA: INJURY

November 1944, Gdańsk

I'm about to turn the key in the lock when I hear a noise from the left corner of the veranda. My hand freezes. It's dark, so I can't see anything. "Who's there?" I ask.

"It's me," someone whispers. "I just need some bandages."

"Felek!" I gasp. "Are you okay?"

"Yes, I've got a small wound." I can hear pain slipping through his strained voice.

"Come inside," I say and turn the key.

"No, please, I don't want to put you under any risk. I will come another night."

Since the summer, I've still been passing any information I get through Pan Alojzy, but Felek visits me every few weeks at night, when everyone is asleep. Pani Genowefa's neighbor, Frau Wolf, has been calling on her quite often. She can't stand that Pani Genowefa married a German and thanks to that is treated with respect. This woman is a piece of work.

I open the door and look around. "Now, please get inside," I whisper, hoping that he will listen. Thankfully, he does.

I take his coat off and examine his right arm. "It's bleeding. Does it hurt?"

"Nah, it's just a scrape, but I was afraid that if it isn't cleaned it might get infected."

I can sense his shyness in admitting to needing my help. He's always so brave and self-dependent.

"I'm glad you came in," I say and kiss his lips.

He kisses me back and butterflies flutter in my stomach. For a moment, I forget that we're still standing in the foyer.

But when I hear Mama clearing her throat not once but twice, I jump away from him. "Mama, this is Felek. His arm is bleeding, so I invited him to come over, so we can help him."

Mama stands with her arms crossed at her chest, but the moment she registers my words, she ushers Felek to the kitchen and instructs him to take a seat at the table. The whole time she doesn't question his presence in our home any further but focuses on helping me.

Lately, I've been thinking how wrongly I judged her all these years.

She cleans his wound with cold water and soap. "Thankfully it's not a deep wound and there isn't anything stuck in it. How did this happen?"

A pinched and tension-filled expression covers his face, but when he speaks his tone is calm, "It's from a knife fight."

"I can see that it just happened, so that's good that you came here," Mama says. "I will make a solution of vinegar and warm water and hopefully it will be enough to kill any bacteria."

An hour later, we all sit at the table with Sara and the children and devour Mama's pickle soup. After she wrapped Felek's arm in a clean bandage, he wanted to leave, but we insisted that he spend the night and gain some strength before going back into forests.

I look at her from across the table and can officially say that my mother is a true heroine. She's been supportive to

Sara and Rebekah. Despite the current food shortage in Gdańsk, she makes sure that we have a warm meal every day. And now she didn't put Felek outside the door the moment she was done taking care of his wound, or even the moment she caught him kissing her daughter in the dark; instead, she stood firm that he stays for dinner and gets a decent amount of sleep.

"Have you heard anything new from the front, Felek?" Sara asks.

"Enough to know that the war will be over soon," Felek says and grins. "The word is that the Allies have liberated most of the occupied territories and the Germans are being pushed back more and more."

"I knew that we would win when they lost in their advances over the Soviet Union," Mama says and thrusts her chin forward. "They've been losing their control of the Eastern Front since, but this isn't something that you would read in their propaganda gazettes."

"Well, the war isn't over yet and I have a feeling that there is still a lot ahead of us," Sara says.

"Don't forget that the Allies liberated Rome in June, and then pushed German troops east from Normandy. This is huge," Felek says. "*Szkopy* already lost this war but they're still doing everything to prolong the suffering. Now they are even more dangerous because they are desperate, they are cornered like a—"

Our conversation is interrupted by Maciek who jumps into Felek's lap and settles into immediate sleep. "Like a frightened cat," he finishes, and we all laugh.

"My cat likes you," Kornel says, his smile reaching his eyes. "Do you care to play chess with me?"

"Kornel, honey, Felek must rest. Why don't you play with me?" I make sure to sound enthusiastic though chess isn't something I feel up for right now.

"You're no fun, besides I always win with you," he says and exchanges a knowing look with Felek.

Felek coughs a bit, and his pinched expression makes me suspect that he's doing everything to not laugh. This is new to him because the Felek I got to know usually doesn't have trouble expressing his amusement. He's trying not to hurt my feelings.

"I can play," he says. "But you may have to remind me of some of the rules as it's been a while."

"Sure, but I will have to collect some chocolate from Gdańsk in return." Kornel smirks and tilts his chin up.

"Kornel, enough of that nonsense," I say. The fact that he remembers the story with Napoleon Bonaparte warms my heart.

"I was kidding. Relax, sister."

"I'm sorry, buddy, but I don't have any chocolate. Your best bet is your sister, she's the one who works at the factory." Felek's voice is apologetic.

Kornel claps his hands together. "Aha, you don't know the tale that I heard from my sister. Well, my friend, I'm glad to tell you this important story." Then, as he arranges the pieces on the old wooden chessboard, he fills Felek in with the details of the old story.

At bedtime, Mama insists that I allow Felek to sleep in my bedroom, while she can share hers with me. It's the most sensible option in this situation, so I agree.

But, of course, once my mother's snoring is regular, I sneak out the bed and tiptoe to my bedroom. As I suspected, Felek isn't asleep, because the moment I open the door he leaps to his feet and enfolds me in his arms.

"Oh Kasia, how I missed you," he whispers. "Come here, my *Kochanie.*" Darling.

THIRTY-FOUR
FELEK: BETRAYAL

January 1945, Mirachowskie Forest

I take a seat at an oak table and continue sipping my beer, after meeting with one of the Resistance members. The tavern owner cooperates with our movement to free Poland from German clutches.

My next mission is extremely dangerous, one that may require the ultimate sacrifice. It's why I must see Kasia before setting off tomorrow. If it's God's will, He will let me stay alive, despite all the odds being stacked against me.

The atmosphere of the place appears to be friendly for Germans as the village band sings German old folklore songs and the menu consists of German cuisine. All of this is done to fool them; it's the most effective way to fight them: pretend while doing everything to continue the work underground to liberate our Poland.

"I knew I would find you here." Adka's voice brings me back to reality. How would she know if I rarely stop here? Something isn't right, I think immediately.

I gaze around but don't notice anything suspicious. Because

of the late hour, the tavern is already closed and there are no patrons here beside the bearded owner who busies himself with instructing his workers in efforts to clean up the place. I was about to depart too for my bunker in the forest. Every time I go there, I think of Zofia and how I miss her.

I force my mind back into present and ask, "How did you get here?"

"The owner is a good friend of my father."

"You followed me," I say, instilling a note of firmness into my voice. "Why?"

Since that day when Kasia smuggled cyanide to Zofia, Adka hasn't said a word to me, nor has she looked at me. I tried reasoning with her that she deserves someone who will love her and that I could never offer her that. I only got the silent treatment, so I ceased my attempts.

She sits on the opposite end of the table. "Yes. I need to talk to you and since you don't come to my house anymore, I had no choice but to look for you."

"How did you find me?"

"I followed my father the other day when he met here with you."

"I take you have an important matter on your mind, since you've gone to such trouble to see me."

"I didn't want to part on bad terms," she says, causing my muscles to relax. "I know I wasn't too friendly when we saw each other last."

"True. Listen, Adka, I need to apologize to you, too, for giving you false hope. I trust that one day you will forgive me." I drink the last of my beer, feeling glad that she decided to communicate with me, so we can clear the air between us.

To my surprise, tears come down her cheeks, so I fish out a handkerchief and hand it to her.

She takes it and wipes her tears away but keeps silent while gluing her soft gaze to my face. "You don't want me even though I gave you my heart," she says.

"Oh, Adka," I say gently. "You deserve so much more than what I can offer you, but you will always have my friendship."

"Let's run away together from here." Her pleading eyes unnerve me, and I feel even more guilty.

I choose to disregard her remark. "You're beautiful and witty, and so smart. I'm certain that one day you will meet a man worthy of you. Just keep your expectations high as you are one of a kind." I smile at her, but sense that my words are falling off her like rain from a duck.

"What do I need to do for you to want me as much as you want the other woman?"

"Please, forget about me. This is best you can do for both of us right now."

"She gets up. "Don't worry, I will not bother you anymore. You won't see me ever again." She touches my cheek with her fingers and settles her intense gaze into mine. "I'm sorry, darling." Then she marches away, her stance full of a heart-breaking attempt at dignity.

I'm baffled by her last words, but I also know so well that when people hurt, they often say things they wouldn't in normal circumstances. I get up and after saying goodbye to the owner, I walk out, fully embracing the awakening effect of the bone-chilling air. While I feel sorry for Adka, I suspect that she doesn't truly love me. She's just acting this way because her womanly pride has suffered. I don't judge her for it, but she hasn't stayed away from other men, even before I rejected her. I saw with my own eyes, and Zofia told me so.

Just when I lurch through the falling snow and walk around a wooden barn that belongs to the tavern, someone leaps at me from behind the building. There are so many of them and everything happens so fast that I don't even get a chance to reach for my gun and defend myself. It's a set-up, I know it is. I've been ambushed.

"Is that him?" a gruff German voice rings out—a man.

"Yes, that's Felek." It's a woman's voice, cold as ice, also in German. "He works for the Polish resistance."

It takes me a split second to recognize it, but when I do my spine stiffens.

The voice is Adka's.

THIRTY-FIVE
KASIA: MISSING IN ACTION

January 1945, Gdańsk

As we wait for the tram to the city center, I glance at a poster with proclamations to Danzig citizens from Georg Lippke, the mayor of Gdańsk, and Albert Forster, the Nazi gauleiter and deputy. They call on us all to stay calm, work hard and help refugees.

"If not for the Reich Germans and their sick love for the Nazis, we wouldn't be in this mess," a woman beside me in a floor-length mink coat snaps.

"True," I say and bite my tongue not to throw in her face that Danzigers supported the Nazi regime as much, or even more, while indulging in their comfortable, well-upholstered lives. Now, when the Soviets are on their way to liberate the city, they panic and suddenly declare themselves to be ardently opposed to Hitler and his regime. Well, that's way too late.

January has been very chaotic, with an atmosphere of panic and distress engulfing the city as columns of carriages with refugees from East Prussia arrive; they are fleeing from the Soviets—the very people who are about to march into our city, possibly as our *liberators*. The trains are overcrowded with people heading west. Gdańsk is only their temporary stop, the place from which they frantically try to secure spots on trains or ships going west. In the meantime, they camp out in tents on the city's squares or parks, stranded in basements, carriages, schools, or flats abandoned by people who have already left the city. Yes, it's chaos.

The panic within the city's population started in the middle of this month, since the Red Army began their powerful offensive on the entire eastern front. That's when the chaotic flight of Danzigers set in and they have been going on ever since. In this turmoil, some run away, and others arrive... while the air raids have intensified since the start of the year.

"I don't remember when last we had such a severe winter," Malina says and rubs her raw, scarlet cheeks with her gloved hands. Both sisters accompanied me today for the chocolate delivery to the SS Headquarters in the Oliwa Manor.

"Don't complain, sister, it could be worse. Besides, when frost stings our fingers, we know we're still alive," Alina says and sighs. "I hope Papa feels the same." They haven't heard from their father for a very long time now.

"No one can take our hope away," I say and stroke her arm.

"True. I wanted to ask you about the Oliwa Manor."

"What about it?"

"Every time we go there, you cross yourself before we enter the building. I noticed it again today. Why?"

Malina nudges her sister. "Alina, please stop being so nosy," she rolls her eyes," she's like that with everyone. One day she will get herself in trouble because of it, and this time we will not be able to help her."

I slowly smile. "I don't mind answering. You see, every time I enter the threshold of that manor, I get cold sweats running down my spine at the thought of what happened there in the seventeenth century. But I'm sure you've heard of it too."

"Is this about Jakub Schwabe, the Gdańsk city official?" Malina asks.

"Yes."

"What about him?" Alina frowns. "I've never heard anything about this man."

I nod my head at Malina, so she tells the story to her sister as we stomp our feet to stay warm at the freezing tram stop. "He got rich enough to buy the manor and the surrounding property where he lived with his wife, a woman of extraordinary beauty. For the first four years, the property bloomed under their supervision, and he even surprised his beloved wife with a new winery. But one day Schwabe was accused of fraud in the city of Gdańsk treasury. The scandal attracted so much publicity that his wife left him. Unable to bear the loss of his wife and the disgrace that surrounded him because of the accusations, Schwabe took his own life: he hung himself in the main entrance of the manor."

Alina lifts her chin and says in a serious tone, "Do you think his ghost is still living there because of the trauma he endured?"

"Alina," her sister says, disapproval marking her face.

"I do think so," I say, exchanging knowing glances with Alina.

"I believe in ghosts too," she says, her chin trembling for a moment. "I often feel our mother's soul present as if she keeps visiting us."

I look at her in sympathy. Their mother died from a complicated case of pneumonia when they were still only toddlers.

The rattle of the arriving tram disrupts our conversation.

"Finally," the woman swathed in mink says. "Listening to your prattle gives me goosebumps."

"Go on, lady," Alina says and smirks at her, earning another nudge from her sister.

I can't suppress my laughter. Alina is the most spirited girl I've ever met and the fact that she isn't afraid to stand up for herself warms my heart, except when it gets her in trouble like that time when Sebastian had to save her from the Gestapo.

When we get off the tram and navigate toward the factory among crowds of exhausted, disorientated families with their belongings, I say to these two sisters of whom I am so fond, "I'm not sure how much longer the factory will stay open, so I wanted to tell you that if you ever need help, never hesitate to come to my home." I take their hands, each in turn. "Once the Soviets intensify their attack, it should be safer in Wrzeszcz than in the city center."

I spend the rest of the day helping to stud chocolates with caramel as the department is shorthanded today. I enjoy the practical monotony of the task, the repetition that creates trays of identical sweets. After an hour or two, on the way to the lavatory, I pass Alojzy who's cleaning the corridor floor using a long stick with a rug on the end.

"I got a word yesterday about Felek," he whispers, glancing both ways, making me halt. "He never reported back after his last mission; no one knows what's happened to him. He's missing in action."

THIRTY-SIX
FELEK: STUTTHOF

January 1945, Stutthof concentration camp

As I lie on the lice-infested pallet atop a rickety bunk bed, I can't stop thinking of how fast my life has changed within the last few weeks. It's already past midnight and the wooden barrack is swathed in darkness, but I can't fall asleep. I would give everything to see my Kasia, feel her touch, smell the sweet and sensual jasmine perfume she likes to wear. I pray that she's safe. My life without her is meaningless.

After Adka's betrayal I was brought to Gestapo Headquarters where I expected the worst. But the following day they brought me and other prisoners to this camp with its low wooden barracks, barking dogs and perimeter of electrified barbed-wire fence.

After they shaved my head, they threw me under a cold shower, and then I was ordered to put on an old shirt and trousers, marked with a red cross, which indicates that I'm a political prisoner. I received a camp number and was sent to one of the wretched wooden barracks.

Later, I learned that I'm among the lucky ones. Selected transports of prisoners go straight to gas chambers, even women and children are not spared. They simply murder *undesirables,* and anyone unfit for labor by poisoning them with carbon monoxide, injecting phenol into their hearts, executing them by hanging or just shooting them where they stand... I witnessed it myself when they hanged a teenage boy who tried to escape. Every prisoner was forced to watch his agony. I will never forget the haunted look in that young boy's eyes.

The first two weeks were the hardest, and the weakest among us quickly died due to the severity of the conditions which offer not the slightest human comfort, harsh and prolonged beatings with sticks and whips, murderous labor and meager food rations that consist of watery slop with rutabaga and black bread with sawdust, plus dirty drinking water. I had bloody diarrhea for a long time, but it somehow went away before it killed me as it took so many others.

I was immediately assigned to work at Focke-Wulf aircraft factory's assembly department, which operates in the camp to produce the Fw 190 Würger single-seat fighter plane for the Luftwaffe. We slave under constant guard and gun barrels pointed straight at us, but it's much better than cutting down trees or other merciless, life-destroying labors.

The never-ending exhaustion from hunger that twists my insides drains me to the point of giving up, but in the hardest moments, I think of Kasia and how much I yearn to see her again.

I do everything I can to appear strong during the selections in barrack number thirty, named as "the death barrack". The SS men and the camp doctor have people marching in single line while they look for *candidates* for the gas chamber. It's hard to watch the faces of the old and sick so full of despair and begging for mercy. The Germans usually attempt to calm them down by claiming that they're merely selecting those who will be sent to work in better conditions. Unfortunately, the flipside of this lie is that for them, people unsuitable for work are unnecessary ballast to be eliminated.

Before those roll calls in barrack thirty, we try to hide the weakest ones, as many we can, under pallets and blankets.

We also try to remember the numbers assigned to the prisoners who were already chosen for the gas chamber. That's because during those selections Germans have a rule to write down only the numbers of the ones who were doomed for death. When another prisoner dies of sickness or starvation during the night before the gas chamber, his number is taken by the one who is going to be gassed by replacing the armbands with their numbers on. This desperate ruse only has a chance of working because here in Stutthof the numbers the Germans give us aren't tattooed into our skin like they are in Auschwitz.

Our unspoken rule is not to lose heart, to help and protect each other, and to skillfully harm the occupier whenever possible. Cunning and conspiracy help in survival: some of us constantly look for ways to weaken our enemy.

We're in the midst of an ongoing typhus epidemic and we've even found a way to transfer that typhus to German soldiers at the front thanks to the fact that Polish prisoners work in different workshops within the camp. It's almost unbelievable, but one of those workshops maintains uniforms for Wehrmacht soldiers. Including their underwear.

So, a Polish nurse who's assigned to work in the infirmary collects lice from patients infected with the virus into ampoules under the guise of laboratory tests. Then the nurse passes the ampoules to the camp writer who smuggles it into the tailoring workshops where the lice are thrown into uniforms and underwear before it is shipped to Wehrmacht soldiers, even hundreds of thousands of kilometers from the camp.

The greatest consolation is the news about the defeats of the Germany on the front that come through the grapevine. It often brings tears of joy, hope and comfort to tired faces, even in the worst misery of this camp. It motivates us to do the impossible and survive another hour, another day, another month...

THIRTY-SEVEN
KASIA: THE TRUTH

February 1945, Gdańsk

On my way to the factory, I pause and look at a poster in the shop window of a bakery. It appeals to civilians to keep calm and reminds the soldiers about severe punishment for desertion. The Nazi-driven radio station in Gdańsk still spreads the sick propaganda from Berlin, just like their newspapers.

Since Felek's disappearance last month, I can't focus on anything. I wait every night hoping to hear him calling outside the house or sneaking into my bedroom. Last week I went to the Gestapo Headquarters on Neugarten with a chocolate delivery, though we stopped these at the end of January. I was hoping to convince Hauptsturmführer Abt to tell me if Felek is held in one of their prison cells, but the guard informed me that Abt had left for Berlin. And with him, I thought, went my only chance to get to Felek, even if he was still in that prison.

I hope he isn't there, that he's still free on some other mission, or in hiding. Everything is possible and I try to keep optimistic, trusting God that one day he will bring my Felek back to me. If I lose hope, I know I will simply lie down in the street and weep.

Two days ago, Sebastian received an order to close the factory as the building will now be used to shelter refugees from East Prussia. There was nothing he could do, so I'm on my way to grab my few personal belongings from Papa's office, like the framed picture from his desk. Sebastian is hoping that once the madness ends and the war is truly over, we will be able to reopen the factory.

Well, once the Soviets enter, we will be living in a different world, I'm certain of that. I have nothing to worry as I never collaborated with the Nazis, but Sebastian's situation is different. Hopefully they will be convinced by his arguments that he had no choice, that he went along with the Nazis' commands so that the factory could stay open and provide people with safe jobs.

Since that day on the beach when he proposed to me, he hasn't shown me the same warmth as before. He keeps his distance, but there have been a few occasions when I realized that he's followed me or sent one of his trusted people from the factory to spy on where I go and who I see.

I still wonder if he had a hand in my father's demise, although there is no way to prove it. I contacted Dr. Fischer, but he only confirmed Mama's words that Papa suffered from a heart disease that progressed rather fast.

The factory is so quiet, and I can't even spot Pan Alojzy anywhere. No secretary in the office either but I wonder if Sebastian is still there and when the refugees will arrive. What will happen to all the expensive machines at the factory and our stocks of cocoa beans?

I enter the office and get busy packing, making sure to take everything that has sentimental value. Felek was right when he said that nothing will change the fact that my father will be always my papa, though I'm ashamed of his deeds. As I look at the photo of us at the beach all those long years ago, I pray for God to grant him mercy and forgiveness.

"I received the order to join the Wehrmacht." Sebastian's low voice chills me, but I turn and treat him to a sympathetic look. The only reason he wasn't mobilized before is because of his high connections, but I guess now it doesn't matter. They will take every and any man because they are clearly losing and need more and more soldiers.

"I'm sorry to hear it," I say. "When?"

"As soon as the factory is shut down. You know I never wanted to fight in this war, especially now that Hitler is facing defeat, and the Soviets are almost here. Joining the Wehrmacht now is like committing suicide." He gives an exasperated laugh.

In this very moment I understand what he's trying to tell me—he isn't planning to do as they expect from him.

"What will you do?" I ask, meeting his gaze.

"Bruno has secured seats on the train west. It leaves tonight. There is no point staying here."

"What about the factory?"

"I can't run it now, so there can be no factory for me. I will return once all this madness ends, if the Soviets have anything left here after their purges."

"Well, I wish you good luck then." My tone is brisk, dismissive. I've always known that Bruno is a pathetic milksop of a coward, but I thought Sebastian might have enough courage to withstand the worst and not run away with his tail between his legs, but I keep my thoughts to myself. It's best that we part on decent terms.

He drops to Papa's chair, making me wonder why he would do that. Does he want to prolong this farewell conversation?

"I always respected Dietrich, and you know it. At first, I took care of you and your family because I felt like I owed it to him, after all, he taught me with such generosity about the chocolate business. But then, I fell in love with you." His gaze penetrates mine as if he's trying to read my thoughts.

I swallow hard, trying to find the right words. "One day you will meet the right woman." That's all I can offer right now, unable to declare that I love him too. I've lied enough to him through those years.

"Bruno has passes for the train for you, too. Please come with me, Katharina. I dream of nothing more than marrying you. My life has no purpose without you in it."

I turn away, avoiding his gaze. "I can't."

"Why?" His voice is devoid of emotion.

It's about time that I told him the truth. "I love another man." The very act of saying it to him brings so much lightness to my being, but at the same time so many conflicting emotions pull at my heart. It's hard to let someone down like this; unrequited love is heartbreaking.

But Sebastian's response is not one of compassion. He slams his fist into Papa's desk causing me to jump. "You made me your puppet through all of those years." Fury shakes his voice. "You played your games making it sound like you cared when you didn't give a damn about me. Just being honest would have been nice, but no, you chose to be treacherous. You are a snake."

Shaken, I hold my nerve, determined to defend myself against his foul words. "I never promised you anything. For God's sake, I didn't even let you take me to bed," I say through my clenched teeth. "If you think that I'm naïve, then you're very much wrong. If you didn't act as if you hold the safety of my family's lives in your hands, and just behave like a decent man would, I would have told you a long time ago that I don't love you."

My words only inflame him. He slams Papa's picture frame into the floor causing the glass to shatter into particles. My heart goes through excruciating pain as if every one of those pieces delves into it. At the same time, I feel terrible fear. I have noticed in the past that one of Sebastian's flaws is that when he's driven to extreme anger, he seems to lose control over his actions.

"Stop it, Sebastian," I say, not caring for the tears running down my cheeks. "For the memory of my father." My voice is soft and my gaze pleading.

The fury in his face intensifies even more while droplets of sweat form on his forehead, but I can see that he is trying to grasp for control. After a long moment during which the only sound in the room is that of our breath he speaks again, and his voice is as soft and pleading as mine now. "Please, come with me. I have enough love for both of us. The true feeling will emerge in you too, once you understand your place in my heart. One day you will feel the same as I do, just give us a chance."

"My heart belongs to another man," I say carefully. "You deserve honesty and I'm giving it to you now, I'm sorry it's so late though. You will find your happiness one day, with someone else, and then you will forget about me." I force a reassuring smile.

"Who's that man?"

"Please, for the sake of my father's memory, let's part in peace." In this very moment, I see in his glassy eyes that he fully understands that I don't want him. I also detect a hint of bitter acceptance.

"I don't give a damn about Dietrich's memory," he spits out the words. I feel a shift in his attitude, as if he's done pretending, but this might be a product of my imagination. I've always thought that I have a gift of sensing when people's intentions change. "This idiot you call Papa let me manipulate him, like a schoolboy." He laughs low in his throat. "I used him to my liking while he squirmed like a snake."

A taste of bile fills my mouth. "Did you kill him?"

"Why would I do that?" He sneers at my question.

"Besides, he died of a heart attack, you can ask Dr. Fischer: he was there when it happened. The old fool got upset when Bruno kept winning in poker and taking all his money."

"I know about the Pervitin," I say. "Did you add enough to kill him?"

If he's surprised that I know, he doesn't show it. "Those were just orders I had to fulfill for the government. Nothing else. Your father neglected his health and it's why he's dead now. I had nothing to do with it." His tone is final.

"I had to ask."

"I'm the one who hired the private detective to get information on you when you lived in Warsaw. I lied when I said that it was your father that did it. What I learned regarding your connection with the Polish Resistance was enough to blackmail Dietrich to do as I pleased. He knew that if he refused to listen to me or Bruno, I would denounce you to the Gestapo and you would be tortured to death."

I flinch at his revelations as Pan Alojzy's words that Papa was a decent man play in my head. "Why are you telling me this?"

"Well, since we are being so honest toward each other, you deserve to know the truth. Bruno received this assignment to camouflage explosive in the chocolate bars, and only Dietrich's brilliance could make it work. Once I threatened to give you away to the Gestapo, your precious father did as we pleased, and quickly forgot about his repulsion toward serving the Third Reich. Thanks to that we made a handsome amount of money. If you married me, we would be set up to live very comfortably for the rest of our lives."

So, this at last is the truth. Blackmail. "You're a self-serving bastard. You disgust me."

"Oh, stop it, Katharina, don't play the good girl. You lied to me all these years to take advantage of me. I'm not stupid. I allowed you your fairy tale life in this factory because there were advantages for me too."

"You wanted to get to the Polish Resistance," I say, my pulse speeding.

"Precisely. If I succeeded, I would be rewarded greatly by the Führer himself. But I was too soft with you, I see it now, and because of that, my mission failed. Now it's too late."

This man appalls me, his systematic manipulation of my father and targeting of me. But I also feel a wild, almost delirious relief sweep over me that I never gave in to him—not my body and not my morals. "I hope to never see you again," I hiss as I turn away from him.

"Ah, my dear Katharina."

His dangerous voice makes me swirl around.

"Not so fast." To my horror, he's holding a pistol in his right hand. It's aimed directly at me.

A cold hand of fear catches at my heart. "What are you doing?"

"If I can't have you, no one else will," he says.

Before I have a chance to reply, his finger presses the trigger releasing a sudden but deafening sound followed by a silence and a whiff of metallic scent in the air.

I look down at a red spot spreading through the front of my cardigan. I feel excruciating, shattering pain and this weird cold stillness... Is this the end of my life? I slowly fumble to my knees and realize that he's aiming his pistol back at me.

"I'm sorry, my love, but if there is something else beyond this, we will reunite, I promise." His voice is so soft it's almost a purr. "Close your eyes and go to sleep now. I will send another bullet through you, so you don't suffer prolonged agony. I love you, my princess."

I want to scream at him, but the word "No" is stuck in my throat. Then there is this heart-shattering and air-splitting boom in the air. He drops his pistol and crumples to the floor, his head shattered by another bullet.

Another bullet. Another bullet.

I am struggling to keep my eyes open, so I stop fighting.

"Stay strong, child, you will be alright," a kind, familiar voice assures me. Pan Alojzy. "The bastard is dead; he won't hurt you anymore. Stay strong, child."

THIRTY-EIGHT
KASIA: OUT OF BODY

February 1945, Gdańsk

I feel so light, like I am floating.

There is no pain in my chest anymore and I don't shiver. Instead, I'm overtaken by immense peace, untamed happiness and love. I've never felt this good before, such a strong sense of being loved.

I'm surrounded by rays of light but even though I try to look around, all I can see is a tunnel with more light ahead of me. So, I decide to go toward it, but it's like someone holds me back.

"It's not your time yet, Kasia. You must go back because you aren't done living on Earth." There is no speech or signs, only this soothing voice in my mind.

I know it's God who is telling me this, I just feel it. At the same time, I don't want to go back to the misery down there if I can feel the way I do over here—so loved and at peace, without all the burdens I left behind, without pain, heartache and cruelty.

"Please, don't send me back. I want to stay," I beg in my mind unable to make sounds, then I attempt to move toward that tunnel with the light, but the faces of my loved ones flash in my mind...

"Go back, my child. They need you there. When the right time comes, you will be back home with me."

In this very moment, waves of trust and acceptance wash over me. It's not my time yet, God told me so. Who am I to question Him? "Lord," I say in my mind, "please forgive my father and surround him with your love."

"My mercy has no limits," he says.

It is maybe a second later or maybe a day, I don't know, but I find myself floating up to the ceiling in a room with white walls.

Down there, three people hover at a body lying on top of an operating table.

"We're losing her," a nurse says, her voice panicked.

"I told you she wouldn't make it," a younger doctor says, and I can hear the tension in his tone. "We're wasting our time here."

"I'm the one making decisions here, Dr. Koch." Somehow, I recognize Dr. Fischer's stern voice; I notice how the front of his white apron is all caked in blood. "Please, continue your duties or I will not hesitate to use the revolver that's in my pocket."

His words seem to work for now because they both focus again on the operation. Curious about who the patient is, I float down and gasp. The woman lying on this operating table is me.

"Fight, Kasia, fight," I instruct myself. And I do.

THIRTY-NINE
KASIA: THE SIEGE

March 1945, Gdańsk

Dr. Fischer carefully removes the stethoscope from my chest and pushes his glasses back up his nose.

"Thank you for saving my life, Dr. Fischer," I say. After almost a month in hospital, today I'm finally being discharged.

"You're welcome, dear. Your heartbeat is fine and lungs clear. It's time for you to leave though you must take it easy and rest. Considering the way the Soviets keep advancing toward Danzig, we will be evacuating this hospital soon anyway." He sighs and rubs his white beard.

I've known this good man my entire life, and I always liked him, never detecting any bad intentions. He proved his humanity when he did the impossible and saved my life, later simply stating that it was a miracle.

"Can I ask you something, doctor?"

"Of course, my dear. What is it?"

"That day when you were operating on me, did you tell Dr. Koch that if he didn't continue his duties, you would use the revolver in your pocket?"

He creases his forehead. "I see gossip spreads fast in this hospital."

I touch his arm. "No, not at all, please rest assured that no one told me about this." For a moment I decide on the right words, and resolve to tell him the truth, even though I'm sure he will deem me insane. "You see, I heard it while my soul, I assume, was floating up to the ceiling. It's like it separated from my physical body. I heard every word you said and saw what was happening. I know this sounds unbelievable but I'm telling the truth. Thank you for not giving up on my life."

He frowns. "I admit, this does sound unbelievable. I did apologize to Dr. Koch for my threat. He agreed to keep it between us, and we asked the nurse that whatever happened in that operating room must stay between us." A look of confusion covers his face.

"I didn't hear it from any of them, or anyone else. What I told you is the truth, though there are moments when I think that it was just a dream."

"You definitely weren't able to hear us because you were completely unconscious," he says.

It doesn't look like I will be able to convince him. "Well, when I floated above you, I saw a brown file folder on top of that medicine cabinet that reaches almost the ceiling. Can you please get the ladder to see if it is truly there? I'm curious myself, because if it's not there, then I just had weird dreams."

His face turns white. "I don't have to check because I know it's there."

"The only time I was in that room was when you operated me, so I could not make this up."

"I believe you, my child, I believe you. Your words are proof that there is more to this life and our existence than what is here in front of us. I've always believed in eternity. Thank you for sharing your experience with me." He smiles gently. "It brings me hope, and I trust it reassures you too."

Our conversation is interrupted by Mama who comes to collect me. The day I woke up for the first time after the surgery, Mama and Kornel were sitting at my bed. It's when I understood why God sent me back—they need me, and I need them. I wished that Felek was there too.

When we get out the hospital, Pan Alojzy is waiting for us next to a rickshaw, a bike with a small carriage. I'm puzzled; I've never seen it before.

We settle in and Pan Alojzy pedals away into the gray streets of Gdańsk, toward our villa in Wrzeszcz.

"Where did Pan Alojzy take this rickshaw from?" I ask. I'm thankful that he did because I still feel dizzy at moments and haven't gained anything like my full strength back.

"He says it was abandoned in the streets." She sighs. "So many German people have left the city, afraid of retaliations from Soviets. But since yesterday there are no more ships sailing from Gdańsk, nor are there any trains."

"You should have left without me," I say.

"I tried securing a passage for all of us on a ship and taking you out of the hospital early, but I had no luck."

During the coming days the situation changes rapidly, and it feels like the Soviets will attack our city soon. The SS, Wehrmacht and Luftwaffe troops work on preparing defenses, especially focusing on bridges, roads and railway stations. Something tells me that it's going to be a fierce fight.

Since the eighteenth day of March, the Russian air raids happen every night. More and more buildings are destroyed, like industrial factories in the New Harbor, or regular houses in Wrzeszcz, but the biggest destruction happens in the city center where fires spread in dense buildings after every bomb explosion. The beautiful Dutch-style buildings of our Old Town lie in blazing ruins, their ornate soft-hued facades nothing but rubble.

On the twenty-fourth day of March, I phone Pan Alojzy

and Pani Jadwiga, who moved back to their old flat after the occupying German family left Gdańsk, and I contact Pani Genowefa and her husband too, convincing them to come shelter with us. It's too dangerous to be staying in the city center right now. The phones still work, some shops are open and the trams are running.

But it all changes the next day, after a massive bombardment that night.

I can't stop thinking of Malina and Alina. I couldn't call them because they don't have a phone, so in the early morning I decide to head toward the city center. Everyone is still asleep, so I have no problem sneaking out of the house. Mama would stop me if she knew.

It's not an easy walk as bomb holes and piles of rubble block my path, while the wind carries clouds of smoke. The closer I get to the city center, the more my heart shatters at what is around me. The wooden buildings of the city center are in flames after last night's air raid. People are trying to bring the fires down but it's a Sisyphean task, especially given that the Soviets cut off the water supply to the city. It's extremely dangerous to be here right now as the artillery fire could begin any time.

When I arrive at the tenement where the girls live in the cellar, it seems like the building is abandoned. Maybe they already left but how were they able to secure passage out of the city? I feel so bad that I didn't check on them earlier. Not knowing what to do, I bang on the door and scream their names, but when I push hard it opens. After going through the entire house, I'm sure there is no one here. Things are out of order, a muddle of clothes and blankets and hairbrushes as if someone was in a rush to flee.

I come back home with my heart broken, but I choose to think that they're far from Gdańsk or hiding somewhere in a safer part of the city. Both girls are savvy, and they make a perfect duet working together. They will survive the hardest times. I just wish that I knew for sure their whereabouts and that they're fine.

That evening we all go to the basement as the firing and bombardment is constant now. The Soviets' attack against the Germans is ferocious, and I pray that we'll survive this battle. The villa's walls and floors shake with every explosion. The shrieking sounds of bombs make me hold my breath, while praying that it doesn't strike our villa.

For the sake of the kids, we try to keep positive. Pan Alojzy plays the harmonica and Pani Genowefa tells us Kashubian stories. Kornel sits between Mama and me, Maciek on his lap, and little Rebekah clings to Sara.

For some reason, Jadwiga can't take her eyes off the little girl. "Why didn't you tell us?" she says staring at Sara.

"Darling, it's not the time for this now. We will talk once all this madness ends," Pan Alojzy says.

If we survive, I want to add.

"I tried looking for you, but you didn't live in your flat anymore, then we were moved to the ghetto," Sara says, ignoring Pan Alojzy's words, tears coming down her cheeks. "Everyone from my family is dead. We are the only ones left."

"I'm sorry," Pani Jadwiga whispers. "Please, let us be in your life. We will help as much we can. She's Marek's daughter too."

Sara closes her eyes, then nods. "Rebekah, darling, this nice lady and gentleman are your grandparents."

The girl gazes at the older couple with interest, then she walks to Pan Alojzy, takes the harmonica from his hand and brings it to his lips. When he plays, she swirls around as if dancing for a short moment, before clinging again to her mother. This is so heartwarming. Sara has been worrying that she doesn't say any words, but I'm sure that once things go back to normal, she will talk.

"She has Marek's eyes," Jadwiga says, so many emotions slipping through her face. This is the first time I've seen her talking about her son without crying. The fact that Rebekah is their granddaughter is so unexpected. I feel such relief that Sara and her daughter will now have these good people in their lives

Suddenly, a terrible roar pierces the air, and everything shakes, then cement dust falls from the ceiling.

Rebekah's cry rings out but Sara cradles the little girl in her arms, and soon there is only muffled sobbing. Kornel on the other hand puts his head on Mama's lap, his eyes closed.

I simply pray that we all survive this and that my Felek has enough strength to go on, wherever he is, and that he will be restored to me once this nightmare ends.

The attack is so intense and prolonged that we stay put underground for the next two days, while the ground constantly shakes from the impact of bombs and artillery fire. The stuffy air in the basement brims with cement dust and mold. Thanks to Mama's forethought we have enough food and water, but we must ration it as we don't know how long we will have to stay here.

On the third day, the firing and bombing stops, now replaced by a mayhem of shouting in Russian. Through the whole time in this basement, I've been shutting down my emotions, focusing instead on keeping my expression positive and cheerful for everyone around, especially the children. But in this very moment, my will refuses to obey as panic and fear sets in, then the thrilling feeling of excitement that the Germans have been defeated.

Still, if the liberation was by Poles, we would be jumping in happiness right now; instead we worry about what is going to happen next. We have all heard the many, bloodthirsty stories of how Soviets treat Germans as part of their retaliation. Kornel and I have German blood; Mama was married to a German man; Pani Genowefa's husband must be worrying the most. It's all so complicated. Tension in the air grows with every second and I don't think explanations would be enough here, as the Soviets probably treat everyone they find here as Germans.

"Any pretty ladies here?" A slurring voice in Russian rings out from the kitchen just above us, followed by malicious, self-amused laughter.

FORTY
KASIA: CHOLERA

March 1945, Gdańsk

"It's better they don't find us here right away," Pan Alojzy whispers. "Let's keep silent and wait a little longer to see how things go."

"You're right," I whisper back and swallow hard, unable to control my trembling. I could not agree more with him. The entrance to the basement isn't easy to find, my grandfather made sure of that when building this villa, but they will eventually discover us, and my stomach feels rock hard at the thought of it. I hate feeling helpless.

We stay in silence for the rest of the day, and to my relief, there is no commotion upstairs anymore.

"They took what they found, and they left," Pan Alojzy says, "but others will come too, so we must stay put longer until they burn off their drunken stupor."

"We can't sit here forever," Pani Genowefa says and sighs. "I can't breathe here."

"Pan Alojzy is right," I say. "Probably by tomorrow they will move on to liberating other parts of the city and it will be safer for us." I'm not sure if I believe my own words but one must have some hope.

"They will find us sooner or later, so I think we should go up there and say that we're Polish," Mama says.

"And what about Pani Genowefa's husband?" I ask, feeling sad for the good man that right now would most likely receive horrible treatment at hands of Soviets because of his German nationality. We must protect him. He did so much for the Polish Resistance.

"For God's sake, Kasia, he isn't a woman, so he will be fine." There is an edge to Mama's voice. She expects the worst right now too. "He must pretend to be mute until things calm down and the retaliations stop," she continues.

"That's a brilliant idea," Pani Genowefa says and proceeds to translate it into German for her husband, just as the sound of clinging footsteps comes from outside the entrance of the basement, in the back of the villa hidden behind shrubs.

As my heart rate speeds up, a quiet voice says in Polish, "Please open, good people, I overheard you and I'm here to help."

I exhale with relief when realizing it's my mother's tongue. "We should let him in," I whisper, "he's Polish and I don't hear any accent. He must truly have heard us talking."

"I will go check," Pan Alojzy says and slips to the entrance. "Who are you?"

"I'm from the Polish armored brigade," the man says and Alojzy lets him in.

When he enters, he runs his flashlight over us. "Poles?"

"Yes," Alojzy says.

"That's good. I don't speak any German, but I wanted to see who's here before more Soviet drunkards arrive in the morning and begin their orgy. I see you've been lucky so far."

"Is Gdańsk all liberated?"

"No, not yet, but this district is free from Hitler's forces." A note of elation reverberates through his voice. "The city center and the Old Town, and other parts, are still in German hands, but not for long. Anyway, you must be careful. Some of the Soviet soldiers aren't sober at all right now, and they are looking for revenge after what Hitler put them through. You must protect your children and women." He changes his voice into a whisper, so I instinctively get up and go nearer so I can hear him. "They are engaging in drunken violence, rape and looting. They enter cellars, basements or shelters, and they will soon come to you too. You're lucky that your home is on the outskirts of this district, so many of them didn't get here yet."

A shiver of terror runs down my spine. "Should we try running away?" I ask.

He turns to me, surprise painted on his face while he keeps his flashlight on. "No, you wouldn't survive, not right now. You must immediately put up a sign out front that you are Polish and find a way of informing the incoming troops that you all are suffering under the cholera outbreak. This should scare them away and save you from this unthinkable violence. Also, please do not interfere with their looting and let them take what they want. Your life is more important than material things."

"We're so thankful for your kindness," I say. "God bless you."

"I'm doing what's right. I separated from my brigade on the outskirts of Gdańsk only hours ago to look for my sister who lives in Wrzeszcz. What I've already seen, turns my stomach sick. Those drunken primitive brutes should be punished for their violence and cruelty. Please, be careful and do as I tell you."

"Have you found your sister?"

"No, but her neighbor told me that she left Gdańsk at the beginning of February. Thank God."

"That's good for her."

He nods, lifts the flashlight, and before walking away, he salutes. "Long live Poland."

We echo his words.

"I will go upstairs and try to make the sign," I say.

"You should stay here," Mama says from behind; she must have been standing there the whole time. "You heard the soldier—they have no mercy. Let me go."

"You both stay here," Pan Alojzy says with finality in his voice. "I will take care of that and stay up there to inform any incoming soldiers that we have the cholera epidemic here."

"Do what's right, Alojzy," Jadwiga says. "We must save our granddaughter and Kornel's lives."

The ploy works well, because in the following days whenever the Soviets see the sign that there are Poles here suffering from the cholera outbreak, they don't bother stopping.

∽

The city is officially liberated on the thirtieth day of March. When we finally emerge from our shelter, I have a hard time looking through the brightness of sunlight and the smoke from the ruins of the city.

Our house was looted of all valuables, furniture and even Mama's piano, but at least it still stands while so many of the other city buildings are in ruins, especially in the central part of our own district, but the most damage is in the historical heart of the city. Ruins are all around; this city is bleeding like never before.

The most painful thing to look at is so many human bodies in the streets. I saw a woman who hanged herself from the door lintel. Streets are covered with debris from the battle, torn tramtracks, dead horses and abandoned wagons and automobiles.

Our city that was once called the "Jewel of the Baltic" has

been turned into a city of roaring bonfires and the rubble of broken buildings and people.

FORTY-ONE
FELEK: THE EXECUTION

April 1945, Stutthof

At the end of January, many inmates were forced-marched out of the camp, but I was among the ones kept here. Since then, the typhus epidemic has claimed lives at a terrifying rate, leaving us clinging to less and less hope despite the news that Soviets keep advancing and have already liberated Gdańsk.

In March, Soviet aircraft bombed the camp several times, killing so many prisoners. We've been forced to work on building underground shelters in the forest for the SS crew and other Germans stationed near the camp. The damn *Szkopy* have gathered a lot of troops and heavy military equipment within the camp, so I'm guessing that's why the Russians are carrying out their air raids on us.

The rumors are that the Germans are getting ready to evacuate us via the sea since there is no way out through the land because of the Soviets encircling us. We are supposed to reach the Vistula River and then the Hel Peninsula from where we would be sent by sea to Germany. It sounds absurd to me, impossible. But who knows how much truth there is in all of this.

This morning, we are summoned for a roll call, but they aren't counting us like they have done other times. This feels different. The guards seem anxious, like they're desperate or afraid of something, especially one heavy-set German near me who keeps glancing to his wristwatch. They must be afraid of the Soviets, who, we all know, will get here soon. I dread what will happen to us before then.

To our astonishment, each prisoner gets a half loaf of bread, a quarter of margarine and a piece of dry meat, then they divide us into two groups. I'm among the ones rushed on foot outside of the camp's perimeter.

Some men eat their food rations right away. I chew on the dry meat and a small piece of bread, but the rest I hide in my pockets. We might be starving now, but who knows when we will get something again.

The guards keep shouting to hurry while our column moves forward on the dirt road. We're too weak to walk fast. I'm at the end of the column, so if not for the two Germans right behind me, I would not think twice before fleeing into the woods. One of them breathes loud and sweat covers his red face, while the other moves with no effort at all thanks to his athletic physique. They have both treated us at the camp ruthlessly, and if I could only get my hands on them... But they have weapons and I'm too weak. Our column is surrounded by guards all the way through, so trying to do something now would mean certain and immediate death.

"I'm telling you that when the time comes, those Polish pigs will hand us to the Soviet barbarians like pigs for slaughter," the older German says in a slow but panicked voice. "One, after another, before we even get to the Vistula."

I realize it's the same man that kept looking at his watch during the roll call. He makes me nervous as I know so well that the biggest cowards do the most stupid things under fear. His conscience is stained with ugly deeds. He knows none of us would show him mercy if fate changed the power balance between us.

"The Russians have no chance with us," the younger guard says. "Don't fret, Karl, our noble German race always wins."

"What a fool you are," Karl snaps with a harsh cough. "This war is already lost to us, and it's only a matter of days or even hours now before the Soviets get here. And then they'll rip us to pieces."

After a longer break, the younger man says, "It's not like we can run away from all of this."

"We should do what Fritz just did."

"He left before us, so how do you know what he's done?"

Karl sighs. "If you knew how to look, you would see bodies in the old courtyard. Fritz gave orders to shoot those Polish crooks, so they don't point their fingers at him if it comes to the Soviets capturing us. At the same time, he got rid of the useless rats."

"Best solution to the problem," the younger guard says and laughs.

"We must do the same with our group and flee to the Reich," Karl says. The determination in his malicious voice sends a shivery rush of adrenaline to my brain. "I'll tell our boys to round these Polish bandits up for execution."

FORTY-TWO
KASIA: COME BACK TO ME

October 1945, Gdańsk

The war ended five months ago, but Felek hasn't returned. I've contacted the Red Cross, but they don't have any information about him. Deep in my heart, I feel that he's alive and that fate will bring him back to me one day.

Alojzy thinks Felek was arrested during the Resistance action and brought to the camp in Stutthof, but there is no way of confirming this. Rumors are that after the camp was liquidated, inmates were sent west, walking in a death march column. But we have no way of knowing if Felek was among them. I can only pray that my beloved comes back to me.

After our city's liberation, we lacked food, electricity, gas, running water... but most of all we seemed to lack civilization. Danger not only came from drunken Soviet soldiers, thieves and looters, but also from buildings that could collapse anytime or outbreak of fires and unexploded bombs. We left home only when necessary.

After the amber boutique was burned during the Russian siege, Pani Genowefa and her husband moved to live with her nephew in Rybno, the Kashubian village. Alojzy and Jadwiga still live with us because their tenement didn't survive either. Mama offered for them to stay permanently. Alojzy was hired as watchman in the shipyard and Jadwiga took over our kitchen once more, with Mama's blessing, spoiling her little granddaughter Rebekah and Kornel with baking special treats. Sara found a position in the hospital as a nurse; it was her occupation before the war.

I, on the other hand, have attempted getting back our factory, which survived, as it rightfully belongs to our family. But things aren't easy because now Poland is in the hands of Stalin. After months of being sent back and forth, I was officially informed that it's going to be nationalized and that my family has no rights to it, and unofficially, I was given the advice that if I wish for myself and my family to stay alive, I must drop the subject. I have no words for all of this, nor the power to do anything. The factory is lost to our family for good...

My whole life I knew that one day I would be running the chocolate business, even if by my future husband's side, and it was something that I truly desired. So now it isn't possible, I feel lost as if I do not have a place in this world anymore.

But we aren't the only ones. The same thing has happened to the chocolate factory in Warsaw where I worked. It was nationalized and the ownership taken away. I know this thanks to Ciocia Lucyna who visited us last month.

Without the factory to keep me busy, I spend most of my days helping to clear the city of rubble. Around ninety percent of the city center has been destroyed by air raids and artillery fire, but also by Soviet troops after the liberation of the city.

My heart hurts to look at it. It was built by the greatest masters of the Renaissance and Baroque, and it was one of the most beautiful historic complexes in northern Europe. Now it's a pile of ruins.

Now German citizens leave the city while more and more

Poles, who have nowhere to live, arrive. Since July, the new authorities organize transports aimed at displacing Germans, but sometimes also Poles, who were citizens of the Free City Gdańsk and are deemed to be untrustworthy.

Because Kornel and I are half German, and Mama was married to a German, we had to report for a new verification procedure. This time we were lucky because the man that interviewed us has known Mama since their childhood. They grew up in the same village and they recognized each other right away. Thanks to him, we avoided any issues and were spared the threat of transportation to Germany. The ones that ended up being transported had to start their lives from scratch, something that we are lucky to be able to avoid.

Things have slowly stabilized here. In April, the most important communication routes were cleared despite streets strewn with rubble, human corpses and horse carcasses, and at last the first hospitals were open. In June, the first tram line was launched, and Polish Radio began transmitting from Gradowa Hill.

Kornel was happy when we told him that schools were reopened, though he still cries at night for his old friends. I understand him so well...

So many people perished in the war; we will never see them again. It's hard to accept this...

It's impossible for me to keep moving on without Felek, without knowing what happened to him. The only thing that gives me strength is hope that there will be a day when I see him again, either in this life or the next. My heart belongs to him, and I will never let anyone else take his place. If he isn't here any longer, I would rather spend the rest of my days alone.

∼

"You sure don't look like you're dressed to clean up rubble today, sweetheart," Pani Jadwiga says one morning when I enter the kitchen. She's making rolled pancakes stuffed with my favorite apple marmalade.

I inhale the sweet aroma of vanilla mixed with cinnamon, thinking of my chocolate mixtures. "I have a job interview," I say and take a sip of the strong black coffee she's prepared.

Mama looks up from her *Dziennik Bałtycki* newspaper spread on the table, her brow arched. "Where?"

For a second, I wonder if I should tell the truth, but knowing them they will find out sooner than later anyway. "At our old factory."

Mama touches her throat. "Are you sure this is the right decision?"

I sigh. "I don't know, Mama, but I need to start bringing in some income too, and they are looking to hire people." The way I view my mother has changed. While growing up, Papa was my hero, and I feel like I took Mama for granted. The war struggles showed me that she is a strong and incredible woman.

"You know you don't have to. We are managing just fine," Pani Jadwiga says and puts her hand on my shoulder. "Give yourself more time."

"Jadwiga is right," Mama says quietly. "You've been working so hard every day helping re-build this city, even though you should be careful with your heart and health. You remember what Dr. Fischer said after the surgery; your heart will never function in a normal way. Rushing into a decision like this one might prove to be too much."

I'm lucky to have such loving people in my life who truly care for me. But the truth is that since the war ended, I put my life on hold while waiting for Felek, like he's going to knock at the door any moment.

"Everyone contributes here beside me. Sara works at the hospital; Pan Alojzy at the shipyard; you, Mama, spend all your days sewing; Pani Jadwiga shopping for food, cooking and caring for Rebekah; Kornel is busy with school; and I feel like a misfit." I close my eyes and choose my next words carefully. "I need to start living again. I'm hoping to one day enroll into university classes again to continue the studies I started before the war. But for now, I plan to find a job, and working at the factory seems right up my alley, even if it might be hard at the beginning."

Pani Jadwiga sighs and gets up to resume working at the stove while Mama's soft gaze stays on my face. "Promise me that you will not take this position if you aren't comfortable with it. Your health is everyone's priority here."

Out in the streets, the October air is crisp and feels refreshing on my skin. But the sky is gray and gloomy, making me feel even more resigned. After trying to find out for months about what happened to the prisoners in Stutthof, yesterday I learned that some of them were shot during their march west. I force myself to believe that Felek was among the ones who were left alive but it's impossible to chase the dark clouds away. The news of this dreadful mass execution drained all energy out of me while I cling to the thought that he's alive.

I take a tram and watch my beloved but destroyed city with a sinking heart. The old city which remembered the times of the Polish kings, Napoleon Bonaparte and patriots dying in the Polish Post Office, but also Teutonic Knights and Prussians, is gone. The new Gdańsk has returned to Poland, although it's not a free Poland.

By the time I enter the cobbles of the chocolate factory courtyard, raindrops run like a ghostly touch over my skin. Before, I always took comfort in the fact that Pan Alojzy was here, busy with his broom; now I walk through it with an empty feeling inside as an unknown group of men busy themselves unloading bags from a truck.

This place has been always my second home. Even during

the war, I felt at home here despite Sebastian's presence and the function the factory played in supporting German soldiers. But today, I feel nothing. It's as if something in me has died for good. Maybe because I know that we lost it, and it will never be ours again. There is nothing I can do about it. I can't win against the system we're now living under.

When I enter the area where the offices are located, a middle-aged secretary with her hair in a tight perm looks at me from under her glasses that fall down her nose and says, "How can I help you?"

"I have an appointment for a job interview." It's so weird to be hearing Polish being spoken here, when before it was forbidden. Even before the war, the main language here was German. My father never learned Polish; instead, my mother mastered his native tongue to perfection.

After the secretary confirms my information, she instructs me to take a seat on one of the chairs placed against the wall. It surprises me that there are no other candidates waiting here to be interviewed. Ten minutes later a phone rings and the secretary tells me to go into Papa's old office.

After I knock, a gruff voice says, "Come in."

I swallow and brace myself as I step in and close the door behind me. Then I look up to the man sitting at my father's desk.

FORTY-THREE

KASIA: YOURS, ONLY YOURS...

October 1945, Gdańsk

"Poldek? What are you doing here?" I say making sure to sound friendly though this man is one of the worst scoundrels. He's the one who denounced Felek while pretending to be working for the Resistance. Because of him, my beloved was tortured in the Gestapo Headquarters on Szucha Avenue and went through hell. When his treachery got discovered, he was already gone, and no one could find him.

Now he's sitting here in his perfectly tailored suit, looking like a highly intelligent and cultured man. He still looks young with the same glasses and coal-black hair despite a huge receding hairline.

"Kasia, my comrade," he says and spreads his hands to the sides in a gesture of welcoming me, "I'm honored to see you again. Please, take a seat."

Damn Stalin collaborator, I think but obey his request, stopping myself from grinding my teeth. Seeing this cad in my father's chair angers me even more, to the point where I'm having a hard time controlling myself.

"I was assigned to put this factory back on its feet." He gives me a knowing look, rolling his eyes in a theatrical way. "I know it was taken away from your family, but we all must contribute for the greatest future of the Republic of Poland. The only right way is to nationalize everything—even a chocolate factory—for the good of all."

I nod, not knowing what to say—besides, I don't trust myself to speak right now. After the arrival of the Red Army and the Yalta agreements, I was afraid of the new communist government, and so far, I've been proved right. Crime and terror against innocent people have been unrolling across Poland. Stalin's Secret Police along with *UB*, the so-called Ministry of Public Security, commit mass arrests and murders of officers and soldiers of the *Home Army*, the Polish Resistance members, because they resist the communist authorities and continue the fight for an independent and sovereign Poland, while staying in hiding. This awful man represents that new regime of terror and oppression.

"I was thrilled when I saw your application for a position at this factory. You helped your father running it, correct?"

At this point I do not want to work here anymore or have anything to do with what the factory stands for now, or this disgusting traitor. It was a mistake to come here. "Not really, I only helped with some menial tasks until I moved to Warsaw to study business."

"Oh, do not diminish your merits. The people we questioned confirmed for us that your input into this place was substantial and your father valued you. When he died, you returned to the factory which at the time was under the Germans, and you were responsible for deliveries to the Gestapo and SS institutions. You also worked on chocolate recipes. Please correct me if I'm wrong?" His mean eyes drill into mine while his mouth folds in self-amusement.

"I see you did your homework." I had no idea that I was of

such interest to the communists. I realize with a lurch of horror that they must want something from me since they haven't arrested me like so many others.

"What's important is that we move forward and leave the past behind. I know what you did in Warsaw, but, please, rest assured that you're safe if we decide to hire you here."

What a bastard... I look Poldek straight in the eye and say, "Don't forget that I know what you did in Warsaw, as well."

He narrows his eyes and tilts his head down. "No one will believe the daughter of a German criminal. You engaged in activities with the idiots from Warsaw and later you were in a relationship with that lover of Nazi ideology. And let us not forget that your blood is half German. You might be deep into espionage, and as far as I know, people are receiving death sentences because of such behavior." He glares at me. "On the other hand, my comrade, they will believe in every word I say, so if I was you, I would be cautious."

Realizing that by coming here I have cast myself in a deep hole without a way out, I have a dropping sensation in my stomach. Then, it hits me that in fact the only reason I'm here is because someone left at my door a leaflet with information about job openings here. This was his game right from the beginning. "What do you want from me?"

"Don't be so serious, my comrade. I have a solid offer for you as I always liked you, even back then in Warsaw. I always cherished your smile and politeness. You only need to show your commitment to us."

I want to shout at him to stop calling me his "comrade" but I swallow my anger and say, "What offer?"

The irony... Before, I had to pretend to agree with Hitler's cruelties and now with Stalin's brainwashing. It's hard to imagine which is worse. Why can't I live my life the way I feel is right?

"I would like to make you our production and quality

manager," Poldek intones, as if this were a perfectly ordinary interview. "There is no one better fitting for this position than the daughter of the founder of the factory. You will be supervising what we manufacture and sell to our clients, making sure that no one else offers the same variety of products as we do. Your job will be to make us the number one chocolate brand in Poland and Europe."

"You are asking for the impossible."

He looks at me as if I am a little slow at understanding. "We will provide a separate room for your use with equipment to work on and test new products that will guarantee our success. For all the people, you're the only one with such genius and experience thanks to your father."

We both know that I'm not in a position to reject his offer, he was clear about it right up front. I must protect my family, so I say, "When will I start?"

He nods with approval. "I knew you're clever. Once you sign some documentation declaring your loyalty for comrade Stalin, you will be able to start right away." He claps his hands together.

Alarm tingles at my spine. I could never sign such garbage, but I must stay calm and continue pretending. Always pretend.

He takes my silence as agreement because he gets up and walks around the desk, then he shakes my hand after I rise from my chair. "I will have all paperwork ready in no time. Why don't you return in two days at the same time?"

"Well, since today is Wednesday already, would it be okay for me to come back on Monday? I would use a few more days to relax," I say in a pleading tone of voice. I guess I would make an exceptional actress because the two-faced snake Poldek agrees.

∼

"There is no way that I will sign any of their documents," I say in the evening to Mama while walking back and forth across our family room. "By going there, I've put myself into this mess."

"Something tells me that they've already been keeping an eye on you," Mama says, distress painted on her face. "Even if you didn't go there today, they would have visited you here sooner than later."

"Yes, that's obvious."

"The good thing is that they do need you, and that will secure our safety."

"I can't do it, Mama. I can't sign any of this." I stop and hold her gaze. "How could I?"

"It's just a piece of paper, who cares?" she says and shrugs. "You must think of Kornel."

"That's the same thing you told me when it came to Sebastian." I drop to the sofa next to her. "I can't play the game again. I'm drained."

"Don't forget that thanks to this game, as you call it, we survived."

"We must leave Gdańsk. It's the only sensible option in this situation; I will not sign any of their papers."

"And go where? You think that Warsaw isn't the same as here? They will find you over there too, and everywhere else in this country."

"Abroad. I will find a way," I say impulsively, but with determination. I don't know how I will do it, but I'm desperate to try any possible way to get away from here.

She sighs. "When are you scheduled to go back over to the factory?"

"On Monday."

"So, you do have a few days," she says and takes my hand. "The only way to secure a passage on a ship from here is by bribing the right people. Since Alojzy works in the shipyard, he might be able to help you connecting with them."

"Me? I'm not leaving without you and Kornel."

"We will see what we can do." She gets up. "Why don't you follow me? I need to show you something."

We are home alone as Pani Jadwiga and Pan Alojzy took the children to the cinema, and Sara hasn't returned yet from her shift at the hospital.

To my astonishment, Mama takes a shovel and leads me to the garden in the back, all the way to the apple tree in the far corner. Then she starts shoveling the soil.

"What are you doing, Mama?" This woman will never cease surprising me.

"Shush," she says, "or the neighbors will hear us."

I find another shovel and help her, and only when we both are covered with sweat and our breathing is heavy do I hit something hard.

"What is it?" I whisper.

"American dollars that your father buried before the war. He made me promise that I would only look for it in a critical situation when nothing else could help." She puts her hand on my shoulder. "Now is the right time to use it."

Once we get back in the house, I realize that the wooden box contains enough to get us out free and still have enough to settle in another country. This is incredible.

I clear my throat as emotion sets in. "Thank you, Mama."

"I left it alone through the war because I knew that it would be useless. But now it's time that we let it help us. Let your father help us." She wipes her tears away. "He believed that if he was here, he could protect us, even at the highest sacrifice, but he couldn't stand the thought of what would happen to us if he was gone. It's why he hid all these dollars."

"He truly loved us," I say, unable to deny it anymore. "He never stopped loving me. I understand now."

"Yes, darling, he loved you right to the end. He regretted hurting you. Please, forgive him, despite all his mistakes."

"I already have, Mama. I just wish that he never signed the pact with the Nazis. If he only gave up the factory, knowing that in the end it all would be fine as long as we were together. Look at us now—we lost his precious factory anyway, but we are fine if we stay together and support each other. If he did just that, I would never have drifted apart from him."

"I tried reasoning with him, but your father would not listen. He built the business with his own hands from the very beginning, so he did everything to keep it for his children. I know that nothing will change what he did, but in the end, he's my husband and your father."

"Yes, Mama. I will never stop loving him."

∼

In bed that night, I twist and turn unable to get any sleep. Pan Alojzy already agreed to connect me with the right people to secure us a passage to Sweden via sea—of course, we must pay a handsome amount of money. I pray that it will all go in the right direction and soon we will be free from the impossible situation I find myself in here.

But what really takes the peace of sleep away from me is the thought that Felek might come back one day, and I will not be here. This breaks my heart into a million pieces. I've dreamed of the day when he returns to me, but if I flee as I must, it will never happen. My body and soul are completely numb.

All night, I cry and cry, and cry, unable to grasp at the sadness that creeps into my soul. But at dawn when I have no more tears left, I freeze at the sound of a little object hitting at my windowpane.

Without thinking I leap to my feet, jump forward and open the window, all while my heart pounds beneath my rib cage.

Cold air hits my skin, but I couldn't care less, focusing on looking down. "Who's there?"

"Are you still mine?" A voice comes from the darkness sending bolts of electricity through my entire being.

His voice. My Felek.

"Yours, only yours," I whisper, letting elation spread through every particle of my soul and body.

In no time I fly downstairs to let him in, and without caring about the entire world, I run into his embrace.

"My Kasia," he says with a catch in his voice and pulls me closer, then his lips touch mine bringing heaven to me.

A combination of elation and mind-blowing sensation that he is truly here pours over me. My Felek, my beloved, my soulmate, my calm is here. His kisses are tender and fervent, full of the relentless longing that we've both endured.

I draw him closer and brush my hand over his hair unable to believe that I'm touching him, as currents of heat rush through me.

When he lifts his head, his heartfelt eyes reflect such strong emotion that it feels almost foreign to me. "I love you," he says.

EPILOGUE
FELEK: I DON'T REGRET ONE THING...

Seventy years later, England

Why? My God, why did you take her away from me? How am I supposed to live the rest of my life without her? You gave us twenty beautiful years together, to end it so rapidly, without warning. Why? Please, tell me why this had to happen to us, to our children?

That's what I've been asking for the last fifty years... I feel like I'm stuck in an empty bottle without the way out. But we do have children and grandchildren for whom I've kept going and living my life, until I reunite with my beloved.

At the time of her passing, Jagoda was eight and Nela was six. Our two precious daughters were waiting so long for their mother to come back to them... I have no doubt that she's been watching over us. When I close my eyes, I feel her presence stronger with each day. My beloved wife hasn't died, her soul is alive, but as a human I long for her touch, to hear her voice, to have her beside us. It's been so hard...

It all began in May of 1965 when she was given a cancer diagnosis. She fought against the terrible beast, but in

December of the same year we lost the battle. Even the war couldn't defeat her, only cancer could, and had.

That October day when I returned to her seventy years ago, was the happiest moment in my life. I swore to always love her and treat her with tenderness and respect, and to bring happiness to her. After they evacuated us from the camp of death at Stutthof, the Germans took us by sea to northern Germany. It was one hell of a trip to get there on a small and overpacked boat, but I somehow survived inhuman conditions and near starvation.

Since my arrest and placement in Stutthof, my only hope was to go back to Kasia, to see her once more, so having her again in my arms, felt like true heaven. We found a way of leaving Gdańsk and heading for Sweden and then England. Her mother and brother joined us.

Through the first years, Kasia manufactured a homemade chocolate and soon opened a small business, which later bloomed. After many courses, I got a license to work as an electrician, just like my father and grandfather... Kornel became a doctor and worked in the hospital where he did everything to help his sister. But *everything* wasn't enough.

Her mother already lived with us, so she helped me raise our daughters.

I travel to Poland once a year, but everything has changed there now. My parents and sisters are long gone, and so are most of my friends from the Resistance.

My Kasia visits me in my dreams, always floating in light, and I know it's really her. Don't ask me how I know, I just do. We hug and kiss and talk and are together again. Every night that she's with me, I beg her to never stop coming back.

Through the years she's been telling me to take strength from our children and grandchildren, and that my purpose on this earth isn't over yet, that I still have things to do. But, God, you know how much I yearn to be with her.

Now, at the tender age of ninety-six, I'm ready to reunite with her when the right time comes. I never re-married or was with any other woman. I lived for my children, then grandchildren, while my beloved wife's spirit has never left my heart, my mind... Some say I'm a fool for not living my life to its fullest, but in my definition, the life that I have had is the truest it could have been, after she transitioned to the other side.

I don't regret one thing knowing that the pain and loneliness that've become my faithful companions are the price for loving her eternally. I will not reach true happiness until I join her in the life after this one.

A LETTER FROM GOSIA

Dear reader,

I want to say a huge thank you for choosing to read *The Wartime Chocolate Maker*. If you did enjoy it and want to keep up-to-date with all my latest releases, just sign up at the following link. Your email address will never be shared, and you can unsubscribe at any time.

www.bookouture.com/gosia-nealon

Gdańsk (German Danzig), a port city on the Baltic coast, has a rather complicated history. The city was found in the tenth century by the Polish king Mieszko I, but in the fourteenth century, the Teutonic Knights took it over, killed the locals and brought over a colony of German settlers. Gdańsk returned to Poland in the fifteenth century but was populated by German residents. By the eighteenth century, the city was known as the most flourishing port on the Baltic coast, but that's when it landed in the hands of Prussia, due to the second partition of Poland between Prussia and Russia.

After the Great War, Poland finally gained its independence, returned to the world maps and got its own access to the Baltic Sea, which was called by the German propaganda as the "Polish corridor". The Treaty of Versailles also created *Wolne Miasto Gdańsk* (the Free City of Danzig) situated to the east of the "corridor". The city was independent, neither part of

Poland nor Germany, but with around eighty percent of its population being German and the other twenty percent Polish.

The beginning of the war in 1939 brought tragedy to Jews and Poles in Gdańsk. Civilians were dragged out of their homes and arrested, many killed or sent to a nearby camp in Stutthof... The Germans officially began World War II by attacking the Polish munitions depot in Gdańsk's harbor and the Polish Post Office on Hevelius Platz. But they were met by a strong resistance...

While writing this book, as a lover of chocolate, I was delighted to learn about the history of chocolate in Gdańsk, which as a port city, was open to new and unknown flavors. And so, chocolate arrived in this city on sailing ships as early as the seventeenth century. Because of that, the people of Gdańsk drank chocolate before it was fashionable in the rest of Europe. At first, chocolate was treated as something that only the richest could afford, but over time, it found its way into the homes of the less wealthy residents. The first chocolate factories in Gdańsk appeared in the nineteenth century.

There is no doubt that Gdańsk is a city of rich culture and history, famous not only for ships and amber, but also excellent chocolate.

I hope you enjoyed *The Wartime Chocolate Maker*, and if you did, I would be very grateful if you could write a review. I'd like to hear what you think, and it makes such a difference helping new readers to discover one of my books for the first time.

I love hearing from my readers – you can get in touch through my social media or my website.

Thanks, Gosia

KEEP IN TOUCH WITH GOSIA

www.gosianealon.com

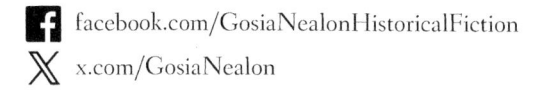

facebook.com/GosiaNealonHistoricalFiction
x.com/GosiaNealon

ACKNOWLEDGMENTS

This novel was inspired by the incredible strength of my sister, Kasia. My protagonist doesn't only have her name, but I also tried to instill in her the values that so perfectly define my sister: strength and resilience, the will to fight through the worst times, compassion for others, intelligence and a wise approach to life situations, a hardworking nature... My sister was a classy woman with a lighthearted sense of humor, as well as beautiful taste and style. She never hesitated to speak up even when others lacked courage, or to stand up for her family and friends in their lowest moments. There was something about her that made others feel safe with her, it's how I felt when I was with her. Love was at the center of her earthly life, and she would do everything for her children, for her family.

Kasia was also a brilliant and compassionate Mathematics Teacher. One of her high school students wrote a beautiful tribute to her, so I'd like to cite here a short part of it: "...*You never failed to make any of us smile, to help us at times of difficulty, you were just the kindest, most sweetest, most thoughtful soul I've ever met on this earth... You loved every single one of us, and went above to help us succeed...*" It's how my sister was here and it's how I know she continues to be in Heaven. I'm eternally thankful for her unconditional support.

Love is also at the core of this novel. I believe that it was the power of love that helped so many people survive through the worst of times, through war. There are different shades of love in my book: the innocent love between two people, the unconditional love of a parent and child, unrequited love, and finally the eternal love… Love didn't cease to exist during the war because it's when it was needed the most.

I'm lucky to have my loving and supportive family, especially my parents Elżbieta and Zdzisław; my husband Jim and my sons Jacob, Jack and Jordan; my nephews Matthew and Ryan; my brother Tomek who's an exceptional History Teacher; my brother Mariusz with his lovely wife and children; and the rest of my family and friends. Thank you for always being there for me.

I'm thankful to my amazing editor, Natalie Edwards, whose encouraging approach and constructive insights help me grow as an author and significantly improve the quality of my work. I'm lucky to be able to work with her.

I'm thankful to the brilliant team at Bookouture and the wonderful editor Emma Hargrave for their hard work and support.

I'm thankful to the historian, Dr. Jan Daniluk, for providing very useful information about Gdańsk during World War II.

I'm thankful to my lovely cousin Cathy Gustafson for reading my every book and sharing her thoughts.

I'm thankful to my friend Ania Albrecht who proves that a true friendship stays forever…beyond time.

I'm thankful to my friends Iza Pszeniczny and Ania Pierwocha for their awesome support.

I'm thankful to my readers for reading my books, writing reviews, sending encouraging messages and comments on social media. They inspire me to keep writing.

PUBLISHING TEAM

Turning a manuscript into a book requires the efforts of many people. The publishing team at Bookouture would like to acknowledge everyone who contributed to this publication.

Commercial
Lauren Morrissette
Hannah Richmond
Imogen Allport

Cover design
Eileen Carey

Data and analysis
Mark Alder
Mohamed Bussuri

Editorial
Natalie Edwards
Charlotte Hegley

Proofreader
Claire Rushbrook

Marketing
Alex Crow
Melanie Price
Occy Carr
Cíara Rosney
Martyna Młynarska

Operations and distribution
Marina Valles
Stephanie Straub
Joe Morris

Production
Hannah Snetsinger
Mandy Kullar
Jen Shannon
Ria Clare

Publicity
Kim Nash
Noelle Holten
Jess Readett
Sarah Hardy

Rights and contracts
Peta Nightingale
Richard King
Saidah Graham